CH00735259

# The Cormabite Maneuver

## A Lighthearted Murder Mystery in Space

Galactic Detective Agency
Book 6

Gary Blaine Randolph

i

This is a work of fiction. Names, characters, businesses, events, and incidents are the products of the author's imagination. Any resemblance to actual persons, living or dead, or actual events is purely coincidental.


Copyright © 2022
by Gary Blaine Randolph


All rights reserved. No part of this book may be reproduced or used in any manner without written permission of the copyright owner except for the use of quotations in a book review.

ISBN: 978-1-7379299-4-9 (paperback)
ISBN: 978-1-7379299-5-6 (ebook)

# Contents

Chapter 1  The Date of a Lifetime ................................................................ 1

Chapter 2  Fly Me to the Moon ................................................................... 6

Chapter 3  What Lucas Did .......................................................................... 12

Chapter 4  The Rheged Edge ....................................................................... 16

Chapter 5  Carry On, My Wayward Son ...................................................... 20

Chapter 6  A Stowaway's Guide to the Galaxy ........................................... 25

Chapter 7  Blue's Clues ................................................................................ 29

Chapter 8  Cliff Hanger ............................................................................... 35

Chapter 9  The Occasion of the Body Snatchers ........................................ 41

Chapter 10  Not the Evening Any of Us had Envisioned ........................... 47

Chapter 11  Room and Bored ...................................................................... 54

Chapter 12  The Search for Lucas ............................................................... 58

Chapter 13  Lifestyle of the Rich and Famous ........................................... 64

Chapter 14  Lucas's Run .............................................................................. 71

Chapter 15  Crookland Nine-Nine .............................................................. 74

Chapter 16  Born to Run ............................................................................. 80

Chapter 17  Mother and Child Reunion ..................................................... 84

Chapter 18  Dak Tracy Meets Oren Vilkas .................................................. 90

Chapter 19  Returning to the Scene of the Crime ...................................... 95

Chapter 20  The Gallery .............................................................................. 100

Chapter 21  A Few Answers and a Lot More Questions ............................. 107

Chapter 22  Lucas Helps Fix the Shaymus, For Real .................................. 113

To Daniel and Rachel, who tolerate me eating into their Gabe time to read this nonsense with him.

Chapter 23  The Missing Assistant....................................................118

Chapter 24  Cormabite Confab ........................................................125

Chapter 25  The Lineup....................................................................130

Chapter 26  The Question of the Carafozzio.....................................134

Chapter 27  The Sewer King in the Study with the Cane...................140

Chapter 28  A Long Shot..................................................................147

Chapter 29  The Body in the Morgue...............................................154

Chapter 30  Dial P for Pardiun........................................................158

Chapter 31  The Daffy Dumonts......................................................164

Chapter 32  Rendezvous with Rumble..............................................171

Chapter 33  The Galley Infirmary....................................................177

Chapter 34  Oren Acts All Smug......................................................181

Chapter 35  The Stakeout.................................................................187

Chapter 36  Nobody Pays Any Attention to Kids..............................194

Chapter 37  The Setup .....................................................................198

Chapter 38  I Love it When a Plan Comes Together..........................205

Chapter 39  The Fight Scene............................................................211

Chapter 40  Oren Takes the Stage....................................................216

Chapter 41  So Where's the Painting? ..............................................222

Chapter 42  Date Do-Over ..............................................................227

Last Word and Free Stuff................................................................232

Other Books by Gary Blaine Randolph .............................................233

# Chapter 1

# The Date of a Lifetime

*Gabe*

I had been preparing for this for weeks, and nothing was going to mess it up. Or so I thought at the time. I mean, when you propose marriage to someone, you want to do it right, right? And as a guy who occasionally works for an outfit called the Galactic Detective Agency, I knew I could pop the question in a way that would be out of this world. Literally.

I was over at Sarah's place. We had watched an animated movie with Lucas, her seven-year-old son. When it finished Lucas ran to his room to get ready for bed, and Sarah snuggled into my shoulder. Her blonde hair cascaded across my chest, and I caught a whiff of her perfume. This was the moment to launch the plan.

"This is nice," I said, "but I was thinking it was time you and I went out on the town. Someplace special."

"Something more special than the living room?" I loved her sarcasm.

"You bet."

She sat up, eyes aglow. "Where? St. Elmo's? The Eagle's Nest? I've heard good things about Peterson's on the north side."

"I was thinking someplace not in Indianapolis."

"Where?"

I pointed toward the heavens with my eyes, finding myself momentarily distracted by an odd spot on the ceiling. Was that a water leak? Somebody ought to check into it. I shook off the thought and caught Sarah's eye.

She bounced like a toddler. "A date up in space? We're going to visit another planet? Is that what you're saying?"

If you aren't familiar with my previous stories, you might be even more surprised about all this than she was. The fact that I sometimes travel among the stars as an operative of the Galactic Detective Agency is not common knowledge on Earth.

Neither is the fact that there are aliens out there at all since Earth is subject to a galactic quarantine. Apparently, the human species doesn't yet measure up to their exacting standards for making first contact. I can't imagine why.

The only reason I knew anything about life on other planets was because a year and a half earlier Oren Vilkas, the boss of the Galactic Detective Agency, had recruited me to help with a case of an alien hiding on Earth. One thing led to another, and now I'm on call so to speak.

Sarah and Lucas are the only other people on Earth who share my little secret. They even accompanied me one time on a trip to another planet to drop off an alien we had apprehended. And Sarah had helped on another case out in space.

She slugged me in the arm. "It's about time you arranged to take me out on the *Shaymus* again, Gabriel Lake." The *Shaymus* is the spaceship used by the Galactic Detective Agency.

Both Sarah and Lucas had been bugging me to take them on another spaceship ride ever since spring when I had come back from my last case with a mysterious black cube that could contact my alien co-workers any time I wanted.

I had delayed making the call precisely because I knew a date out among the stars would be the perfect place to ask Sarah to marry me. Of course, that's a huge step. All summer I dithered about whether I was even ready for marriage, whether I thought Sarah would say yes, how this whole thing might impact Lucas. After stewing through all that and finally deciding to do it, I then had to steal one of her rings and buy a diamond in a matching size.

It all took time. It wasn't until now, in early October, that I was ready to pull the trigger, light the candle, start the ball rolling.

"Can you find a sitter to stay late?" I asked.

"I can on a Friday night."

"Then let's go all out. Make it an unforgettable evening, the date of a lifetime."

She cocked her head and pulled her glasses down to peer at me over them. "What's this all about anyway?"

Uh-oh. I may have said too much. "Nothing. I want to show my girl a good time, is all." I hoped I was convincing. "Now let's figure out which Friday."

When I returned home that night to my bungalow in Indy's Fountain Square district, I retrieved a cardboard box from under my bed and took out the cube given to me by Oren Vilkas. I pulled out the note I had placed in the box and read it again: *Square Blue Button*. Oren had told me that button would summon them. The cube had a bunch of other buttons too, but he had implied that pressing some of them would do things I wouldn't want to do. Which is why the cube had spent the last six months safely in a box under my bed.

I placed the cube on my bedspread, the square blue button facing up, and sat cross-legged in front of it. I reached out a finger, hesitated a moment, and then pressed.

A low rumble started up, not from the box but from all around me. The bed shook. The nightstand quaked. A picture of Sarah and Lucas began waltzing across the top of the dresser. I jumped up and grabbed it before it jittered off and crashed onto the floor.

The rumble resolved into a musical note, starting out like a thrumming bass guitar, gradually rising in pitch until it became a shrill ringing. The sound pulsated inside me. I jerked my hands up to cover my ears, but it didn't help. Then all fell silent except for sounds of barking around the neighborhood as the tone apparently moved on up into the dog whistle range.

A blue pinprick of light appeared in the corner of the room near the ceiling, twinkling like a star. An envelope I had left on top of the dresser levitated into the air, spun around in a circle, and with a sucking sound disappeared into the blue pinhole. Great! Now I would have to go online to pay the electric bill.

"Hey, Gabriel!" a voice drawled out from the blue light.

"WALT?"

WALT, an acronym for Wormhole Atomic Long-Range Telecommunications, is the communications AI on the *Shaymus*. He communicates at faster than the speed of light, which you have to do if you want to talk to someone in another star system and not wait years for a reply. WALT pulls off that trick by opening and sending messages through tiny wormholes, hence the name.

"At your service, Gabriel." For reasons I never understood, WALT sounds a lot like the actor Owen Wilson.

"So, WALT, I take it this blue twinkling thing in my room is a wormhole?"

"Bingo! You've been paying attention."

"How come one doesn't appear on board the *Shaymus* when you're doing your thing there?"

"On the ship I open them inside a containment unit for safety purposes. For some reason, you don't have a molecular containment unit in your bedroom.

Which reminds me, don't get too close to the wormhole. You do *not* want to be sucked into one of those things. Anyway, how can I help you today, Gabriel?"

"Yeah. Oren said I could call sometime and request a pickup. I want to take Sarah on a date to another planet."

"Ooh! Sounds romantic. Where are you taking her?"

That was the question I had been asking myself. I had visited a handful of worlds, but selecting one for a date was problematic. Bononia was the one planet she had seen, so that was out since I wanted to take her someplace new. Cunedda and Delusia both had ridiculously heavy gravity. Donovio was humid and mucky. Malt had no atmosphere, and by that I don't mean the place was boring. It literally had no oxygen or air pressure to keep you alive, which isn't romantic at all. Diere was nice, and they owed me a favor, but the planet wasn't all that safe. The women there are twenty-feet tall and have on occasion sat on people by accident.

I tentatively settled on Rheged Prime, Oren's home world. The part of the planet I had seen was green and lush. There was a painting in Oren's office of the mountain that the *Shaymus* had been named after. Mount Shaymus had an incredible view of the sea. I thought that might be a fitting place to ask for the hand of my intended.

"I'm working it out," I told WALT. "Can I speak to Oren?"

"Sure. Coming right up."

"Yes, Gabriel." The sonorous voice of Oren Vilkas came through the wormhole. Oren owned the *Shaymus* and the Galactic Detective Agency. It was up to him to say whether this plan was going to happen.

"Hi, Oren. I was wondering if it would be convenient for you to pick up Sarah and me. I want to take her on a date across the galaxy."

"We should be able to make that work. Where did you want to go?"

"Someplace beautiful. I was thinking about Mount Shaymus from the painting in your office. Is there somewhere there we could eat?"

"There are no restaurants allowed on the mountain, but picnics there are beautiful. Our ship's food replicator can provide any kind of meal you want."

"That sounds perfect!"

"As it happens, we will be heading to Rheged Prime for a case."

"Then good timing, I guess." That should have been a red flag on this whole idea, but I was so caught up in date planning that I missed it.

"We have been asked to recover a stolen painting."

"An art heist, huh? Cool! Though it sounds tame compared to our usual cases of murder and mayhem."

"That was why I didn't call you in. I know how much you enjoy the murder and mayhem."

"Whatever gave you that idea? Granted, our adventures have generally ended up with a murderer punching me or shooting a blaster at me. But I'm a man of peace. You'd be surprised how rarely anybody ever shoots at me when I'm doing software development." Which was my day job here on Earth.

"You are welcome to sit in on the case."

"Thanks. But this trip is all about Sarah."

"Do I detect that this is an auspicious occasion, Gabriel?"

"If I work up the nerve, I'm going to ask her to marry me."

"Indeed! What is your Earth custom? Do I say congratulations or best of luck or what?"

"I only want to hear you say you can come this Friday night."

I had no idea of the pot I was stirring, the bear I was poking, all the things I was setting in motion. I mean, if I wanted someplace exotic, I could have taken Sarah to that new Ethiopian place downtown. But no, I had to take her to another planet. I bet nobody who went out to Chili's that weekend ended up being swept into a web of art heists, kidnapping, and murder.

# Chapter 2

# Fly Me to the Moon

*Gabe*

In the noir detective movies I love to watch, the hero rarely ends up with the girl in a happily-ever-after ending. Sometimes it turns out that the girl the detective had fallen for is the murderer, and he (sorry, no female protagonists in these old movies) has to send her up the river for it. Definitely not the kind of thing to get you feeling all romantic and wanting to settle down.

Maybe that's why up to now I haven't been willing to commit to a relationship. I hate to even commit to a two-year contract with a cell phone provider let alone plight my troth til death do us part.

But I always remember what my grandfather said. When he and Grandma were celebrating their sixtieth anniversary, I asked him how they managed it. He handed me a cookie, one of the chocolate chip cookies my grandma was famous for, and said, "I have been eating these cookies for sixty years, and they're always delicious. I must've owned a dozen or more cars, lived in seven different houses, but eaten this one cookie. And I'm glad to do it. Once you find the best, it isn't a limitation. It's a comfort."

Of course, Grandma made other kinds of cookies too, so I'm not sure what he was talking about. But I understood the sentiment. Those words were on my mind that evening when I arrived at Sarah's house to pick her up.

"What do you think?" She twirled in front of me in a sleeveless sundress with a wide skirt that seemed to flow around her. A wide-brimmed straw hat perched over her blonde hair. "Does this look right for a picnic? You said it would be warm, right? Gabe? What's the matter? Close your mouth."

I hadn't realized my trap was open. What did I think? I had thought I looked cool in the new summer sports jacket I had bought for the occasion and my detective fedora — I couldn't board the *Shaymus* without my beloved fedora — but next to her I was a slob. She looked like she had stepped out of a magazine.

"Um … that's what Oren says — warm, balmy. It's the height of summer on that part of Rheged Prime."

Sarah called out, "Lucas, Gabe is here. We're getting ready to leave."

His voice filtered out from behind his bedroom door. "Okay. Have fun."

"Aren't you going to come out and say hi to Gabe?"

"I'm busy looking for a Lego piece."

Sarah looked at me and shrugged. "I guess he's growing up."

"Are you ready to go?" I asked.

"Is it chilly outside? Here it is October, and I'm wearing a sundress."

I pulled off my sports jacket and draped it around her shoulders, my hands coming away clammy as I belatedly remembered the ring I had secreted away inside. I reached out and took her hand so she wouldn't slip it into the pocket. Then I remembered that the ring box was in the other pocket and awkwardly switched to her other hand.

Sarah turned to the babysitter, who was on the couch buried in a textbook. "Jenna, you have the food, movie and bedtime instructions, emergency numbers. Anything else you need?"

"I'm good," the babysitter said, flashing a brief smile before returning her gaze to the book.

"We should be back by …" Sarah glanced to me with the question on her face.

"The wee hours, I guess."

"Will you be fine until then, Jenna?"

The babysitter's expression was almost condescending. "Don't worry."

Sarah gave me a what-are-you-going-to-do face. "Okay. Let's go."

We walked out the front door and down the walk to my car. As she settled into the seat, she gazed back at the little rental house with a crease between her eyebrows.

"They'll be fine," I said. "WALT is set to forward all texts to you across the light years. And we'll be back before morning. C'mon. How often do you get a chance to picnic on another planet?"

"Not often. Hard to believe, but this will be my first time."

"Well, thank you for sharing it with me."

I pulled away from the curb and headed toward Garfield Park where the *Shaymus* had landed in a clump of trees that afternoon. I had been there an hour before making sure everything was ready for our special night.

Just my luck, East Street was blocked by a utility truck working on a gas main or something. I ducked down a gravel alley full of ruts and holes, coming out on the next street, which turned out to have a stop sign at every intersection.

"Ugh." I wasn't in the mood to have things mess up my evening. Of course, in retrospect, this was nothing compared with what was to come.

Sarah reached over and patted my leg. "Calm down."

We made it to the park, and I found a spot for the car on the street. We walked across the grass, hand-in-hand again to keep her from sticking her fingers in *the* pocket. With my mind buzzing with all the plans for the evening, our conversation lagged.

"Why so quiet?" Sarah asked.

"Hmm?" I shook myself out of my thoughts.

"You've barely said a word."

"Oh. Sorry … um … how are the martial arts classes coming?" She had started training after our space adventure, which had ended in a skirmish.

Her eyes danced. "Fantastic!"

"You'll have to demonstrate some time."

"Sure. Should I do a leg sweep on you right now?"

"You've already swept me off my feet," I said, pleased with the play on words.

The conversation lagged again as my mind once more started running through the date ahead of us.

"Is something the matter, Gabe?"

Dummy, I thought to myself. This *is* the date. Get your head in the game. Be in the moment.

"No. No … I'm overthinking, I think. I'm trying to make everything perfect tonight." We were now at the edge of the trees. I stopped and pulled her toward me. "Have I told you how great you look?"

"Actually, you haven't. I was beginning to wonder."

"Oh. Sorry. My synapses are bouncing around like toddlers on a playground."

She leaned in and gave me a quick kiss before patting me on the chest. "Focus, Gabe."

Right. Focus.

We stepped through the trees, and there it was — my home away from home — trillions of miles away from home most of the time.

Imagine an egg lying on its side. Add some struts underneath and small wings extending out the back. Now paint the whole thing red, add a black stripe running horizontally around its middle, and stick a clear dome on top. Then upsize the whole thing to make it large enough to hold three decks with quarters for a handful of people. That's the *Shaymus*.

We approached, and I said, "Open ramp."

With a *whir* the ramp began to lower from the side of the hull as dramatically as in the scene when Klaatu first appears in *The Day the Earth Stood Still*.

I said, "See how it responds to my commands? Cool, huh? Like Han Solo. Star Lord."

She smirked. "More like Star Nerd."

Jace, the engineer on the *Shaymus*, was waiting for us inside, his blue-skinned face beaming. "Hi, Gabe. Hi, Sarah. We're ready to go whenever you are. Are you going up to the office or to your cabin or what?"

Now, if you're new to my adventures, you may be wondering how a blue-skinned Rhegedian alien like Jace spoke English. The answer is that he didn't. He spoke in his language. Sarah and I spoke in ours. Inside each of us, tiny nanobots called translator bots attached to our auditory cortices and translated any known language directly into our brains. This is the kind of amazing tech Earth is missing out on because of the quarantine.

I took another glance at my date and easily decided for some alone time with her. "How about we pass the ride in my cabin? I'll say hello to Oren over the view screen there."

"Suit yourself."

Sarah handed me back my jacket. As I slid it on, my hand patted the ring for about the hundredth time. We circled around the gleaming white crew deck hallway to my cabin, cabin eight. The door slid open. Oren's face greeted us from the view screen. "Welcome, Gabriel and Sarah. May I say it is a pleasure to see you again, Ms. Gallo."

"Hi, Oren," Sarah said.

"Gabriel, we will be arriving on Rheged Prime early to allow me to meet with our client on the art theft case. If you are so inclined, you are welcome to sit in on the interview. I would appreciate your observations even if you won't be working the case with us."

"Thanks, Oren," I said. "Put me down as a definite maybe. As you can see, I'm here with a beautiful woman, and I wouldn't want her to feel abandoned."

"Of course not," Oren said. "I hope you enjoy Mount Shaymus, Sarah. I spent many happy hours hiking along the clifftop. Of course, that was when I had a corporeal body."

"Thanks, Oren," she said. "I'm looking forward to it."

Oren nodded once and the view screen went blank.

Sarah's eyes met mine. She moved in and wrapped her arms around me.

We were interrupted by a smooth, synthesized voice coming over the speakers. "Hi, Gabriel. Welcome back, Sarah. It is good to have you with us again." This voice was Kah-Rehn's, the AI pilot for the *Shaymus*, super smart, sometimes temperamental, and apparently not overly tuned in to when people want some privacy. I broke off the embrace.

"I must say," Kah-Rehn said, "you look lovely, Sarah, according to my data on Earth standards of beauty."

"Thanks, Kah-Rehn … I think," Sarah said.

"You two need to strap in for take-off."

"Sure thing," I said. "We will. Hey, Kah-Rehn, would you show us the flight on my view screen?"

"Certainly, Gabriel."

Now where to strap in? Sarah could take the spacious lounge chair in the middle of the room, and I could strap in on my bunk. But this was a date. This was *the* date. I said, "How about we both squeeze into the chair? It will be cozy."

Sarah looked at me skeptically. "I don't want to be stuck in an uncomfortable position for twenty light-years."

"Which will only take a few minutes to traverse."

"I know. I know. All right, let's give it a try."

We slipped into the chair. It took a little wiggling about for a minute to find comfortable positions. I put my arm around her and gave her a squeeze.

"Are you okay like this?" I asked.

"I'm not complaining."

A five-point harness snaked out of the chair and wrapped us in. Then a rumble started up from the engineering deck, and the ship took off. The view screen showed the ground falling away below us. A *whump* followed by a *clang* sounded from somewhere else in the spacecraft.

Sarah lifted her head. "What was that?"

"The noise you mean?"

"Yeah."

"Beats me. I guess something wasn't strapped down."

# Chapter 3

# What Lucas Did

*Lucas*

Hi. This is Lucas. Gabe said I could write part of this because … well, you'll see why. But, boy, writing sure is a lot harder than talking. Thanks to Gabe for some writing tips and to Mom for helping me with spelling and stuff.

I've heard grownups tell stories about things that happen to kids. And you know what? It's always about what the grownups think. Nobody ever tells the kid's side of the story. That's what I'm going to do.

Now this whole thing starts out with me breaking like all the rules, which I want to say isn't generally like me. But seriously. Ask yourself what you would do if you were in my place.

That night after the movie when I went to my room to get ready for bed, I heard Mom and Gabe talking about calling Oren to go on a date out in space. I rode on the *Shaymus* once, and it was awesome. But that was one single, measly time, and I really, really wanted to go again. But Gabe had never offered to take me. So when they said they were going, I knew I had to do something.

First, I tried playing it cool. The next time Gabe was over I said to him, "Remember that time you introduced me to Jace and Zastra and Oren, and we flew to another planet?"

"How could I forget?" Gabe said, "Did you enjoy that?"

"Yeah! I'd like to go again sometime."

I was hoping he would say something like, "Hey, they're coming by, and I'm taking your mom for a ride. Would you like to come too?"

But that isn't what Gabe said. All he said was, "Maybe I can get you a ride out in space again sometime, sport."

My stomach dropped, and I played my last card. "When?"

"I don't know. Sometime."

Sometime. That was almost the same thing as never.

Gabe didn't exactly lie to me. But he wasn't entirely honest either. And I couldn't figure out why they weren't taking me. Maybe Oren didn't want a kid on his ship. Maybe Zastra or Jace had said something like, "You can bring Mom along, but not Lucas." I had thought they liked me, but you can't always tell.

If only Gabe had been honest and explained it to me. But that's grownups for you. They only tell you what they want you to know, not the things you want to know. For all I knew, this could be my last chance ever. I decided I had to take matters into my own hands.

It was obvious when they were going to take their ride on the *Shaymus*. Mom said she was getting a babysitter for Friday night because she and Gabe were going on a date. Generally, she tells me where they're going, but she didn't this time — like it was some huge secret.

"Can I come with you?" I asked her. I figured it was worth a try.

"I don't think so this time, baby. Gabe said this would be a special evening."

"I like special evenings."

She shot me a mom look. "This is an evening for Gabe and me. But I'm giving Jenna …" She's my usual babysitter. "I'm giving Jenna money for pizza. And you and I can rent a movie for you to watch."

Yeah, great. Another pizza and a kid's movie. Like I haven't done that a thousand times. Luckily, I had a plan.

Thursday at school, I made a deal with Noah to borrow his jacket and Colts cap in exchange for my pudding next time they have it in the cafeteria. He wore them Friday, and we traded. This was going to be my disguise.

Friday night when Jenna got there, I acted all happy and excited about the evening. After saying hi, I said I was going to play in my room until the pizza came. I had already hidden Noah's jacket and hat under my bed. When Gabe came, I slipped them on, opened my window, and jumped outside, glad that we had moved in the spring. My bedroom at the old apartment was upstairs, which would have ruined everything.

As I hit the ground outside my window, my first thought was that I was going to be so grounded for this. But my second thought was that they had pretty much forced me into it. How else was I going to ever get back on the *Shaymus*?

I ran around to the front of the house. I checked to make sure Mom and Gabe were not heading out the door. Then I ran to Gabe's car and climbed into the backseat. I huddled down on the floor as low as I could and pulled the jacket over my head. I tried to look like something thrown into the back, which wouldn't be out of place in Gabe's car.

Our front door squeaked open. Gabe and Mom's voices approached. They got into the car and drove off. I tried to hold my breath, to not make a sound.

Gabe said, "Are you ready for this?"

Mom said, "Sure! It's not every Friday night a girl gets to go to another planet." And they were planning to go without me.

They drove around a while. At one point they went down some bumpy alley that knocked me around. I hit my head on the part of the floorboard that juts up. It hurt, and I had to close my eyes and bite my lip to keep quiet.

They finally parked and climbed out. I stayed where I was and counted to one hundred. Then I scrambled to my knees and peeked out the window. We were at a park, and Mom and Gabe were walking across the grass toward a clump of trees.

I opened the door on the other side as quietly as I could. I shut it, and the door made a *thunck* so loud I figured they had to hear it. I ducked behind the tire and counted to thirty. When I sneaked a peek over the trunk, they were still walking away. I started to follow. Once, when they looked back, I dropped to my knee and pretended to tie my shoe. They didn't recognize me in Noah's jacket and cap.

They stopped at the edge of a clump of trees and kissed, which was gross. If they were going to do that the whole time, I wasn't sure I wanted to go with them. Then again, they were flying out in space. So, holy hotdogs, yeah, I wanted to go — even with the kissing.

I ran to the trees in time to see them walking up the ramp of the *Shaymus*. I was hoping they would leave the ramp down after they went in, and I could run up into the ship, but it started rising as soon as they disappeared inside.

Right beside the spaceship was a tree with a fork in it low enough for me to jump and reach. I climbed up the tree and looked down at the ship. I knew jumping to it wouldn't do me any good. You can't exactly ride on the outside of a spaceship through space. You would die.

I spotted this funny black bump on top of the ship right behind the dome. I remembered Gabe told me once that the *Shaymus* had a docking port. That could be my way in. A red lever stuck up beside the docking port — or what I hoped was the docking port. From the end of the branch, I could jump and grab hold of the lever and then open the port and drop in. I hoped so anyway.

I sidestepped along the branch. The further out I moved, the more it bent and creaked. I was afraid it was going to break. Out there on the bouncy branch, the black bump and red lever looked a long way away. But this was my only chance. I had to make this jump. I took a breath and leaped for the ship.

My body didn't quite make it to the black bump, but my fingers reached the lever, and I grabbed and held on tight. The lever slid back with my weight, and I was afraid I was going to keep on sliding all the way off the ship. But I got a grip with my sneakers and hung on.

A rumble started up from below me, and I realized the ship was taking off with me hanging off the side. I pushed with the toes of my sneakers and pulled myself up on top. The lever, when it slid, had opened a small cubbyhole beside it. Inside the hole was a red button.

The *Shaymus* rose into the air. The trees around the ship started to drop away. Wind whooshed past my face.

Before I had started any of this, I imagined it would be like in a kids' movie where the kid does something heroic. But this wasn't a kids' movie, and it wasn't heroic. This was crazy dangerous. I was going to die!

I reached in and pressed the red button. The sides of the black bump spun away to reveal a tube with a ladder inside.

I reached for the top rung and pulled myself in, flipping over with a sharp pain in my wrist, losing my grip, sliding down the tube. I landed hard on the bottom of the tube — on my bottom too, which hurt so bad I had to hug myself to keep from yelling out.

A door at the bottom of the tube swooshed open into a hallway of the ship. I scooched away from it, and it closed again. Above me the docking port spun shut as the sky faded from blue to black.

I had made a lot of noise when I fell down the tube, and I was sure someone would come and yell at me. I sat there in the dark, waiting, holding my wrist, willing away the pain, wiping my eyes. Nobody came.

# Chapter 4

# The Rheged Edge

*Gabe*

Not that I knew anything about what Lucas was up to. I was snuggled up with Sarah in the large, comfy chair in my cabin as we soared across the galaxy courtesy of the *Shaymus's* chrono drive.

As you may have heard, the universe is enormous. Most people, however, don't grasp just how unbelievably, immensely massive it really is. You know the term light-year. It's the distance light can travel in one year. The nearest other solar system to Earth is more than four light-years away. Some stars in our galaxy are more than fifty thousand light-years away, which means the light you see from one of those distant stars began its journey when your ancestors were still hunter-gatherers. Before cows or pigs or dogs were domesticated. Before the first cities were built. Long before any world history you studied in school ever happened.

If light, which is the fastest thing in the universe, took all that time to travel across the galaxy, how long do you think it would take you to reach even the nearest star? The answer is much more than your lifetime. That's why all the sci-fi shows use hyperspace or warp speed or whatever.

But all that is made-up stuff. The real way aliens travel among the stars is with what's called a chrono drive.

See, back billions of years ago, shortly, in relative terms, after the Big Bang, the universe was considerably smaller. The chrono drive works by first going back in time thirteen billion years to that tiny primordial universe, then moving across that smaller space to the place where a planet will someday form, and finally coming forward in time. And that, friends, only takes a few minutes.

Don't press me for details on how it does any of that because I don't have them. Jace tried to explain it to me once, but it didn't take. I only know it requires an advanced AI, like Kah-Rehn to do all the calculations, taking into account the universe expanding, galaxies spinning, planets orbiting, and whatnot. Try to run the numbers yourself, and you might end up inside a star or a black hole or even inside your target planet instead of sitting in a cozy orbit around it.

Sarah and I were nestled in the chair as Earth glowed below us on our view screen, blue and fragile, the continents rolling past. The dawning sun blazed in a halo of orange from the horizon. Then a buzz vibrated through the ship as the chrono drive kicked in.

As we orbited the globe and moved back in time, the electric lights all over the world blinked out. Ice ages came and went, continents drifted. Down there somewhere dinosaurs plodded across the ground, flew through the skies, swam in the oceans.

As we continued moving faster and faster backward in time, Earth broke up. Stars deformed and reformed. Space itself morphed from black to blue to orange and finally to a dense red soup of quarks and electrons.

"Remind me again what all that is out there?" Sarah asked.

"It's everything. All the matter in the universe before gravity started pulling it into galaxies and stars."

The buzz stopped, the ion drive ignited, and we began moving across the primordial space. Then the buzz began again, and we watched the whole show again in reverse as we came forward in time to the present.

Only this time a different planet formed below us, a world less blue and more green. Not a planet of continents scattered amid vast oceans as on Earth, but a world with a single continent stretching all around the globe, interspersed with huge inland seas. A bright sapphire ball shone above the horizon, the star of this solar system.

Sarah said, "You say this is Oren's home world?"

"Yeah. Jace's too. Rheged Prime."

"Does the Prime part imply the existence of a Rheged the Second or something?"

"Rheged Minor. It's in this same solar system. You probably wouldn't like it, though. It rains all the time there. Ooh. Look up ahead."

We had descended into the atmosphere and were coming in low over one of the inland seas. Something the size and general shape of a giant marlin, nose sword and all, leaped out of the water in front of us. At the apex of the leap, it unfolded wings and flew off into the clouds.

Sarah gaped at me open-mouthed.

"Flying fish," I said.

"Uh-uh. Except flying fish on Earth only leap a few feet and return to the water. That guy took off like a bird."

"Yeah. Imagine trying to land one with a rod and reel. Those guys could tow you up into the air."

A shoreline approached, a huge rocky precipice stretching out of the deep blue water toward a sky the color of a robin's egg. The cliff was a dead ringer for the picture in Oren's office.

"I think that's where we're going," I said. "Mount Shaymus. Jace said it's nearly a mile down the mountainside to the water, twice as tall as any sea cliff on Earth."

"It's beautiful," Sarah said, "and so lush."

The clifftop was covered with trees and flowering plants blooming in vivid blossoms and huge leafy fronds. We swept past the bluff, gliding over a family of something like deer only with moose-like antlers and a stubby horn like a rhino. The animals grazed in prairie land while a nearby colony of huge red lizards sunned themselves on a mossy rock.

We passed on inland over green fields and thick forests. Slowly houses and roads began to appear, the built-up districts becoming more and more numerous as we traveled. In the distance a city loomed.

A few minutes later we sat down in an urban area of low buildings punctuated by towering skyscrapers. Some of the towers were slender cylinders topped by wide domes. Nearly all the buildings had landing pads. Flying cars filled the airspace as a monorail snaked through the streets.

"What city is this, Kah-Rehn?" I asked.

"This is the city of Tikal," the AI answered. "It is the fifty-third largest city on Rheged Prime with a population of two million, seven hundred thousand people. In Earth units it covers two hundred thirty-four square miles or six hundred six square kilo—"

I cut her off. "That's enough, thanks. The name was sufficient."

"So cool," Sarah said. "It's like *The Jetsons*."

"Well, on *The Jetsons*, every building was on stilts."

The straps retracted back into the chair. Sarah scrambled out and stood there, arms crossed.

"Why do you have to do that?" One side of her upper lip had risen into a sneer.

18

"Do what?"

"Correct me."

"I corrected you? Sorry. It's just I could never figure out why they drew the buildings like that. Wouldn't they be unstable?"

"It was a cartoon show. Don't be so literal."

"But here they are literally in front of us."

Her look could have withered grass. "Well, if it means that much to you, you can ask somebody."

I took it as a sign of our deepening relationship that she was now calling me on things she didn't like. Or let's say I hoped that was what it was. It's not easy being in a close relationship, especially when you're an idiot sometimes.

I found myself humming *The Jetsons'* theme song. Oh no, I thought, now the tune was going to be stuck in my head. Maybe for hours unless something jarred it loose. As it turned out, boy oh boy, something certainly did knock it out about a minute later.

"What's next?" Sarah asked.

"I think sunset will be the best time for the picnic. We have a few hours. I need to check on the food plans. We can visit with the crew. We can walk around the city if you want."

Jace's voice sounded over the speakers. "Gabe. Sarah. Can you step out to the central shaft?"

"Sure," I said. "What's up?"

"Um … there's something you need to see."

We exited the cabin and walked around the hall. Beside the central shaft connecting all three decks of the *Shaymus* — engineering on bottom, crew deck in the middle, and Oren's office on top — stood Jace. Next to him on the floor sat someone smaller wearing a Colts ball cap.

Jace said, "While we were in flight, Kah-Rehn notified me that we had an intruder. I got up here as soon as we landed."

From the floor the face looked up. It was Lucas. He darted a sheepish glance in our direction. "Hi, Mom."

# Chapter 5

# Carry On, My Wayward Son

*Gabe*

"Lucas Archibald Gallo!" Sarah's clipped off the words. "What are you doing here?"

My eyes bounced back and forth between Sarah and Lucas. Her jaw was tight. His was trembling. Her eyes were boring holes into him. His eyes were focused on his shoes.

Simultaneously, my plans for the evening were disintegrating as quickly as Avengers after Thanos snapped his fingers. But I reminded myself that my scheme wasn't the main issue at stake here. The main concern was Lucas.

"How did you get on board?" Sarah demanded. She ran a hand across the back of her neck and rocked back and forth.

Lucas continued to stay silent.

Jace said, "I found him in the docking chute. He must have come in through the port."

Sarah pursed her lips and took a breath. She made a 'calm down' gesture with her hands, clearly for her own benefit. "Let's see what we have here." She began counting on her fingers. "One, you sneaked out of the house. Two, you left your babysitter alone. Jenna will be freaking out any minute now. Three, you stowed away on a spaceship. Four, you rode in a spaceship without being properly strapped in. Five, seeing you here, knowing what you did has scared me half to death. What do you have to say for yourself, Lucas?"

His voice came out faint and reedy. "I … I heard you guys talking about taking a ride on the *Shaymus*. I wanted to go too." His whole body stiffened. His voice grew intense, husky. "I know you and Gabe went off together that other time back in the winter. You think I didn't know, but I could tell from things you said and your looks at each other." He paused, sucked in air. I thought he was going to cry, but he ran a sleeve across his eyes and fought it back. "How come I never got to go again? This should be my turn."

My heart went out to the little guy. I wanted to say something, to comfort him. But throughout this whole relationship I had always let Sarah raise her kid her way. I held back and pressed my lips together.

"Lucas …" Sarah stood steel rod straight. "Lucas, this was so dangerous, baby."

Jace said, "Super dangerous. That chute's not meant for travel."

A soft *whir* came from the central shaft. A graceful circular staircase emerged from the smooth sides of the cylinder that runs between the decks of the *Shaymus*. Then came a clanging on the steps.

Zastra appeared boots first, followed by the hem of her long, hooded duster and finally her scaly, green head with its five sweeping ridges. "Hey, Lucas. How are you doing?"

Zastra is a Srathan, a human-sized lizard species. She is Oren's number one operative and probably the last person you would expect a kid to get chummy with … or to get chummy with a kid. She's a no-nonsense kind of person and, with me at least, more grumpy than nurturing. But when she and Lucas had met a year earlier, they hit it off.

She moved to him and took a knee, placing a clawed, scaly hand on his shoulder. "I'm glad to see you again." She peeked up at Sarah and me. "If your mom can spare you, we can hang out together for a while."

It was like in the movies when somebody cuts the red wire right before the bomb's timer hits zero. Sarah took a breath and visibly relaxed. Lucas swallowed. A hint of a smile played across his face.

Sarah clipped off the words. "Good idea. In fact, right now would be an excellent time for you two to catch up. Later, Lucas and I need to talk, but I'm not in a good place for that currently."

Sarah turned on her heels and strode back around the corridor toward my cabin. Zastra motioned with her head for Lucas to follow her, and they climbed up the steps to the office.

I looked at Jace. "What do I do? Should I go to Sarah? Should I go to Lucas? Maybe you could use a hand down in engineering?"

"Nah, I'm good. And I don't know anything about Earthling relationships. You want to be a family man, you figure it out." He descended the stairs to engineering, leaving me alone in the crew hallway.

I decided to give them both a few minutes. "Lower ramp."

The ship's ramp opened, and I headed out into the city of Tikal to clear my head. I needed to figure out what this meant for my plans for a date and for proposing.

The street was packed with Rhegedian pedestrians as if Comic-Con was in town, and everybody had dressed as the Blue Man Group. There were no sidewalks or even any defined lanes for the vehicles. People walked in the streets. Hover vehicles, when they came to pedestrians, pitched up to glide over the top of them and continued on their way. When they met another hover vehicle, one sailed over the other.

I walked along the street marveling at the futuristic buildings and their odd shapes. Sarah was right. This really was like *The Jetsons*.

I came to a street vendor standing on a corner behind a flamingo pink cart full of canisters. I stepped up to check it out.

"What flavor?" asked the blue Rhegedian woman behind the cart.

"What flavor of what? What are you selling?"

"Maerceci."

"Maer ... what?"

She gave me a deadpan look. "You've never tried maerceci?"

I pointed at the non-blue skin on my hand. "I'm from out of town."

"How about a sample? We have plain, crowberry, and sun flavored"

"Yes, please. Anything but crowberry." I couldn't imagine what that would be like.

The vendor took a cardboard stick and held it under the nozzle of one of the canisters which made a whooshing noise. A dollop of something blue appeared on the stick with a consistency halfway between whipped cream and soft ice cream. She held it out to me. "This is the sun flavored."

I licked it. The creamy substance was sweet and fruity and left a tingle in my mouth almost like soda pop.

I dug in my pocket for the finger-sized metal tube, which is what they use for money out in most of the galaxy. This one was tied to Oren's accounts. He had given it to me earlier in the day to use on the date, saying he would deduct whatever I spent from my earnings on my next case. "I'll take a whole helping."

The vendor pulled a cardboard dish from a stack and held it under the nozzle of one of the canisters. She filled the dish and handed it to me. Just the dish. No spoon. No straw.

"Do I … what? Lick it? Pick it up with my hand?"

The woman made a sucking noise with her mouth.

"What?"

She shook her head in disbelief. "Hold it near your mouth and suck."

"You're kidding me."

She shook her head again.

I tried it. A string of the stuff levitated out of the cup and into my mouth as if it were passing through an invisible straw.

"Wow! How does this mercetti—"

"Maerceci."

"Right. Whatever. How does it do that? How does it make it to my mouth?"

"You must not know much about physics, boy."

"Well, I took it in high school." And immediately forgot everything after every test. Except pulleys. I loved pulleys. "This is some kind of physics?"

"Sure." She winked. "String theory."

Was she pulling my leg? Possibly. Even probably. The only way to find out would be to ask Jace. And if it had been a joke, he would make fun of me. I pretended not to hear and backed away.

I returned to the *Shaymus*. As I approached my cabin door, it *dinged*, presumably to alert Sarah, who was inside, that I wanted to enter. It makes that sound all by itself, though not all the time. If no one is inside, my cabin door opens automatically as soon as I approach it, without any dinging. If I pass by someone else's cabin, their door doesn't open or even ding unless I stop outside. I guess the doors have AI circuitry like WALT and Kah-Rehn, but I didn't understand how it worked.

"Come in." Her voice came out flat and subdued.

The door slid open. Sarah was lying on my bunk in the fetal position. "Where have you been?"

"Taking a walk. Are you all right?"

"Aside from raising a juvenile delinquent?"

"Lucas is not a juvenile delinquent."

"Not yet. But sneaking out of the house at seven years old? It doesn't bode well."

I sat on the bunk and put a hand on her side, feeling her stiffen and tense. "Yeah, well, the lure of flying out into space is a powerful temptation. Maybe I should have planned a day trip with him first."

She sat up and eyed me. "Maybe you should have."

"Does this mean our date is ruined? Should we call it a day and have Kah-Rehn take us home?"

Sarah jumped off the bunk and paced across the cabin. "Oh no! I'm not letting this kid ruin my evening. I bought this sundress, and who knows when I can wear it again seeing as how Indiana is heading toward winter."

I went to her and put my arms around her. "Good. We still have a few hours before sunset for us both to get our heads back in the game."

She pulled away. "First, I need to contact Jenna before she calls the cops. Hey, WALT?"

A drawl sounded over the speakers. "Hey, Sarah. Hey Gabriel. What's up?"

Sarah said, "More than I can go into right now, WALT. I need you to send a text for me. You still have all my contacts, right?"

"C'mon. Of course, I do."

"Okay. Send to Babysitter Jenna. Say this, 'Guess what? Lucas sneaked into our car. We'll keep him with us this evening. You can go home. We'll settle up later. Sorry.'"

"Sent," WALT replied.

"Now what?" I asked.

Before she could answer, WALT said, "Oh, here's the reply already. Wow! It's all emojis ... let's see ... gritted teeth emoji, monkey with hands over its mouth emoji, smiley face emoji, thumbs up emoji. Do you have any idea what all that means, Sarah?"

"Close enough."

"Honestly. Most species use words."

"Thanks, WALT," she said, dismissing him.

I tried again. "Now what?"

"Now you go away and let me sit here by myself for a while. Then I'll go talk to Lucas. I'll be all right." She looked down. "My dress is all wrinkled."

I stretched an arm toward a panel on one wall. "May I present the pressing cabinet. All you do is hang the dress in it and tap the button. Want me to show you?"

"I'll figure it out." She jerked her head toward the cabin door.

I stepped toward it then turned back. "He's a good kid, you know."

"I know he is. I think the trouble is you're rubbing off on him."

"Well, what can I say? I'm a role model."

# Chapter 6

# A Stowaway's Guide to the Galaxy

Lucas

"So, Lucas, you stowed away." Zastra's yellow eyes blinked at me slowly. "Gutsy thing to do."

I didn't know what to say to that. I couldn't tell if she was yelling at me or giving me a compliment.

"Um …"

She had taken me to the upper level of the ship, the office, which, unlike the rest of the *Shaymus*, doesn't even look like a spaceship. The office has dark green walls, wooden desks, and leather chairs.

One time Mom took me to a ritzy office in downtown Indy where she had to drop off something for a guy. The office on the *Shaymus* was just as fancy, except it didn't smell weird like that other place.

Zastra told me to sit in the chair at Gabe's desk. She took a seat in hers facing me. The whole thing was awkward, but it was better than being talked to death by Mom.

A chirp sounded from Blan across the room. "You know, Lucas. If Klistines find a stowaway, they'll toss them out an airlock … during flight."

"Hey, don't scare the boy," said Buad. He ruffled his feathers as he perched beside Blan inside their habitat. "Listen, kid, most people won't airlock you, leastwise not nowadays. But you can get yourself thrown in jail for pulling a stunt like this."

Buad and Blan look like little yellow birds, but they aren't. They're brothers from the planet Avan. Like Zastra and sometimes Gabe, the Avanians work for the Galactic Detective Agency solving crimes and such.

"Who are the Klistines?" I asked.

"Blue ridged heads. Humongous black bug eyes. A lot of teeth. You know."

"No, I don't. I don't know anything about aliens except you guys … and well, a couple of others"

Zastra said, "The point is, Lucas, you need to be careful about what alien spaceships you board. You're lucky you stowed away with us."

I flopped back in Gabe's chair. "I don't think you have to worry about me climbing on random spaceships. Aliens don't ever come to Earth. That's the trouble. That's why I had to do this. This was my only chance to go out in space again."

Zastra eyed me. "Gabe has talked about bringing you along, but it's tricky. Sometimes our cases are dangerous."

"Are you kidding?" Buad said. "They're always dangerous … especially for Gabe. Remember the time he launched himself into space?"

Blan cackled. "Oh, yeah. I'm surprised he lived to tell the story on that one."

Zastra said, "Your mom wouldn't want you to get into any kind of trouble, Lucas."

"I can keep out of trouble," I said.

"Can you? And yet here we are after you climbed aboard a spaceship through the docking port."

I didn't dare tell her the *Shaymus* was in the air at the time. I didn't need another lecture in addition to the one Mom was going to give me. "How much trouble am I in?"

Zastra shrugged. "No clue. I'm not your mom. I do know Gabe has been planning this date with your mom for some time, and you threw a wrench into it."

I let my head drop back and stared out the dome in the ceiling at the blue sky of whatever planet we were on. Not only was I in trouble, I had also messed stuff up for Mom and Gabe. They were both going to be furious with me.

Zastra said, "It doesn't do any good to dwell on it now. Let's talk about other stuff."

"Okay. Like what?"

"Anything. Do you have any questions for us?"

I had a ton of questions about space travel and planets and what their lives were like. "Do you have any kids?"

She threw back her head in a lizardy laugh that sounded like air escaping from a car tire. "Me? No way. I'm too young for egg laying. Srathans don't have offspring until we're about seventy years old."

I sat back up. "No kidding? That's like super old on Earth."

"It gives us time to live our lives first and then focus on family afterward."

"What about brothers and sisters?"

"Now those I have — hundreds of them."

"Hundreds? Really? Does everybody get their own birthday party?"

"Well, since I don't know what that is, I'm gonna say no."

"And you have parents, right?"

"Yeah, my mom commands a battalion of soldiers."

"Whoa! Cool!"

Zastra opened a drawer in her desk and pulled out a piece of polished red metal. The thing was a rectangle except for odd shapes cut out of the corners. She handed it across to me. I turned the shiny object over my hand. An emblem like a coat of arms with spears and blasters was stamped into one face.

"This is the badge for her battalion, the Krohlyan."

"This is awesome," I said.

"You can keep it."

"No! Seriously?"

"Sure. But you can't tell anybody on Earth what it is."

"Right. I understand. I'll say the badge is from some Earth army. So that's your mom. What about your dad?"

"I haven't heard from him in a while. He's somewhere out among the stars."

"Same for me. Well, not among the stars, but he just as well be." I ran a thumb across the battalion badge. "I don't even have any memories of my dad."

I had a fuzzy picture in my head from when I was little of Mom being sad and telling me everything was going to be fine, which must have been after my dad left. I guess that was kind of a memory about him, but that was it.

And Mom had been right. We were fine, just the two of us. She always said we were a team. I thought about Mom down in Gabe's cabin being mad at me for ruining their plans. Some teammate I was.

I said, "I messed stuff up good this time."

"Listen, Lucas, don't worry about it. You can hang with me while they have their date. Rheged Prime is a great place with lots of fun things to do."

"Is that where we are?"

"Yeah. Jace and Oren's home planet. Have you ever ridden in a flying car?"

"No!"

"Didn't think so. Have you ever tasted maerceci?"

"What's that?"

"I'm not sure myself. But Jace always talks about having it as a kid, so it must be good. We'll check it out."

"Maybe we ought to do it soon before my mom decides it's time to talk to me and grounds me forever."

Zastra stood. "Valid point. Let's go."

As I slid from Gabe's seat, the video screen on the front wall of the office came on. Oren Vilkas was on it.

"Hello, Lucas," Oren said. "I was unaware you would be coming along."

"I ... I wasn't supposed to."

"Oh?" The word came out super long.

Zastra said, "Long story. We were heading out to the planet to show Lucas some sights, keep him busy while Sarah and Gabe ... do what they need to do."

Oren said, "Have you forgotten the client is coming in? In fact, she is due any minute. I would like you here for the interview, Zastra."

"Oh," Zastra said. "Right. Too bad. Lucas could really use getting out for a while. But—"

Buad said, "Hey, Chief. How about I take the kid out? Anything I miss, Blan can fill me in on later."

Oren said, "That should be satisfactory."

Zastra said, "What do you think Lucas?"

I mean, walking around with a little yellow bird wouldn't be as cool as hanging out with a lizard warrior. Then again, Buad was still an alien, and that was plenty awesome.

"Sure," I said.

Buad flew out of the cage and perched on my shoulder. "Let's go, kid. I want to try some of that maerceci stuff myself."

# Chapter 7

# Blue's Clues

*Gabe*

I was back in my cabin after spending some time in the galley where I indulged in a replicated glazed donut to assuage my disappointment about the mess descending over my carefully planned date night. Sarah was with me in the cabin, dealing with her own feelings, which, whatever they were, she wasn't sharing with me.

The door dinged.

"Come in," I said, grateful for the diversion.

Zastra stared back at me from the doorway. "The client is here."

"Where's Lucas?" Sarah asked. "I thought you had him."

"He's fine. Buad is taking him out on the town. Why don't you both sit in on the interview? You have time before evening, and it will take your mind off the kid."

Sarah asked, "Is it all right with Oren if I sit in?"

"It was his idea."

Sarah pulled herself out of the chair. I popped on my fedora to feel more like an old-timey detective, and we climbed with Zastra to the office. We found the client standing there, perusing the artwork on the office walls, her hands clasped behind her back. She looked up as we entered.

Until that moment, I had envisioned our art owner client as an old man or a white-haired widow with glasses the size of safety goggles. Turned out I was as off-target as a *Star Wars* stormtrooper in a blaster fight.

She was young, slender as a flower. Her hair was a bright shade of lemon, flowing to her shoulders, a stark contrast to her blue skin. This was the first Rhegedian I had met who didn't have black hair. I think I gawked a little but quit when I noted Sarah eyeing me.

"Sorry for the delay," Zastra said. "These are our associates, Sarah Gallo and Gabriel Lake from the planet Earth. Sarah and Gabriel, this is Bella Balok."

I held out a hand. Bella grasped it with one of hers and stroked it with the other.

She caught my eye and flashed a warm smile. "Gabriel, such unusual skin. What do you call the color? Amber? Coral?"

"Coral? No, I don't think coral."

I glanced at my hopefully soon-to-be fiancée, who returned a steely gaze over the tops of her glasses. I snatched my hand away, glad that I was going home later this evening and leaving the others to deal with this one.

"You're currently turning a bit more coral," Zastra said with a smirk.

"And I love your hat, Gabriel" Bella said, gazing at the fedora. "It suits you."

"Um … thanks."

"Will Mr. Vilkas be joining us?"

"Of course," Zastra said. "Have a seat."

Zastra led Bella to one of the red leather chairs placed in front of the view screen before sitting at her desk. I perched on a corner of my desk, waving to Sarah to take my seat.

The view screen came on showing the face of Oren Vilkas. Technically, I should say *a* face of Oren Vilkas. He can choose any face he wants, though generally he goes with a slightly blue-skinned version of Dwayne "The Rock" Johnson. This time he was looking bluer than usual, probably since we were on his home planet where everybody shared his native skin tone.

"Good day, Ms. Balok. I am Oren Vilkas."

She paused for a moment, twisting her head to one side. "You are … digital?"

"I am."

"That explains it."

"Explains what?"

"I looked you up on the network. Your career spans five centuries. I wondered if perhaps Oren Vilkas was some sort of title passed from detective to detective."

Oren made a slight bow with his head. "I assure you I am the only one who has ever been. A little more than four hundred and twenty years ago, I was a living and breathing Rhegedian like yourself. However, on the verge of my death I had my consciousness uploaded to circuitry."

"A bold move."

"Indeed, but I preferred living digitally to dying."

"Have you been happy with the decision?"

"Obviously, I have. Were I not, I would not still be here. I admit there are many things about a corporeal existence I miss — the savor of food, the touch of another person. Of course, I wouldn't have those things if I were dead either. All those losses are more than amply compensated for by a vibrant mental life. But perhaps we should turn our attention to business. Tell me about this painting that was stolen."

"Yes. It is the *Self-Portrait* by Pollock Cormabite. The artwork has been in my family for generations."

"Indeed! I have seen images of her *Self-Portrait*, but I don't believe I have ever seen it in person."

"You wouldn't. The painting has always been in private hands, never in a museum."

"It's value?"

"It is the only self-portrait — or any kind of portrait — of Cormabite. And one of the few paintings from what is known as her green period. It must be worth millions. But, of course, the sentimental value to me is beyond measure. I remember it from my childhood, my grandfather gazing at it for what seemed like hours. He told me he could almost glimpse in it the soul of the celebrated artist."

Oren closed his eyes. "Ah, yes. Great art can have that effect. Tell me about how the painting was stolen. When and how did it happen?"

"Two days ago I was away from Tikal for an overnight trip. Someone broke in and stole it."

"This was at your home?"

"Yes."

"Are you positive it happened that night?"

"Of course. I was gone for only the one night."

"Is it possible the painting was taken at an earlier time, but you failed to notice?"

"I would have spotted it. The staff would have as well."

"Of course. Was anyone in the house at the time of the robbery?"

"No. The servants were either with me or sent away for the night."

"What staff do you have?"

"A maid, a driver, a chef, and my assistant-slash-publicist."

"We should interview them," Zastra said. She held up an electronic device. "Can you give me their addresses?"

Bella pulled out a device of her own and tapped it a few times. A *ding* sounded on both gadgets.

Oren asked, "Does the house have a security system?"

"It does. Somehow it had gotten switched off. I assume the thieves must have worked out the code."

"Or obtained it from one of your employees."

"I am the only one who knows the passphrase. I set the system myself every night and turn it off every morning."

"Do you remember setting the security system before you left on the night of the robbery?"

"Yes, I do."

"You said thieves. Do you have reason to suspect there was more than one thief involved?"

Her head jerked up. "Why, no. No reason. I suppose it was more of an assumption. The robbery simply seemed like the sort of undertaking that would require more than one person. As in one for the security system, one for the actual theft, one as a getaway pilot. Something along those lines."

"You may be right. Though if the thief had all night and there was no one around …" Oren let the statement finish itself. "Tell me, is your home isolated?"

"Somewhat. I have neighbors, but the tracts are … spacious."

"And how many people knew you owned the painting and were cognizant of its value?"

Bella crossed her legs. "It hung in one of the public rooms. I am a firm believer that great art should be displayed and enjoyed. I also believe in entertaining. Thousands of people would have seen it over the years. As to how many were aware of its value, it is difficult to say. Certainly, art critics and collectors would know."

"And art critics and collectors have been in attendance at your parties?"

"Oh, yes."

"Have the sentries examined the crime scene?"

I whispered the word sentries to Zastra as a question. She muttered the word police back to me.

Bella shook her head. "No. I called you instead."

"Why not the sentries? I am sure you understand my services come at a price."

"Yes, a high price." Her eyes were earnest, focused on Oren. "Three reasons. First, these thieves are intelligent. I do not believe they will be apprehended by sentries, who are competent but plodding and unaccustomed to this type of crime. It will require a genius, such as yourself. Second, I heard about another painting you once recovered, a Dolly. And third, as to your fee, I'm sure whatever you charge is bound to be trivial compared to the value of the painting."

Oren showed no reaction to the mention of his fees, which normally were anything but trivial. "I am surprised you learned about the Dolly. The story was kept hush-hush at the request of the client. In any event, if the sentries have not been there, then our first concern is to have my operatives examine the crime scene. It is getting late today. If it is convenient, I will send them in the morning. Now, turning to the next topic, is there anyone you suspect of having taken the painting?"

"No."

"Not any of the people who came to your parties?"

"No. Certainly not any of my friends."

"But …" He let it hang.

Bella was silent a few moments. "But an art collector friend of mine, Dun Luce, had an assistant named Mot Vagis. I never trusted this Vagis."

"You said he *had* Vagis as an assistant? Past tense?"

"As I understand it, Vagis has now disappeared."

"Since the theft?"

"That's what he told me when I talked to him about the robbery."

"That is certainly suggestive," Oren said. "We will want to pay a visit to Dun Luce to ask about Mot Vagis. Who else should we talk to? Who would possess the knowledge of how to fence a painting of this value?"

"You might talk to Trub Nurke. He owns a prestigious art gallery."

"Anyone else?"

"The other well-known art collector in town is Udra Danril."

"He is a friend of yours?"

"I don't think he has friends."

"What else can you tell me about these people?"

"Hmm. How to describe them? Mot Vagis is more or less my age. Intelligent. Scheming, I would say. Or that was the impression I got. The other men are all older. Dune Luce is fun to be around. Loves art. Loves food, which shows." She cradled her hands out several inches in front of her tummy.

"Trub Nurke is my advisor in all things art related and has been for years. His gallery is top-notch. He has a skilled eye for art. Udra Danril I mainly know by reputation. I understand he has an impressive collection and an equally prickly personality."

Oren looked around the office. "Does anyone else have a question?"

"I do," said Blan from the habitat.

With a start, Bella whipped her head in that direction. "Oh! I'm sorry. I didn't see you there."

Blan said, "Understandable. I'm not gigantic like the others, and that gives me an advantage. I can tail a suspect without the guy ever seeing me. Anyway, my question. Do you have any family?"

She answered in a monotone. "No. I was an only child, and my parents are both gone."

"Our condolences," Oren said.

"It was a long time ago."

"Any other questions?" Oren said.

There were no takers.

"Well, thank you, Ms. Balok. You have given us more than enough to begin the investigation. Expect my operatives tomorrow."

Bella Balok rose. "Thank you, Mr. Vilkas. It has been a pleasure meeting you and seeing your ship. I look forward to putting this unpleasantness behind me."

Zastra stood and said, "Deploy stairs."

The staircase *whirred* out from the side of the central shaft, and Zastra escorted our guest out.

I turned to Oren. "What do you think?"

"It is an interesting case. What do you think of our client?"

I said, "She seems awfully young to own a painting worth a fortune. But I suppose that's old money for you. Clearly the loss is weighing on her."

Sarah gawped at me as if I had proposed drying the dishes, not with a dish towel, but by rubbing them down with the family cat. "What? Are you telling me you believed all that baloney?"

# Chapter 8

# Cliff Hanger

*Gabe*

I looked at Sarah and blinked. "Baloney? You mean you don't believe Bella?"

"She's hiding something. I don't know what, but she is."

Over the years I'd known her and the time we had dated, I had come to trust Sarah's intuitive insight into people. She seemed to be able to read my friends better in five minutes than I had in five months. Still, this was our client, the person paying for our time, and we had to give Bella the benefit of the doubt, right? Or was this about something else?

"Is this because she stroked my hand?"

Sarah's eyes flashed. "No, that's another thing altogether. And the flirting with you. Babe, you're cute and all, but ..." She didn't finish the sentence.

"But what? What are you saying here? I'm not flirt-worthy?" I knew the moment I said it that the comment would come back to haunt me. It didn't take long.

From his habitat, Blan cackled. "Aw, sure you're flirt-worthy, doofus. Some people like goofy-looking nitwits."

For reasons which I never understood Blan and Buad loved to make fun of me every chance they could. I ignored him and turned back to Sarah.

With a smirk on her face, she lowered her voice and in breathy tones said, "I love your hat, Gabriel."

Great! Now everybody was riding my case. "Hey, it's a nice hat."

"All I'm saying is the flirting was a smokescreen for something she's hiding."

I turned to Oren who had been watching all this with an amused expression. "Did you think Bella was lying?"

"I always proceed on the assumption that everyone lies or at the minimum withholds information."

"Well, that certainly makes things more interesting. Be sure to tell me how it all turns out. It's about time for Sarah and I to go on our date."

"Yes, have a wonderful time." The view screen switched off.

"Are we okay?" I asked my date.

She answered in the breathy voice. "Such unusual skin."

Blan chortled in delight.

"All right," I said. "Enough. Are you ready to go?"

"I'd like to have my talk with Lucas first."

Blan said, "I think he's still out with Buad."

She pushed her lips to one side in that adorable way she does when she's thinking. "Right. Maybe it's better this way. Let's do it."

We descended the steps to the crew deck and walked to the galley to prepare the picnic basket. An egg-shaped capsule with a carrying strap sat on the counter beside a folded blanket where I had placed them earlier. I dug a piece of paper from my pocket with a list of goodies I planned to make with the replicator, a few of which I had newly programmed that afternoon.

I stepped to the replicator panel. "One baguette. A dish of Maltese mingo fruit. Three ounces of Dubliner cheese, sliced. A bottle of Bononian light wine. Two Rhegedian crimsaw salads."

The magic food machine went to work, fetching the molecular recipes from its database, and creating the dishes out of a supply of quarks and electrons — the building blocks of all matter — that it keeps on hand. The food materialized on the counter, and I loaded each item into the capsule.

"You've sampled all these things?" Sarah asked.

"Not the salad, but it looks good, right?"

Blan flew in. "Can I use the replicator?" I waived permission. He said, "One seed cake."

A hockey puck of pressed seeds came into being. Blan picked it up in his talons and hovered midair. "I'll leave you guys to it. Good luck, Gabe."

"Thanks," I said, impressed by the atypical lack of sarcasm on his part.

"Though I still think she's way too smart to fall for it." There it was. With a hoot, Blan flew out.

"What was that all about?" Sarah asked. "Who's too smart for what?"

"Never mind. He's only squawking. All right, I think I have everything."

"What about a bottle opener?"

"Right. Replicator, one Bononian wine opener, please."

It appeared on the counter, and I dropped it into the carrying capsule.

"Anything else?" I asked.

"Are you planning to drink from the bottle?"

"Ah. Replicator, two wine glasses."

They came out as real glass with delicate stems. I loaded them gently into the capsule along with the blanket, and we made our way down the ramp out the *Shaymus* to an alien city street.

Most buildings were two or three stories, mixed with towers stretching to the sky. Many of the structures took shapes unusual to Earth eyes — pyramids, cones, zigzags, rooflines like parabolic waves, double-helix towers. It was as if Dr. Seuss served as city architect.

The skies were alive with flying cars, transport planes, and a steady stream of drones doing who knows what. A blue sun hung low in the sky, the evening light bathing everything in shades of indigo.

All the street signs were written in an alien script that looked like a cross between hieroglyphics and Tetris screenshots. Here's the deal, though. If I stared at any sign for a second or two, the letters would start swimming around to rearrange themselves for me in English. That was another feature of translator bots. Not only did they attach to my auditory cortex so I could understand alien speech. They also attached to my visual cortex to translate alien text. Cool, huh?

Because of that, I knew the sign we stood under a few minutes later said: *Pod Shuttle*. That was what Jace had told me to look for. Across the street I glimpsed a person staring at us. The sun was in my eyes, preventing me from getting a good look, but this was definitely not a Rhegedian. The person was covered in golden fur, not blue skin. I know Sarah and I looked out of place on this planet, but no more than that guy. Why stare at us?

A giant yellow drone with a pod cockpit in the middle dropped out of the sky in front of us. Four black arms extended from the base of the pod in an X-shape, a rotor spinning at the end of each arm.

Sarah grabbed my arm and took a step back. "Don't get too close to those things."

"It has to be safe," I said. "C'mon." Even so, I inched my way gingerly forward, side-stepping between the blades toward the open gull-wing door. Inside were two seats.

Sarah followed me into the cockpit. We were the only people inside.

"Who's flying this thing?" she asked.

"Good question. Surely not us."

"Destination, please."

My head bobbed to and fro. "Who said that?"

"Destination, please."

"I think it was the pod," Sarah said.

"Self-flying, huh? Hmm. Well, like I said, it must be safe, right? Jace told me to take it." I said, "Take us to the Mount Shaymus cliff edge."

"Insert payment stick, please."

I pulled the tube out of my pocket and inserted it into a slot near the seats.

"Prepare for take-off," the pod said.

I was half turned in my seat, searching for a seat belt of some kind, when the pod leaped into the sky. The force of the liftoff nearly slid us both out of the seats. Sarah grabbed my knee in a death grip.

We shot up to about the height of a four-story building, then blasted forward, the drone tilting forward to where we were hanging onto the seats while staring down at the ground rushing past us. Sarah screamed. I couldn't tell if it was the exhilarating scream of a roller coaster ride or the terrified scream of an impending plane crash.

"Hey, Pod Shuttle!" I said. "Can we make this ride, I don't know, more leisurely?"

The pod responded by starting to swoop through the air in huge S-curves, left and right while simultaneously bobbing up and down. It was like being in a World War One aerial dogfight. My head began swimming. I wondered who could possibly think of this as leisure.

"Not this!" I yelled. "Slow this thing down. Fly straight … and easy."

The pod straightened out and reduced its speed.

I sat back in the seat, heaving breaths. "Jane, stop this crazy thing."

"See," Sarah said. "Like *The Jetsons*."

We flew on, passing over fields and forestland. In one field a platoon of smaller drones flew through rows of vines, harvesting what appeared to be a kind of large, pale grape the size of golf balls. We skimmed the treetops and watched colorful birds take flight.

The pod landed in a meadow near a dark rock outcropping. As we stepped out, I gave the crazy aircraft instructions to return in a couple of hours. The pod buzzed off, and we were left with the scent of the sea and the cries of seabirds sounding on the air.

A gust of warm wind whipped at Sarah's hair and nearly blew the fedora from my head. Keeping a grip on my hat, I one-handedly set to work unloading our supplies from the capsule. Sarah spread the blanket, and it was a picnic.

The view was amazing. The grassy clifftop at our feet. Dark sheer cliffs curving around the bend of the cove. The thin strip of sandy beach far below with waves crashing on it. Even so I found it difficult to pull my eyes away from my date.

I opened the wine and poured us glasses. "To us."

She raised her glass. "To us."

We tucked into the bread, the cheese, the salad while the scenery of Rheged Prime put on a show just for us.

We chatted about work projects, the weather here and at home, people we knew. We gazed at the birds and the small furry creatures who hopped through the grass near us.

"What's that?" Sarah pointed along the cliff toward a patch of blue wildflowers. Bubbles were rising from the blooms and floating away in the breeze.

We scrambled to our feet and hurried over to take a closer look. The bubbles shot out with a barely audible *pop*. I managed to catch one on the tip of my finger. It glistened like a soap bubble, a tiny black dot of something suspended inside.

"This must be how they spread their seeds," Sarah said. "They must make the bubbles somehow from water they take in plus some chemical."

I picked a flower and handed it to her as we strolled back to the blanket. "Here. To remember this evening."

The sapphire sun dipped toward the distant waves, turning the sky cobalt, the water a sea of ink. Somewhere out over the waves the silhouette of a bird with four wings flew across the setting sun.

I took a sip of wine and a deep breath. Now, if ever, was the time to find out if she was willing to have and to hold. My hand moved to my jacket pocket to reassure myself that the ring was still there.

"Sarah?"

She turned to me, the evening light coloring her skin nearly as blue as a Rhegedian.

"Having a good time?"

"This has been wonderful, Gabe. Such a beautiful place."

"I'm glad. I wanted to talk—"

She cut me off. "Of course, my son is wandering around a strange alien world with a little yellow bird as a babysitter instead of being home in his bed with a responsible human in charge of him."

"Well … How about we don't think about that right now?"

"Easy for you to say."

"Um. Right." I took her hand in mine. "You look fantastic tonight." It came out like a weird non-sequitur.

"Thanks?"

The inflection in her voice threw me. Had I said something wrong? "Not … not that you don't always look great. I'm not saying that. I mean … Well, what I'm trying to say is … um … I've grown close to you since we started dating … and to Lucas too … yeah, he's amazing. Well, even before we started dating really. I mean, we're almost like a family."

With her free hand she reached into the bowl for a handful of fruit and began popping them one-at-a-time into her mouth. "Ooh! These Maltese fruits are delicious. I can't stop eating them. Maybe we should have gone to that planet."

"Well, Malt hasn't had an atmosphere for five thousand years, so we would have to wear spacesuits. Although there is a nice hotel there where a robot pal of mine works. But that's not important right now. What I'm trying to say is—"

"This cheese is awesome too. You say this is Earth cheese? I'm going to have to check it out at the store."

"What I'm trying to say, Sarah, is I'm ready for our relationship to … um—"

Buad's voice cut in over our translator bot connection. "Hey, Gabe, Sarah."

I squeezed my eyes shut. "What is it, Buad?"

"Yeah, well … I … um … I don't know how to say this. I can't find Lucas."

# Chapter 9

# The Occasion of the Body Snatchers

*Lucas*

"Well, Lucas," Buad said, "welcome to Rheged Prime."

I was walking through the streets. And I mean *in* the streets. Blue people were walking and riding two-wheeled scooters right beside hover cars and other vehicles going every which way. Everybody just went around or over everybody else. A monorail skimmed overhead. Talk about strange new worlds.

"So what do you want to do, kid?"

"Beats me." It was all so weird and different that it was hard to even focus. "What do you think?"

"What I like to do first thing when I get to a new planet is check out the worms."

"Ooh! Gross!"

Buad bobbed his head and laughed in a high-pitched chirp. "Eh, I was only messing with you. I know worms ain't for everybody."

"I guess they're okay for birds."

"Hey, watch it. I ain't a bird, got it? I'm a winged person."

"Sorry."

"You know, you can learn a lot about a world from their creepy crawlies. Now take the worms you have on Earth — fat and juicy. That's 'cause your planet has a lot of good soil. On the other hand, Sratha is mainly rock and sand and scrubby plants. Their worms are stringy and scrawny. Plus you gotta be careful going for them lest a boasaur grabs you."

"What's a boasaur?"

"A reptile. Huge teeth. Like one of your crocogaters."

"You mean crocodiles?"

"Yeah, yeah, that's what you call 'em. But with about fifty tiny legs on a super long body. Those guys are humongous, like longer than the *Shaymus*, if you can believe it. They burrow in the sand with only their three eyes sticking out and jump out at you."

"Is there anything like that here?"

"Nah. This here is a safe planet … mostly. Hey, I got an idea. Wanna fly like me?"

"Um …"

"Fly kinda like me, I mean. Don't worry. It's nothin' your mom would call unsafe. Leastwise, I don't think so."

I nodded with no idea of what he was talking about.

"I think the place is a few blocks from here. Wanna take the monorail?"

"Sure."

We found a set of stairs up to the monorail platform. While I climbed, Buad flew to the top. As I was passing the second landing, he flew back down to check on me.

"How're ya doin'?"

"I'm getting there. Sorry I can't fly."

"No problem. You're gonna fly, and you're gonna love it."

Buad flew back up and had the tickets purchased by the time I reached the platform. A minute later a white train with a red stripe running along the side pulled up with a *whoosh*. We stepped inside one of the cars. Only one other person was on board, a guy reading from a tablet who never looked up. I took a seat, and Buad perched on the armrest beside me.

"How come nobody else is riding?" I asked.

"Beats me. I guess people like hover taxis better. Jace told me the monorail was kind of a boondoggle. Some fast-talking salesperson in a straw hat breezed into town and sold them on the scheme with a catchy song."

A voice sounded over the speaker, "All aboard!" With a lurch, the monorail pulled out.

The ride was great. We looked down on the city as it whizzed below us. Every few blocks, the train stopped, the doors opened, and nobody got on. Then it would start again and go another few blocks. I don't know why more people weren't riding. I loved it.

Finally, we reached the station Buad wanted. We left the car and climbed down into a park. The trees all looked like umbrellas. Branches of yellow leaves were bunched at the top in neat circles with skinny trunks sticking down to the ground.

I pointed at something on one of the trunks. "What's that?"

"A tree."

"No. The animal climbing the tree." While we watched, the creature slithered up and around the trunk another inch. It was long and furry like a ferret, but it had no legs.

"Oh. That's a … a whatchamacallit, a legless mammal."

"It's called a whatchamacallit?"

He waved a wing. "Nah. But I can't remember its name. I can't be expected to remember the moniker for every species on every planet, can I? Hey, here's the place. Right over here."

Buad flew to a group of blue people clustered around a yellow bird — or a winged person — like him, who was standing on a table.

The winged guy said to the crowd, "Step on up. Listen, folks, here's your chance to soar like an Avanian. Feel what it's like to fly. No wings? No problem."

Behind the table, three other Avanians were strapping about a dozen drone rotors to the arms and legs of a Rhegedian woman. When they got the rotors secured, they flew back, and one of them said, "Right. Let 'er rip."

The drones started up with a buzz and the woman began rising into the air. At first, she waved her arms around while she struggled to find her balance. Then, as she steadied herself, the rotors lifted her above everyone's head.

"Whoa," I said.

"Neat, huh?" Buad said.

The woman hung midair. Then slowly one of her legs floated out in front of her. She stared at it a few moments before jerking it back. Immediately she flipped upside down. She thrashed around trying to right herself but only ended up somersaulting through the air. The Avanians flew in and brought her down while the crowd applauded. The woman wobbled to her feet and wandered off.

"As you can see with your own eyes," the Avanian on the table said, "it's tremendous fun. Who's next?"

Buad said, "You ready?"

I flashed a cautious thumbs up. Buad paid using a tube he had tied to one leg while the other Avanians attached the rotors to me.

"So, kid," one Avanian said, "when it starts up, try not to tense. Stay loose, and let the rotors do the work."

I nodded. "Stay loose."

They finished strapping me up and started the drones. I tried staying loose, but it was easier said than done. First, my arms rose above my head. Then my legs began lifting. I had to fight the urge to keep my feet on the ground. As my arms and legs went up, the middle of me sagged between them. I must have looked like a sloth hanging from a tree branch.

"How do I straighten up?"

An Avanian called, "Spread your wings. I mean, your arms."

I widened my arms and got myself to a sitting position. The heads of the people in the crowd were now below my feet.

Buad yelled, "You're doing great kid! Try standing. Push down with your legs."

All that did was flip me upside down. "Oops! Help!"

The Avanians swarmed around me and helped me back to the ground. The crowd again burst into applause.

"What did you think?" Buad asked when they had freed me from the propellers.

"It was a blast. I bet with some practice I could really fly."

"Absolutely. There are some wingless people who can use those things to zoom around like a hover car … but without the car."

We walked through the park with Buad perched on my shoulder. He explained stuff to me about Rheged Prime and other planets he had visited.

"What's it like on your home world?" I asked.

"Oh, Avan is beautiful. A great place to nest. The weather is warm most of the time. Trees everywhere."

"Do all the species there fly?"

"Nah. Only the smart ones. We have bugs and worms that crawl around."

"So you eat them, the bugs and worms?"

"Some of them. We also use food replicators."

"I don't think I'd like eating bugs."

Buad shrugged his wings. "You never know. I like some of the Earthling food Gabe programmed into the ship's replicator. Waffles are good."

"Waffles are awesome. When we get back, can I have a waffle?"

"I'm not gonna tell ya no. Speaking of, it's probably about time we returned to roost. It's getting dark."

"What about this maerceci stuff Zastra was talking about?" I was starting to feel hungry, and I wasn't ready to go back to the ship.

"Oh, yeah. I almost forgot. There ought to be a place around here somewhere selling it. You wait here." Buad launched into the air and soared off over the park.

I wandered over to a line of white pods with benches and view screens. They must have been like phones or something because a guy was sitting in one and talking to somebody who wasn't there.

I sat down in the next pod and leaned against the screen. Out on the grass, some kids about my age were playing a kicking game with a mammoth ball the size of small car. It would have been fun to play with them, but I didn't go over. I didn't know them or the rules. Two moons hung in the sky. They glowed a light purple like the lilac bush in my grandma's yard.

"I still haven't gotten a lead on him." The voice came from the next pod. The guy paused for a reply from the other end, which I couldn't hear. "Yeah, I checked with everyone who fences anything like it." Another pause. "No, his place is empty." Another pause. "I already asked at the spaceport. No sign of him leaving. He must still be on the planet somewhere." A longer pause. "Yeah. Yeah. So when I find him and recover the merchandise, and I will, what should I do with him?" Pause. "Oh, I can get him to talk all right. And then?" A short pause followed by the guy lowering his voice. "Fine, he'll disappear where nobody will ever find him."

A *beep* sounded from the other pod followed by noises of the guy standing up. He stepped away from the pod. He was tall, bulky, bigger than Jace or Gabe or Zastra. The guy was so ginormous he totally blocked my view of the kids playing ball.

He turned around like he had forgotten something and saw me. One side of his blue scalp was shaved. Three computer chips stuck out of the bald skin. The eye on the other side was covered by a mechanical black eyepiece. An eerie red light shone out of it.

His regular eye narrowed as it focused on me. "Now what did you overhear?"

I don't think I could have answered even if I had wanted to. And I didn't want to. I didn't want to let on like I had heard anything.

The guy reached in a pocket and pulled out a stubby red tube, like a piece of sidewalk chalk except it had buttons running down the side. He held it out toward me, and for a second, I thought he was handing it to me. But he wasn't.

He said, "Well, we can't let you contact anybody."

I shrank back into the pod as he pressed one of the buttons on the tube thingy. A ringing clanged in my ears like I was standing inside a gonging bell.

When at last the noise stopped, the guy said, "Anors sligaman ar aquso." Or something like that.

He lunged at me, grabbed me by the waist, and picked me up like a suitcase.

"Buad! Buad! Help! Somebody!"

He placed a hand over my mouth and started walking off into the twilight.

# Chapter 10

# Not the Evening Any of Us had Envisioned

*Gabe*

"You what!" Sarah's voice was sharp, harsh. I was glad she wasn't talking to me.

"Look," Buad said over the translator bot connection. "The kid wanted to try maerceci. I flew up to try to spot a stand selling it. When I came down he was gone."

"How could you leave him alone like that? He's a little boy!"

"I wouldn't say little. He's bigger than me."

"He's a child! Did you tell him to stay where he was?"

"Yeah! Sure I did!"

"Then that's what he would have done. Somebody must have grabbed him."

I thought, yeah, like he stayed in the house. I said, "But why would somebody …" I stopped, realizing the why wasn't currently relevant. "Buad, did you call him over the translator bot connection?"

"I tried, but he didn't answer."

Sarah gripped my arm. "What does that mean? You don't think—"

Buad cut in. "Don't jump to conclusions. Those bots sometimes fail. Or maybe he needs to stay quiet for some reason. Or certain kinds of energy weapons can temporarily knock out translator bots."

Sarah said, "Weapons? Lucas. Lucas, can you hear me?"

There was no answer. She glanced at me wide-eyed.

I said, "Buad, where are you?"

"Meeko Park."

"We're on our way. The flying pod thing we took out here won't be back for a while, but there's a monorail station near here, right?"

"Beats me. I don't know public transportation. I fly everywhere."

Sarah let out an exasperated yell.

"Jace," I said.

Jace's voice came through the connection. "Hey, Gabe, I didn't expect to hear from you. How did ... you know ... how did it go?"

"It didn't. Lucas is missing."

"What? Oh, no! What happened?"

"We don't know yet. We're out by the cliffs. Do they have a monorail station around here?"

"Um ... Yeah. Yeah. Head inland from the cliff. It's not far as I recall."

"Got it. Get Zastra and Blan and meet us at the park."

"Which park? Gabe, which park?"

I left it to Buad to answer him as we gathered the picnic supplies in our arms and ran up the hill. At the crest we spotted the station off to the left and dashed toward it. In the darkening evening, the light from the ticket booth shined out toward us. Inside was a Rhegedian wearing a green uniform and a cap shaped like a tambourine.

We rushed to the booth. "When is the next monorail into the city. Meeker Park," I said.

"Don't know any Meeker Park," the ticket agent said.

"Meeko," Sarah said. "Meeko Park."

The ticket agent eyeballed us, then turned to an electronic device, which he tapped. "Next train is leaving in five minutes."

I might mention — for the sake of accuracy and also to slow things down a bit and build the tension even more — that another feature of translator bots is how they translate all units of measure into the hearer's native measurement systems. So while the ticket agent might have said seventeen widgetseconds or however they measure time on Rheged Prime, five minutes was what Sarah and I heard.

"Does that train go to Meeko Park?" Sarah asked.

"Uh-huh."

"Two tickets," I said.

"Single ticket or return?"

"Two tickets. I want two tickets."

"Right. Single or return?"

"What? Oh. I mean, just to there. One way."

"Two single tickets. Twelve bills."

I patted my pockets for the payment stick. I couldn't find it. My head went dizzy, and I felt like I was back in the pod again doing loop-de-loops, which, come to think of it, is probably where it fell out.

"I can't find it. Sarah, check the picnic capsule. Did I lose it in the pod thing?"

Sarah tore everything out of the capsule while I patted my pockets over and over again. A *whoosh* sounded behind us as the monorail pulled into the station — our monorail, that is if we could ever buy the tickets.

"Can I charge them to Oren Vilkas?"

"Don't you have a payment stick?" the ticket guy asked.

"I can't find it."

"Well, let me check." He turned back to the device and started tapping, tapping.

Passengers who had been waiting for the train began to board. Sarah started pacing back and forth. The ticket guy kept tapping and tapping.

"This is an emergency," I said, trying to hurry the guy along. "Her son has disappeared."

The ticket agent stopped tapping, which did nothing for my blood pressure, and turned eyes toward Sarah. "That certainly is terrible. I hope you find him."

With a shaking hand, Sarah made a hurry up gesture. "If you can get us on the train … Please."

The ticket agent blinked, then shook it off and went back to tapping on the device. "You say the name was Orson what now?"

Pressure pounded in my ears. "Oren. Vilkas."

Sarah let out a little high-pitched squeak.

I turned to her. "Go try to hold the train … or talk your way on it. I'll see about getting this sorted."

She grabbed up the remains of the picnic supplies and dashed off toward the platform.

The ticket agent looked back at me with a furrowed brow. "I'm sorry. I don't find any Oren Vilkas in the system."

"But … but surely there's something you can do. This is an emergency. I thrust my hand into the jacket pocket with the engagement ring, ready to barter it away, if I had to, in exchange for the tickets. My finger brushed against the payment stick. I yanked it out and handed it across. Two tickets ejected from a slot, and I ran headlong toward the train.

We huddled together in silence on the stiff vinyl seat as the monorail hummed along. Gone was the casual chatting from earlier.

A sign above us on the wall listed all the stops. I spotted the one that said Meeko, staring at it as if it might disappear should I turn away. The stops lit up on the sign as we approached each one. At last, Meeko lit.

We scrambled out of the car and down a set of stairs to the park. Jace and Zastra met us.

"Anything?" I asked.

"We've called the sentries," Jace said. "Buad and Blan are circling the park. Zastra and I have been asking people if they saw anything."

"Did anyone?" Sarah asked.

Zastra said, "Some kids playing body ball say they saw a beige kid being carried off."

"Carried off? No. No. No."

"Don't worry. We'll track the guy … somehow."

I asked, "Did you get a description of the … the person who took him?"

"Rhegedian. Good-sized guy."

"Do we know which way they went?"

Jace shook his head.

"Do we have any idea why a Rhegedian would kidnap Lucas?" I knew of another species, Thomians, who would kidnap people for the slave trade, but I didn't want to say it in front of Sarah.

"No," Zastra said.

"Excuse me," came a voice from behind us. We turned to find a tall, square jawed Rhegedian with a hawk-like nose and bushy eyebrows. Over a dark suit he wore a pineapple yellow, belted trench coat with a matching hat. The headgear resembled my fedora except it was taller, more like a cowboy's ten-gallon hat. With one arm he brushed back the trench coat, resting a fist on his hip. "Hello, folks. I'm Detective Tracy of the Rheged Prime Sentry Service. Are you the people looking for the missing alien?"

Sarah said, "My son. A boy. Lucas."

"I'm so sorry," Tracy said. "And your names are?"

"This is Sarah Gallo. I'm Gabriel Lake. He's an Earthling. Looks like us but not as tall." I held my hand at about chest level.

"Tell me what happened." Tracy raised his arm and tapped on a device attached to his wrist. A pop-up display appeared in the air above it.

Sarah said, "He was grabbed by someone, a large Rhegedian according to some kids who were playing nearby."

"Rhegedian Primer," Jace said.

"What?" Sarah asked. "I thought they were just called Rhegedians?"

I said, "There are other species on Rheged Minor. Little furry guys and people with eight legs."

Sarah stared at me as if she were trying to take it in and failing to with everything else going on.

"Were you with him at the time, ma'am?" Tracy asked.

"No. He was with an Avanian, though he had flown up into the air."

"Which one flew?"

"What?" Sarah asked.

I said, "The Avanian. Our species can't fly."

"Where is this Avanian now?" Tracy asked.

Zastra said, "Back up overhead looking for the boy."

"I'll need to speak to him."

A knot of half a dozen or so people was starting to gather around and rubberneck at us. Some pointed at Tracy and whispered to each other.

The detective raised a hand to acknowledge them. "Good evening, good citizens. There has been a kidnapping of a small alien boy." Murmurs swept around the group. "If any of you saw anything, my sentries would like to take your statement." The people all shook their heads and started to move off.

Tracy turned back to us. "Unfortunately, most people have gone home already. Tomorrow I'll send more sentries out to canvass anybody who shows up here. Hopefully, they'll find someone who was here this evening and saw something."

"That's it?" Sarah asked. "You can't do anything tonight?"

Tracy knitted his brows. "What can I do? Walk around and interrogate every large person in the city?" He placed a hand on Sarah's shoulder. "Don't worry. We're on this."

Which was precisely what I had told clients sometimes, even times when we didn't have a clue what had happened.

"How can I contact you?" Tracy asked.

Zastra handed him a card. "Contact our ship, the *Shaymus*."

"That's the name of Oren Vilkas's ship, isn't it?"

"Yeah."

"So you are all—"

"Right," I said. "The Galactic Detective Agency."

"Interesting." Tracy stuck the card in a pocket. "You folks try to get some rest and leave the investigation to us. Oh. What about the Avanian? I should talk to him tonight."

Zastra said over the translator bot connection, "Buad, come on down here. The sentry wants to get your story."

"Detective Tracy," I said, "Um … Rhegedians have first and last names, right? I'm wondering. What's your first name … if you don't mind me asking?"

"Gabe," Sarah said with a warning tone.

"In case we want to contact you."

"Not a problem. My given name is Dak."

"It is? Dak Tracy? Dak Tracy? Wow!"

"Gabe." Sarah's expression was not a happy one.

"That's right," said Tracy. "Is there a problem with my name?"

"No. No," I said. "Great name. One I'm not likely to forget."

Buad landed on the shoulder of Tracy's yellow trench coat. He directed a guilty glance at Sarah and said, "Sorry."

All she did was stare at him.

"So whatcha need, detective?" Buad asked.

Tracy nodded a goodbye to us and walked off talking to Buad.

I turned to Sarah, "It appears we aren't heading back to Earth anytime soon. At least with the chrono drive we can stay here as long as it takes and still return to Earth tonight like we planned."

Sarah made a face. "Is that supposed to be a comfort to me or something?"

"No, I …" I stopped talking to keep myself from saying anything else stupid. I put an arm around her shoulder.

She leaned into me for about two seconds before shaking me off. "So what are we doing?"

"Doing?"

"I'm certainly not going to sleep tonight. We might as well do something. Investigate."

"Well …"

Zastra said, "She's right. Let's hit the streets. It's only been an hour since Lucas was grabbed. We might get lucky and find somebody who saw something. Jace and I will go up this way. You two head in the other direction. I'll keep Blan in the sky."

What a spectacular evening this was turning out to be.

# Chapter 11

# Room and Bored

*Lucas*

I struggled to get away from the big blue guy, but he had hold of me tight. He smirked down at me as he kept walking further and further from the park. We passed other blue-skinned people, but they all glanced at us like it was perfectly normal for a guy to be carrying a kid around under his arm. Some even smiled at us.

With his hand over my mouth I couldn't yell for help. I tried to bite a finger but couldn't reach any with my teeth. I spit in hopes it would make him pull his hand away. But he didn't, and I just ended up with my own spit all over my face. Soooo gross!

We walked like that through the darkness until we came to a small house in a street full of small houses. Inside, he tossed me to the floor in a dark room, walked out, and closed the door behind him. The room was as pitch black as a closet. I groped my way to the door and felt for a knob. All I found was a lever, and it didn't move. I was locked in. I moved to a corner of the room and dropped to the floor.

If I hadn't stowed away on the *Shaymus*, I would have been home then watching a movie with Jenna and eating pepperoni pizza. But I did stow away, and here I was sitting on a hard floor in a black room all alone on an alien planet.

I whispered to myself. "They will find me. Mom won't stop looking for me. It will be okay."

I wondered if my mom even knew I had been kidnapped. She was already mad at me. If she thought I had run off from Buad, she was liable to ground me for life.

Was she right now out searching for me? Was she crying because I was missing? I remembered seeing her cry only one time. It was when I had fallen out

54

of a tree. I wasn't hurt or anything, but she said it scared her. I shook the memory out of my head, blinking away my own tears and trying to focus on something else.

"Gabe always says Oren Vilkas is the greatest detective in the galaxy. He'll find me … somehow."

But how? Nobody had paid attention when I was kidnapped. I had no idea where I was. I couldn't even understand what anyone was saying anymore.

It felt like I was going to puke. But I figured this guy wouldn't clean it up, so I forced myself not to. I shut my eyes and did math problems in my head until I calmed down.

I must have fallen asleep because the next thing I knew, sounds jerked me awake. Voices filtered in from the other room. My room was still dark, but now a band of light beamed in under the door. Also, now I could understand what the voices were saying.

"You did what?" asked a voice. The tone was sharp like a question from a mean teacher.

"I grabbed him." This was the voice of the guy who grabbed me. Well, duh! That's what he just said.

"Some alien, you say."

"Yeah. Small one."

"What species?"

"Dunno. None I ever saw before. Looked like a Primer only shorter and skin the color of cheese."

Cheese, I thought? Seriously? I don't look like cheese.

"This makes things considerably more complicated. Now we have to get rid of it."

I didn't like the sound of that.

"Yeah, well, it overheard me talking to you. I couldn't take the chance."

"How do you know this alien understood any of what you were saying? How do you even know it's an intelligent species?"

"'Cause I understood it when it started crying for help."

"That doesn't mean anything. Translator bots will convert dumb animal cries into the word 'help.'"

"Which proves the alien has translator bots, right?"

"No, dummy, it proves you have translator bots. The alien might not. It might not have understood anything you said."

"Oh."

"But we can figure this out. The neural disruption should have worn off by now. Go in there and ask the alien a question. See if it answers."

"What should I ask?"

"I don't care. Ask its name. Ask if it's hungry. Anything."

"Why don't you go do it?"

"Because it hasn't seen me, and I don't want it to. Wait. Shine this on it. I want to get a look at this thing. I'll turn off the lights."

An uneven tapping sounded on the floorboards, *thump tap* pause, *thump tap* pause. The light under the door dimmed. Then the door creaked open, and a bright light beamed in my face. Now I knew why people on shows always shield their eyes from light. I squinted and held up an arm to block the glare. Enough light reflected off the big guy for me to recognize him as the one holding the light. Behind him another person stood in shadows.

The guy in the shadows said, "It's not the color of any kind of cheese I ever saw. More like sand."

Thank you, I thought. No thanks for kidnapping me, though.

The big guy said, "Hey, alien, what planet are you from?"

I hoped if I played dumb and pretended not to understand them, they might let me go. I made a whining noise like a dog.

"Are you hungry?" he asked. "I have some poosha in here."

I was starving, but I didn't know how to communicate that without appearing intelligent. I tried barking like a dog. But then I thought, who knew how the translator bots might translate a bark? I switched to yelling, "Aargh," like a monster.

While they stared at me, my mom's voice sounded in my ear. "Lucas. Lucas, can you hear me? Are you all right?"

I started to answer, "M …" I bit my lip to stop myself. I couldn't let these guys find out I could talk. I squeezed my eyes shut and listened to Mom's voice. She called to me a few more times before giving up.

The door closed. The big guy said, "You may be right. I don't think it understands anything."

"It could be faking," the other voice said.

"Lucas, are you there?" Mom was calling again.

I was afraid to even whisper. I pressed my lips together as tightly as I could to keep from talking.

"So what do I do with it?" the big guy asked.

"Keep it here until the job's done."

"Then let it go?"

"Hmm. Let's think this through logically, shall we? If this alien is intelligent, then it could make trouble for us. If it isn't intelligent, then it won't make trouble. But in that case, does it really matter what happens to it?"

"Um."

"I think you can figure that out yourself."

"Um."

"Better to play things safe."

"Right. Right." The big guy chuckled.

They weren't going to let me go. They were going to kill me. I couldn't wait around to be rescued. I had to find a way to get out of here.

The two talked on about some other guy they were trying to find. They wanted to make him tell them where he had hidden something they wanted. They called it "the merchandise," whatever that meant.

"I've been thinking," the other voice said, "about where he might be, where he would try to lie low. What about his girlfriend?"

"I think they broke up. She dumped him."

"Yeah, well coming into money can motivate people to un-dump somebody. Do you know where she lives?"

"I know where she works."

"Good. Check it out in the morning and report back to me. Lean on her if you have to."

"Will do."

"Oh, one other thing. In case this alien does have translator bots, we don't want it contacting anybody. Hit it again with the disruptor."

No. No. No. I would be alone again, unable to answer Mom.

The door opened. This time old robot eye had the stubby red tube in his hand. I was hit again with the ringing in my ears. And then when they talked, I couldn't understand a word they said.

A little later the other guy left, and everything became silent. I figured that in the morning when my captor left to check out the girlfriend, that would be the time to try to escape. All I had to do was figure out how to get out of a locked room. And then find my way across an alien city. And hope my translator bots started working again. Also, I really needed to pee.

# Chapter 12

# The Search for Lucas

*Gabe*

"His name is Dak Tracy," I said. "I tell you, the galaxy sure is a funny place."

"Can it, Gabe. My son is missing."

"Right. Sorry. But don't worry. Between us and the cops, we'll get him back."

We had been walking along the street, scanning for clues or anybody we could ask for clues. Now Sarah stopped in her tracks, faced me, and searched my eyes. "Do you genuinely believe that? I don't want a pat answer here, Gabe. Tell me the truth."

It would have been easy to be glib, to promise her that everything would work out fine. However, this wasn't the time for glib, and I knew I couldn't promise anything other than to do everything I could. I returned her gaze, took her hand, and squeezed it. "We'll work the case. All of us. I've never seen the Galactic Detective Agency fail. C'mon. Let's find some leads."

Unfortunately, the streets were mainly empty. We passed by commercial buildings all closed for the day. We walked by parking structures designed for flying cars with landing pads sticking out at every angle on multiple levels like a *Star Trek* 3-D chess board.

On one corner we found a Rhegedian juggling balls to a crowd of no one. We approached him.

"Hey," I said, "we were wondering if you noticed a large Rhegedian person coming along here a while ago with a boy who looks like us only smaller."

The juggler eyed me then jerked his head toward a white device about the size of a coffee mug on the ground beside him. It had a payment stick connector in the side.

"Ah, I get it." I fished out the payment stick and gave him a couple of bills. "Now, did you see the kid with the guy?"

The juggler set down the balls. I assumed he was going to talk to us, but instead he picked up three blaster pistols. "Watch this." He started juggling the blasters.

Sarah spoke, biting off the words. "What about my son?"

"Yeah. Yeah. They went down this street right past me. The boy was riding on the man."

"Riding?" Sarah asked.

"Well … in a manner of speaking. The man had his arm around the kid's waist and was carrying him like this." The juggler snatched the blasters from the air. He circled one arm out from his hip like he was starting to do the I'm-a-little-teapot routine.

"He was carrying Lucas on his hip sideways like a bag of potatoes?"

"Well, I don't know what potatoes are, lady, but that's the way he was riding. Pink, the boy was, pink as a Snuul's snout."

I had seen a Snuul's snout, and it was much pinker than Lucas. At least the tentacles at the end of the snout were. Then again Lucas may have pinkened up some from struggling with the guy.

"So they went that way?" I asked, pointing. "What's down there?"

"Here's my exciting finish."

He activated the blasters and resumed juggling, catching each by the trigger, firing shots into the air with each grab. Laser blasts were shooting all around him like fireworks. Sarah and I ducked back around the side of the building.

"Don't worry," the juggler called to us between shots. "The blasters are set on stun."

I peeked around the corner. "I'd prefer to not get stunned. Now let me ask again. What's down that way?"

"Well," — *pew* — "in a couple of squares" — *pew* — "this street turns into a" — *pew pew* — "residential neighborhood." — *pew* — "But I wouldn't go there tonight" — *pew* — "if I were you." — *pew* — "The neighborhood is kind of rough." — *pew pew*.

Sarah stuck her head out. "This is my son we're talking about. We're going after him." She dodged around the blaster fire and took off down the street. I followed, taking an even wider arc. When I caught up to her, she was once more trying to contact him. "Lucas. Lucas, can you hear me? Are you all right?"

She turned to me. "This is so frustrating! Can we go somewhere with a door I can slam?"

"I don't know how the doors work around here. They might all slide."

She punched me in the arm instead. Then she leaned against me and was silent for several moments. "You know, I went freelance after Lucas's father took off. I had to. It was the only way to have enough flexibility in my hours to take care of him."

I knew she had gone into freelance web design three or four years before. I didn't realize how much the decision had been tied up in her failed marriage.

"Best decision I ever made, Gabe, though it took a while to build up my clientele and get my name known. We had some lean months."

She paused, looked up at me. "Lucas is such a perceptive kid. He seemed to realize we didn't have much money. When it was coming up on his fourth birthday, I took him to the store so he could show me what he wanted. And unlike almost any other kid, he was hesitant to say he wanted anything. I'd ask, 'What about this one?' And he'd say, 'Well, if you'd like to buy it for me.' Finally, I said, 'Lucas, baby, I'm going to spend some money on you, and I want to buy things you want.' Then he looked and looked and considered and compared. I thought we were going to be there all night, but I bit my tongue to keep from telling him to hurry. He knew this was his one chance."

She paused. "You want to provide for your kids, to make them happy, to give them everything ..." Her voice trailed off.

I said, "You've given him a loving home, which is what any kid wants most."

She pulled off her glasses and ran a finger across her eye.

"Lucas is all I have, Gabe. If anything happens to him ..."

I wanted to tell her she had me too, that we would face this together. I wanted to promise to take care of them both, to try my best to give them the moon and everything else. But this wasn't the time to say any of those things.

I said, "We'll find him."

She did a slow blink and forced a weak smile.

I said, "What do you want to do?"

"I want to keep walking, searching, asking people. You never know. We might find something."

So we walked the streets for what seemed like hours. I'm not sure what we were expecting to find. It's not like the kidnapper and Lucas were likely to be sitting out on a front step somewhere sipping lemonade.

A few people *were* sitting on front steps. Or working in their yards under lights. Or walking along the street. We asked everyone we saw if they had seen anything.

"A kid with skin like yours?" asked a woman, as she did repair work on a globe-like vehicle under the glow of a streetlamp. "Never seen anybody with skin like yours. How do you do it?"

"Believe it or not, we're born this way," I said.

A man out walking a terrier-sized guinea pig animal said, "Was this an eastern Rhegedian who took your friend?"

"I have no idea," I said. "How can you tell?"

"How can you tell? Sheesh!" He pointed to the back of his hand. "Look, my skin is azure. An easterner's skin is more cerulean."

"Those sound like the same thing to me."

His face dropped. "Well, they're not."

I opted to not waste any more time in conversation with this guy. We moved on. A woman sitting on a porch doing something on an electronic device answered us with a judgy tone. "You let your child out of your sight … alone … at night?"

I took Sarah's arm and pulled her along before she could answer. With darkness, the temperature was dropping, and she wrapped her bare arms around her. I pulled the ring from my jacket and slipped it into a pants pocket, then draped the jacket over her shoulders. After I while her steps grew slower, and she leaned into me.

"Why don't we head back," I said. "It's dark and cold. We can do more tomorrow."

She bobbed her head in agreement, and we turned around. A few minutes later I spotted a hover taxi and flagged it down. The driver turned to ask us where we were headed, flashing us huge all-black eyes and a tall, bald, beehive-shaped forehead.

"Hey," I said, "You're … you're … um … Yutronan?" I met a hotel manager once who was Yutronan.

"Yeah," the driver said, "What of it? You got a problem with that?"

"No. No problem. Only I expected a Rhegedian. Sorry. I ask questions. I'm a curious guy."

"It's called immigration, buddy. It's a free galaxy."

"Sure. Sure."

"People are people."

"Don't I know it. Sorry I brought it up."

Back at the *Shaymus* we met Jace in the crew deck hallway. "Sarah, Gabriel, I'm so sorry. Is there anything I can do to help?"

Sarah nodded, "Can you point me toward some PJs? I can't sleep in this dress, and I don't want to wear it for however many days we're going to be here. Can I get something else to put on?"

"I'll loan you one of my jumpsuits. They're comfy, and you're about my size. I'll bring one by your cabin."

"Thanks, Jace."

We trudged to my cabin where she collapsed on the bunk facing the wall. I sat beside her. She looked small and lost. I didn't know what to say.

"Gabriel and Sarah." Oren's voice came over the cabin speaker. "May I come on screen?"

"Yeah," I said.

Sarah turned over to face Oren.

"First, let me express my condolences, but also my assurances that we will return Lucas to you. I have called in some favors with the government. There is not a spaceport on this planet where anyone could sneak an Earthling boy off world."

"Thank you, Oren," Sarah said. "Why would someone have taken him?"

"I can think of four possible scenarios. The first is that since few on Rheged Prime have ever seen an Earthling, Lucas may have been mistaken for a pet of some kind. If that is the case, the situation will soon be remedied. Lucas has translator bots and will be able to communicate in a way a pet cannot."

Sarah said, "But we haven't been able to contact him. His translator bots may have gone haywire, and if they have, then whoever took him can't communicate with him either."

"They will soon be able to," Oren said. "Those nanobots are self-repairing."

I said, "So this could all be a mistake. What else?"

"The other alternatives are not as benign. It is possible he may have been kidnapped by an enemy of mine who is aware I have Earthlings in my employ. If so, we can probably expect a ransom demand to soon come in. A third alternative is Lucas was taken because he witnessed a crime or something incriminating to someone. In that case there would be no ransom. We will have to search him out."

"And the fourth possibility?" I asked.

"The fourth is that he was kidnapped for the slave trade." Sarah gasped, and Oren held up a hand. "However, that is extremely unlikely. No one has been abducted for slavery from Rheged Prime in two hundred years."

"What can we do to find him?" Sarah asked.

"For tonight we will leave it in the capable hands of the Rhegedian Sentry Service. In the morning I will have Buad and Blan fly surveillance over the city looking for him."

"I want to go out again, too," Sarah said.

"You may. Meanwhile, we must also start investigating the missing Cormabite painting. Since we are short-handed from deploying Buad and Blan in the search for Lucas, I was hoping, Gabriel, that you would accompany Zastra to our client's residence. Sarah, I can send Jace out with you."

"I'd rather stay with Sarah," I said.

"I'm sure you would, but Jace knows this city far better than you do. And I need a detective's eyes at the client's home."

I turned to Sarah. She shrugged.

I answered for the two of us. "I guess it will be all right."

The view screen went blank as a *ding* sounded from the door.

"Come," I said, which was how Captain Picard always said it.

The door slid open to reveal Jace with a gray jumpsuit in his arms. Sarah lumbered off the bed and took it from him.

Jace said, "There's a grease spot on one of the elbows, but otherwise, it's in good shape. Oh, another thing. If you want, you can give me the dress once you're out of it, and if you don't mind letting the replicator destroy it and recreate it, we can replicate other clothes in your size."

"What I want is to have it cleaned," Sarah said.

"We can replicate it clean."

"Thanks. If I end up being here a few more days, I'll bring the dress to you."

She took the jumpsuit and headed toward the bathroom in my cabin. After she shut the door, I took the opportunity to slip the engagement ring into a dresser drawer. I wouldn't be needing it until after we found Lucas.

# Chapter 13

# Lifestyle of the Rich and Famous

*Gabe*

"Are you sure you're going to be okay?" I asked Sarah for probably the fourth time.

She shot me a look. "I'm not a baby, Gabe. You don't have to take care of me. As long as I keep busy, I'll be fine. I'll have Jace with me. You go off and have fun with your blue Bella babe."

There it was again. Sarah didn't like Bella Balok. I didn't entirely trust her myself. But she was our client, and her house was where the robbery had taken place. We had to check it out.

Zastra and I flagged down a hover taxi. We climbed in, and Zastra gave the address. From the back, I could tell that this driver had spindly arms and a round body covered by purple fur.

I said, "You're Donovian, right?"

The vehicle jerked to a stop. The cabbie turned and glared at me. "All right, you two, out of the taxi!"

I said. "What's the matter?"

"The matter is I ain't no Donovian. I'm Fornaxi. Look at my eyes."

"What?"

"I said, look at my eyes, buddy!"

I made eye contact. At second glance the driver clearly wasn't Donovian. Donovians have googly eyes sitting on top of their heads. This guy's eyes were in the front of his face. Less Cookie Monster, more McDonald's Grimace.

"Sorry," I said. "I meant no offense."

"It's true," Zastra said. "He's an idiot."

"Well, I wouldn't say that."

"Too late, Mack," the driver said. "Get out."

I couldn't blame him. I wouldn't want to be called the same species as my old frenemy, Lt. Xox. We climbed out of the taxi, and it sped off.

Zastra scowled at me. "You just couldn't keep your mouth shut."

"I was trying to be friendly."

She stared me down, her eyes slits of yellow.

We caught another hover taxi, this one driven by a Rhegedian Primer, though, believe me, I said nothing about it. We glided up into the hills on the edge of town.

"Can't be a lot of taxis up here. Better wait for us." Zastra said as she paid the driver. She turned to me. "Let's keep this brief. The meter's running."

The house, or mansion more like, was spacious, ostentatious. It sat atop a hill overlooking the city with gleaming white walls and more than enough glass to take advantage of the views. It looked like the kind of place Tony Stark could call home.

We walked up to a grand front entrance that was wider than my whole bungalow back in Indy and rang a bell. An older Rhegedian woman in a black uniform and shaped like a bent stick answered the door, her hair pulled back in a severe bun. She glanced between us.

"We're with the Galactic Detective Agency," Zastra said. "Ms. Balok should be expecting us."

Without saying a word the woman opened the door and headed back into the house. We followed her through to an immense, white-tiled room filled with sofas and settees. Bella was lounging on one of them, barefoot, wearing a satiny, floral print robe.

Without bothering to sit up or even glance at us, she waved an arm and asked, "May I offer you something to drink?"

"We're good," Zastra said. "We need to get to business."

Bella swung her legs around to a sitting position. "Let's see, you're Zastra. Ah, and you, your name is Gabriel."

She reached out and took my hands like she had yesterday. Was she flirting? More like evaluating me, I thought — adding something up, possibly trying to figure out how best to use me for whatever purpose she had in mind. I smiled and pried loose my hands.

"Please sit, both of you."

I sat. Zastra remained standing. "Where was the painting hanging?"

Our client swept a hand toward a bare spot on the wall between two of the floor-to-ceiling windows.

Zastra stepped to it and scrutinized the empty wall. "Did you have security sensors on it?"

"No. My system is based on motion detection. It throws up a force field around anything that moves anywhere on the ground floor."

I said, "So I guess nobody raids the refrigerator at night."

Zastra asked, "Where's the control panel?"

Bella stood and padded across the room to where a sweeping staircase radiated out from a broad supporting column. Halfway up the stairs a keypad hung on the column's side covered with twenty or more buttons, each marked with an alien symbol.

"I had the keypad placed here where it is shielded from the view of anyone either downstairs or upstairs. All it faces is this wall."

Zastra climbed two more steps and inspected a spot on the wall opposite the pad. "What's this?"

Bella mounted the steps and passed a hand across the dark spot Zastra had indicated. "I hadn't noticed that. It's sticky. I'll be sure to have the maid clean it."

Zastra said, "Don't. It may be residue from something deliberately stuck on the wall, possibly a remote-control camera. This could be how they got your security code. I'll stand here. You go pretend to tap in the code."

Bella moved back to the keypad and slid a finger from key to key.

"Yeah," said Zastra, "from here I could see everything."

"But I would have noticed a camera on the wall."

"Would you? You didn't spot the smudge, and the camera might have been less noticeable. It could have been the same color as the paint on the wall and nearly as flat."

Bella frowned.

I asked, "Did you do any entertaining in the nights leading up to the theft?"

"Yes, I had a small dinner party two nights before."

Zastra said, "We need a list of the attendees."

"You don't think ... But those are my friends. None of them ..." Her voice trailed off.

Zastra held up an electronic device. "Can you give me the list?"

"I'll have to prepare it," Bella said."

Zastra handed her a square card with her name and photo. "Send the list here. Include addresses and numbers.""

Bella studied the card. "Do you have a business card too, Gabriel?"

I passed it off with a casual laugh. "Sorry. I'm more of an independent contractor with the agency."

"Part time," Zastra said. "A temp." A grin twitched across her lizard lips.

I asked, "Did any of your guests that evening act strangely in any way?"

Bella giggled. "Have you met my friends?"

"Well, no."

"They always act strangely."

Zastra said, "But no one seemed nervous or upset?"

"I can't recall anything of that nature."

I asked, "What does this painting look like? How would I recognize it if I ran across it?"

"You're kidding me, Gabriel. You have never seen prints of Cormabite's *Self-Portrait*? It is one of the most famous paintings in the galaxy."

"Sorry. Cormabite isn't well known where I come from on Earth with the quarantine and all."

She pulled a device from a pocket of her robe and began tapping and swiping. "I may have a photo. Ah. Here."

She held the device out to us. On the screen was a picture of Bella in a red party dress with her arm around another woman. Over her shoulder a painting hung between the two windows. I leaned in for a closer look.

Bella said, "Enlarge on painting." The device responded by zooming in on the portrait inside a gold-painted frame.

"Huh," I said. "So Cormabite wasn't a Rhegedian?"

"No, of course not," Bella said. "Pollock Cormabite was Axan. The Axans are extremely artistic."

The person staring back at me from the canvas had a head as round as a bowling ball and as dark as a Goth kid's closet. Two huge eyes took up most of the face's real estate. Mouth and nose, if they were there at all, were invisible. Pollock Cormabite looked a whole lot like Marvin the Martian from the Bugs Bunny cartoons. Except instead of a helmet on her head, Cormabite wore a floppy, gray beret, and instead of a ray gun, her hand held a stylized artist's painting palette.

I laughed instinctively. Well, not instinctively, I suppose. It was a learned response from years of watching *Looney Tunes*.

"Something funny?" Zastra asked with a scowl.

I said, "Is this part of a set? Is there another one with Daffy Duck wearing a cowboy hat or something?"

"What?" Bella's face was a question.

I waved a hand. "Never mind. Earth joke. But this seriously is what Cormabite looked like? This isn't like an abstract representation or something?"

"It is Pollock Cormabite herself," Bella said. "Painted by her own hand."

Zastra said, "I assume the piece was insured."

Bella tilted her head to one side. "Yes, but probably not for nearly enough. The policy on all the artwork was taken out during my grandfather's time. Which is why I need you to recover it. Is there anything else you need to see or ask me?"

Zastra said, "I think this will do … for now. We should talk to your staff before we go."

"The only one here is my maid." Bella returned to the couch, stretched out again, and raised her voice. "Koval." The black-uniformed, bent Rhegedian woman shuffled back into the room. "Koval, these people would like to ask you some questions about the robbery."

With her eyes on the floor, the maid said, "What is it you would like to know?"

Zastra said, "I take it you are responsible for cleaning the house?"

"Yes."

"Are you aware of a small smudge on the wall along the staircase at about my eye level?"

Koval glanced up at us and blinked. "No. I'm afraid my back hurts most of the time, which makes it difficult for me to look very far up the walls." She placed a hand on her lower back.

"Sciatica?" I asked.

"No, that's Ms. Balok's assistant."

"What is?"

"Sciatica. She is Ms. Balok's assistant-slash-publicist. My name is Koval."

"Sciatica? That's a name?"

"Yes, sir. Ms. Balok has had Sciatica for years."

"Well, that's too bad." I chuckled to myself.

"Pardon, sir?"

"Nothing."

Zastra glared at me before saying, "I suppose you didn't notice anything stuck on that spot on the wall in the days before the robbery."

"No. Sorry."

"Where were you the night of the robbery?"

She pushed a strand of gray hair behind one ear. "I was at my house in the city."

"Alone?"

"Yes, I live alone except for my pet cesky."

I wondered if a cesky was one of those dog-sized guinea pigs I had seen being taken for a walk.

Zastra asked, "Was the painting here before you left here that day?"

"I … I believe so. I have no specific memory of it. It was hung quite high on the wall."

"And the next day when you came back?"

"Ms. Balok noticed it missing. She pointed it out to me."

Bella called over from the couch. "It wasn't the next day, Koval. You remember, you didn't come in the next day."

"That's right, Ms. Balok. I was feeling poorly that day and stayed home. Must have been the day after."

"Didn't even call," Bella said with an edge in her voice.

"Sorry, miss."

I said, "There was a gathering here a few days before the robbery. Did you work the party?"

"Yes, sir."

"Did any of the guests act oddly?"

"Oddly in what way? It was an art crowd, you know."

"That's what I told them," Bella said.

"Let's say, anything suspicious, furtive."

"I can't think of anything." Koval flashed us an are-we-done look.

Zastra said, "If you think of anything else concerning the party or the painting, Ms. Balok has our contact information."

Koval escorted us to the front door, and we stepped out into a gleaming morning. I moved toward our waiting taxi.

Zastra put out a green hand to stop me. "Wait a minute."

"What? The meter's running."

"Never mind that. Glance around the neighborhood, especially at the recycling truck. Notice anything peculiar?"

Down the street a tall brown, wheeled vehicle was in the process of mechanically picking up and dumping an orange can sitting at the curb.

"Nothing's coming out of the can," I said.

"Yeah. That's because the truck was here dumping that same can when we came in."

"Something else also. The driver isn't a Rhegedian."

"No," Zastra said, shooting a quick glance in that direction. "Pardiun, I think. The person has fur."

"Pardiun. Golden fur. Face and mane like a lion, right?"

"Uh-huh."

"Someone like that was watching Sarah and me yesterday."

"Now that's interesting."

# Chapter 14

# Lucas's Run

*Lucas*

A bad dream startled me awake. I called out, "Mom."

For a few seconds I couldn't remember where I was. Why wasn't this my room? Why was I on the floor instead of in a bed?

Then I remembered, I stowed away on the *Shaymus*. I hung out in the park with Buad. I got kidnapped. The bad dream had been real. I was alone and being held captive on an alien planet. I was hungry. And thirsty. And I still had to pee, only now it was worse.

I clenched my fists. I told myself I was going to get out of there one way or another. Gabe or Mom or Zastra might bust through the door any minute, but I couldn't wait for them. These guys were planning to kill me.

I figured it must be morning because soft light filtered in under the door and from a boarded-up window behind me that I hadn't even noticed in the darkness the night before. I got up and yanked at the boards but couldn't pull them away.

The house was completely quiet. No sounds of my kidnapper or any rescuers. Maybe the big guy had already left to talk to the ex-girlfriend of whoever it was they were trying to find.

The light was dim, but I could see more than I could the night before. I scanned the room, looking for a way out. An open closet stood in one corner. I crawled to it, trying to be as quiet as I could.

The closet was dark, and I couldn't make out anything inside. I felt along the floor and walls with my hands. The closet was empty except for boxes stacked on the floor. I pushed them out of the way to check the rest of the closet wall and floor. No trapdoors.

I pulled the boxes out into the room where I had at least a tiny bit of light. I opened each one. They were filled with stacks of plastic containers. Some of the containers held beads. Some held pieces of electronics. A few had something squishy and gross inside. Nothing seemed useful for getting me out of the room.

Next, I crawled around the room checking the wall and floor. In one corner I found a vent cover shaped like a triangle. It wasn't very big, but I thought I might be able to squeeze through it. I yanked on the cover, but it didn't budge. I felt around the front of the cover and found a bump in each corner.

Those might be the heads of screws holding on the cover. I tried turning them with my fingers, but they were tight. What I needed was a tool. I closed my eyes to picture what I was touching. The heads weren't round. They had sides, five sides.

I remembered the battalion badge Zastra gave me, which had odd cutouts on the corners. There was a chance it would fit. I fished the badge out of my pocket and slid the corner around the screw head. I pulled on the badge, but the screw wouldn't budge. I pushed the badge the other way. The screw started to turn, but then the badge slipped on the head. Apparently, it only kind of fit. I pushed a thumb against it, and it held, turning the screw. Thank you, Zastra!

I removed two of the screws and loosened the third one enough to swing down the vent cover. Now all I had to do was fit inside and follow this wherever it went. Hopefully not into a furnace. I stuck my head in, but my shoulders wouldn't go. I turned my shoulders to the pointy parts of the triangle and slipped in.

The vent was metal. It was warm and damp. It went into the wall a few inches and then turned downward. Everything was dark, and I couldn't tell how far down it went. I whistled and listened to the echo, which didn't tell me much. I had to try it. Only I didn't want to go down headfirst. I scooched back out and turned around the other way. Then I slid through and let myself drop.

I don't know how far I dropped. But my feet landed on another vent cover. Through the vent louvers between my sneakers, I could make out furniture in a room below me. I kneeled as best I could in the tight space and peered through to the room below.

The room was like a basement with small windows high on the walls. For all I knew, it was locked too. But I couldn't stay in this vent forever. The sound of my own breathing was echoing in my ears, and it was starting to feel like a coffin.

I fished the badge out of my jeans again and tried to reach it through the vent to undo the screws. The badge fit through the louvers easy enough, especially since they had bent when I dropped on them, but I couldn't twist the badge around to reach the screws. I was in the process of stretching my fingers when the badge slipped from my hand. It bounced on a couch in the room below and ricocheted off to the floor with a *ting*.

Without the badge I thought I was sunk. Then I thought about how the louvers had bent when I dropped on them. I wondered if jumping on them a few times might break the whole vent cover loose.

I pulled myself back to a standing position, squeezed myself as thin as possible, and jumped, coming down with all the force I could muster. I jumped up and down, up and down, up and down. This was making a huge racket, and I was afraid I was going to get caught. But this was the only thing I could think of, and I needed out.

On the third or fourth jump, the vent gave way, and I fell through to the couch. Shards of the louvers tore my clothes and scraped my skin, but I didn't care. I scanned around the room, hoping to spot a door, if not to the outside, at least to a bathroom.

Stairs in the middle of the room led up to a door — which now started to creak open. I rolled off to the floor, grabbed the battalion badge, and hid behind the end of the couch. Feet clomped down the stairs and over to the front of the couch.

"What?" It was the big guy's voice. "What tore up that vent? Wait! The alien."

That was my cue. I darted around the back of the couch and raced for the stairs.

"Hey!" he yelled.

I dashed up the steps to the clomping of bigger feet coming up behind me. I burst through the door and slammed it shut.

"Ow!" Old laser eye must have run right into the door. From the bumping sounds coming from the basement, he may have rolled all the way back down the stairs. Served him right.

I was in a strange room I had never seen before. I had to decide which way to go, and a wrong choice would be a disaster. It was also going to be a disaster if I didn't find a bathroom soon. But for now I had to put that out of my mind.

I ducked through a doorway. In the next room I saw the front door dead ahead. I ran to it, hoping the door wasn't locked. It wasn't. It opened, and I jumped over a front step and shot out through the little yard at full speed. I glanced over my shoulder as I dashed up the street. The big guy emerged from the house and set off after me.

# Chapter 15

# Crookland Nine-Nine

*Gabe*

Cops. I've run into a few of them on my cases with the Galactic Detective Agency. Whenever we visit Girsu Space Port, the pompous and barely competent Lt. Xox always makes my life miserable. Then there are the run-ins I've had with earthbound deputy sheriffs and FBI agents. What can I say? We don't always work hand-in-glove with law enforcement. I hoped things would be better with Dak Tracy.

Zastra, Buad, and Blan headed off individually to interview Bella's driver, chef, and assistant. I wished I could have interviewed the assistant, Sciatica, just so when I entered, I could tell her to not get up. Or say that my back hurt. Or ask if she knew a guy called Lumbago. So many possibilities for jokes.

But it didn't work out because Sarah and Jace had returned from an unsuccessful hunt for Lucas, and Sarah wanted to follow up with Dak Tracy. I wanted to go with her.

Of course, before we set off, we needed to have some idea of where we were going. I said, "Kah-Rehn, where can I locate this Detective Tracy who's in charge of finding Lucas?"

Kah-Rehn's synthesized voice answered through the speaker in my cabin. "All sentry detectives work out of the central sentry post at Ninety-Nine Bookland Street."

"Ha! You're saying the place is Bookland Nine-Nine? Like the TV show?"

"I'm afraid I do not have much knowledge of Earth television, Gabriel."

Sarah said, "Seriously? Jokes? Let's go."

At the ship's ramp we met Jace heading toward the galley with an empty coffee mug.

"Thanks for taking Sarah around town," I said.

"No problem. It was fun to hover around a Rhegedian city again. Took me back to my youth. Where are you two off to?"

"The central sentry post to ask if they've gotten any leads on Lucas."

"Going to Crookland Nine-Nine, huh?"

"I thought the street name was Bookland."

"People call it Crookland … because they catch crooks, get it?"

I turned to Sarah. "See. Crookland Nine-Nine. That's even better."

She didn't bother to answer. We hailed a hover taxi. The driver of this one had a flat nose and short horns on his head.

Sarah leaned over to whisper in my ear. "Is he what Neep was … or is, I mean?"

Neep Skollie was a galactic alliance planet evaluator and the first alien Sarah had met.

"You mean a Cuneddan?" I said in a whisper. "I think so, but don't say anything." I didn't want a repeat of my earlier confrontations.

The driver turned with dancing eyes. "Did somebody say Cuneddan? I sure am. Have you folks visited Cunedda?"

"I was there briefly," I said. "Nice place." What I remembered most was a hot, dry climate and a whole lot of gravity.

The taxi set off along the streets of Tikal while the driver chatted about his home world and asked about ours. He let us out in a plaza where a fountain stood in front of a huge glass and steel building rising out of the ground in a wedge-shape. The place looked like a giant ramp. Seriously, if the late Evel Knievel were here, he would zoom up that thing on a motorcycle and jump over the fountain plus a line of hover buses parked in front of it, all while wearing red, white, and blue. This was Crookland Nine-Nine.

We walked into a lobby buzzing with activity. Streams of Rhegedians hustled back and forth. Like Tracy, they all wore yellow, though most were not in yellow trench coats and fedoras. Some sported yellow pants. Others wore yellow vests and yellow peaked caps. Though a bit on the garish side, the uniforms were certainly high-vis and a lot less threatening than the blue-so-dark-it's-essentially-black I was used to back home.

Sarah walked directly to a reception desk, while I strolled around and checked out photographs and paintings hung along the tiled walls. They appeared to depict the history of the sentry service. There were pictures of them brandishing everything from spears to blasters, giving the impression of a police force dating back to the Rhegedian Middle Ages.

One painting showed sentries carrying yellow shields atop city walls. Another featured a squad of officers in yellow double-breasted constable uniforms hanging from the running boards of an oldfangled car. Well, not an Earth car. This vehicle was long and tube-shaped, making it resemble the Oscar Mayer Wienermobile.

I was staring at one particularly gory painting of a sentry catching an outlaw — and by catching, I mean on the end of a lance — when Sarah joined me.

"Tracy is in, and he'll be with us in a few minutes."

"Cool. Look at this."

She didn't look. She merely pointed to a grouping of chairs beside the reception desk. "The waiting area is over there."

We sat and watched the activity, during which Sarah alternated between tapping one foot and getting up to pace.

Oren's voice sounded in my ear through the translator bot connection. "Gabriel."

"Yes, Oren."

"Have you learned anything at the sentry post?"

"Not yet. We're still waiting for Tracy."

"Inform me of any clues. While the sentries have more resources and personnel to throw at the problem than do we, we have certain competencies ourselves."

"You mean, we have you, and you're a genius."

"Among many other talents of our team. And one other thing. If your schedule permits, I would like you to accompany Zastra later to interview Trub Nurke."

"Who's that again?"

"The art gallery owner. Ms. Balok suggested he might be able to help."

"Right. Well, Lucas is my first priority."

"Mine too. That's why I want Buad and Blan back on reconnaissance looking for the kidnapper as soon as they finish with the chef and driver. And if they are doing that …"

"Then you need someone to help Zastra. Sure. Makes sense."

"Ms. Gallo." The yellow-capped officer at the desk stood and beckoned us. "Detective Tracy will see you now."

"Gotta go," I said to Oren.

Sarah sprang from her chair. I followed her and the officer through a busy bullpen of desks. Blue-skinned, yellow-clad sentries were tapping on devices or talking on devices or conferring with each other. One guy, apparently a perp, not in yellow and wearing a stocking cap, was handcuffed to a desk.

Dak Tracy stood as we were ushered into his glass-walled office. His yellow trench coat hung on a coat tree in the corner, but he still wore his ten-gallon fedora. "Sarah and Gabriel. How are you folks doing today … under the circumstances, I mean?" He waved us toward chairs as he sat down again.

"That depends on what you have to tell us," Sarah said, taking a seat. "Have you found anything?"

"Well, nothing definite yet."

"Does that mean you have something not definite?"

"I have sentries out in the park interviewing everyone, asking them if they were there last night and saw anyone."

"And?" Sarah's voice was strained, insistent.

Tracy tapped on the device he wore on his wrist like a watch. "Patton, have you found any witnesses?"

A voice crackled through the smart watch. "Not yet, Dak, but we're still talking to people."

"Thanks," Tracy said. He turned to us. "We're looking."

I said, "Last night we tracked the kidnapper into a residential neighborhood."

"I thought we agreed you would leave the detective work to us."

I shrugged. "As you might recall, detecting is kind of our thing too. The word is smack dab in the middle of our agency name."

Tracy scowled. "When amateurs become involved, people get hurt."

"We're hardly amateurs, Detective."

"I suppose. Which neighborhood? What street?"

Sarah said, "We were on Hoban Street, but it could be anywhere in that area. We only found one person who said they saw them."

Tracy thrust out his square jaw like a determined bulldog. "I'll send out some officers to canvass the neighborhood. If anybody saw anything, we'll find out. If anybody is acting suspicious, we'll pick up on it." He tapped the order into his wrist device, then turned back to us. "This is good. I bet we'll have a solid lead by the end of the day."

Sarah said, "I don't want a solid lead by the end of the day. I want my son back now. He's seven years old. He's probably scared to death. For all I know, he may be hurt or ..." Her voice broke.

"Ma'am," said Tracy.

"Don't ma'am me. Find my son."

"We are doing everything we can. By the way, we have a family counseling officer available. Often in trying times like this it helps to—"

She cut him off. "What would help would be to find Lucas."

"Yes, ma' — Yes, Ms. Gallo."

Tracy's wrist device *dinged*. He raised his hand and tapped a button. Text scrolled through a thumbnail-sized projection above the watch. My visual nanites didn't translate the message to English, probably because to my side of the desk it was displayed backwards.

Tracy looked up at us. "We have something."

Sarah leaned forward in her chair. "What?"

"Somebody saw Lucas carried out of the park last night. Or someone being carried out, but most likely him. The witness said the person was small with skin the color of tea with cream. I realize, that's not exactly an accurate color description, but witnesses are notoriously unreliable."

"What about the person carrying Lucas?" I asked.

Tracy tossed a smile in our direction. "That's our lead. The witness says the man had an eyepiece."

"Eyepiece? What do you mean? An eye patch like a pirate? Glasses like Sarah's?"

"No, an implanted cybernetic eye."

"You can do that here?"

"Sure. I take it you don't have cybernetic implants on your planet?"

"No. I don't think so anyway. It's a fast-changing world."

"Well, we do."

"Of course, you do. You guys can upload somebody's consciousness to a computer, so why not? What kind of implants do they do?"

"All kinds," Tracy said. "Some to correct visual or auditory deficiencies."

"You mean like poor eyesight or hearing loss."

"Right. Others provide enhancements — seeing beyond the normal visual spectrum, or night vision, or enhanced hearing. Then there are the neural implants — direct cerebral connection to the network, for instance."

"Wow! That could come in handy," I said. "Unless there were pop-up ads."

"You want to see one?"

Sarah said, "No."

I said, "Sure."

He spoke into his wrist device. "Sam, come in here a minute."

A young detective stepped into the office. "What is it, Boss?"

"Show them what your fingers can do."

Sam held up his right palm. Chips were embedded in the index and middle finger. He made a motion, and a pop-up display appeared in midair. He tapped at a spot in the air to bring up a list, scrolled through it, and tapped again. A picture appeared of the *Shaymus*.

"Now that would be nice to have," I said.

"Thanks, Sam," Tracy said.

"You're welcome, Boss. Do you need anything else?"

Tracy waved him off. "Other augmentations regulate chemical imbalances in the brain or improve focus or boost adrenaline."

"Wait a minute, those aren't performed as some government dictate, are they?" Twentieth century Earth had seen way too many involuntary lobotomies and chemical brain manipulations.

Tracy stared at me, which I couldn't interpret as either yes or no.

"What about Lucas?" Sarah asked.

"Right," Tracy said, "The point here is that all augmentation surgeries are cataloged in a database. We can run a list of all people with cybernetic eyes and cross-reference it against criminal histories."

"Assuming this person has a criminal history," I said.

"Correct. But it gives us something to go on. How many criminals with visual enhancements can be living in Tikal? I'll submit the order now."

Tracy made a series of taps on his wrist device. Sarah reached out and squeezed my hand.

"All right. We have it running," Tracy said. "When we get it, we'll take the list of hits and assign …"

I missed the last part of what he was saying because at that moment Lucas's voice came over our translator bots. "Mom! Gabe! Are you there? Help!"

# Chapter 16

# Born to Run

*Lucas*

Lucas here again. And I bet you're glad to get back to my story since I left it right as the guy with the robot eye was chasing me down the street.

We ran for blocks. The guy behind me had the advantage of longer legs since he was a grown up. But I had the advantage of not having to haul around his bulk. He had to stop and catch his breath every so often, while I kept running.

I eyed the houses as I passed them, hoping to spot somewhere I could duck in and lose him or get protection. But I didn't see any friendly faces — any faces, for that matter — and I couldn't take the chance of running up to a closed door with him on my heels.

And anyway, the houses were too weird to be welcoming. They were all painted in glaring neon colors and made of boxy cubes like a toddler building with wooden blocks.

When I had a little distance on the guy, I turned and dashed between two houses. Unfortunately, I didn't find any promising hiding spots in the backyards. I kept going and came out on the next street with old robot eye still on my tail.

I darted from that street between two more houses. A fence between them blocked my path. A red box sat in front of the fence. I jumped on the box and peered over the fence. Ground cover grew on the other side. It looked soft enough. I used my arms to spring over the fence and rolled on the ground.

As I was getting up, I heard a crash from the other side of the fence. That was encouraging. Whatever had happened, maybe it would slow him down. I kept running, looking back in time to see his blue head emerging over the top of the fence. Criminy! How was I going to lose this guy?

I raced out on the next street and kept running. This street was lined with trees. I thought about hiding behind one or climbing one, but I didn't because that sounded like a good way to end up trapped.

Up ahead I spotted a bridge. Lower ground sloped down on either side of it, filled with clumps of trees. The guy was now a half a block behind me. I figured this was my chance.

I swerved to the right off the street and into the thicket. The ground was soft and covered with yellow leaves. I realized I had no idea what critters might be in a place like this or what the Rhegedian version of poison ivy might look like. But it was too late to think about any of that. I plunged on down the steep slope. Behind me came grunts and the rustle of leaves as the guy plowed after me. Rats! He had seen me.

To my left a drainage pipe stuck out of the hill. The opening was bigger than me, but smaller than the guy chasing me. I ran to it. Light shone from the other end. It ran all the way under the bridge. I pulled myself up into it. The bottom of the pipe was damp, and the water wicked up from my knees as I crawled along through it.

"Hey, kid!" The deep voice echoed behind me in the pipe. I turned and saw his face filling the opening, the cyborg eye glinting red down length of the tube.

I crawled to the middle of the pipe and sat down to catch my breath. Fortunately, the bottom was dry there, so I didn't get my bum wet. The next part would be to wait.

And to call for help. In a whisper I said, "Mom! Gabe! Are you there? Help!"

Mom's voice sounded in my ear. "Lucas! Are you all right? Where are you?"

As I started to answer, I could feel tears behind my eyes. I sniffed and took a breath. This wasn't the time for any of that. Not with the guy's red eye still staring at me. I said, "I'm okay ... I think. I'm running from the kidnapper."

Mom said, "Oh! Lucas! We'll come get you."

Gabe spoke. "Lucas, I'm getting Oren in on this. Oren, can we track his location by his translator bots."

"I'm afraid not," Oren said. "Lucas, you'll need to tell us where you are."

"I don't know exactly. I'm in some drainpipe right now."

Mom said, "What? Are you safe?"

The ugly blue face disappeared from the end of the pipe.

"I can't talk now, Mom. Give me a few minutes."

"Lucas? Lucas? Wait!"

I didn't answer. I figured robot face was doing one of two things. Either he was waiting hidden somewhere for me to leave the pipe or else he was heading over to the other end to see if he could find a way to get me from that side. If his face appeared at the other end in a few minutes, I would know. If it didn't appear, I would have to take a guess. Meanwhile, I needed to count. And I still really, really needed to pee.

When I had counted to two hundred and sixty, the red light from his robot eye flashed from the other end of the pipe. "Hey, kid, come on out. I won't hurt you."

Which was nutso. Of course, he was going to hurt me. He was supposed to kill me. I didn't even take the time to call him a liar. Starting my counting over again at one, I crawled as quickly as my hands and knees would take me back the way I had come.

I was at seventy-seven when I reached the end of the pipe and flipped out onto the ground. I took a second to glance back down the pipe. Only daylight shone at the other end. Which meant he was after me. I bolted up the side of the hill, angling away from the pipe, trying to put as much distance between it and me as possible.

One hundred. I dodged through the trees. I peeked over my shoulder and saw nothing. One hundred and sixty. I reached the edge of the trees and heard twigs snapping somewhere behind me. I crouched low. Two hundred and five. I burst out of the line of trees and headed for the corner of a nearby house. It was orange, and its windows made it look almost like a jack-o-lantern. An "oof" sounded behind me. I hoped that meant he stepped in a hole or slipped and fell.

I turned the corner of the house and saw two Rhegedian kids, smaller than me, playing with a drone. The drone buzzed back and forth between them as they waved their hands to control its movement.

"You have to help me," I said. "A guy is after me."

Their mouths dropped open, and they stared at me. Who knows what they were thinking? Here I was, gasping breaths, with torn, wet clothes and skin not the blue they were used to.

One of the kids pointed at a bush. "Crawl in there."

I scrambled under the bush and made myself as small as I could. A minute later old mech face heaved into view. I shut my eyes and forced myself to breathe through my nose.

"Hey, kids," the big guy said, "um … my pet ran off. Have you seen him? He's about your size but has skin like … I don't know … it's weird. He was wearing clothes."

"Doesn't sound like a pet," said one of the kids. "Sounds like a person."

"No. No. He's a dumb animal. He can't feed itself or nothing. I need to find him before he gets run over or something."

The second kid said, "I saw somebody run past here. But he wasn't dumb. He talked to us. He told us to call for help."

"Yeah," said the kidnapper, "but he's like one of them talking birds. He doesn't understand what he's saying. He repeats things he hears people say."

"He's heard people call for help?" The first kid asked.

"Um … from a vid, that's all."

"If you say so, mister. He ran off that way."

"All right. Thanks."

A few seconds later I heard a whisper. "Stay where you are. He's going away, but he keeps looking back."

I stayed under the bush until they told me to come out. The boys stared at me.

"Where are you from?"

"Earth."

"Is that a planet?"

"Yeah."

"Are you a kid?"

"Yeah. Thanks for telling the guy that story."

"Sure. He seemed creepy. We should tell our dad about you."

"Yeah, and I should tell my mom where I am. Is there like an address or something for this place? Also, do you have a bathroom?"

# Chapter 17

# Mother and Child Reunion

*Gabe*

"Mom! Gabe! Are you there? Help!"

When Lucas's voice sounded in our ears, Sarah jumped from her chair like she was on springs and began pacing in every direction at once.

Dak Tracy, who had not heard Lucas because he wasn't on our nanite network, looked up with bulging eyes at this odd Earthling behavior. "Is she all right?"

"Lucas just contacted us," I said.

The cop rose and leaned across the desk. "Where is he? Is he all right?"

I held up a hand to stop the interrogation so I could hear Lucas. We spoke for only a minute before Lucas said "I can't talk now, Mom. Give me a few minutes."

"Lucas? Lucas? Wait!"

But it was silence. Sarah reached for my hand.

"What's happening?" Tracy asked.

"I don't know," I said. "I think he's still trying to get away from the kidnapper."

The next few minutes ticked by in slow motion until, finally, Lucas spoke again.

I sprang to my feet and said to Tracy, "He's safe. We have an address. C'mon. Let's go pick him up."

Tracy threw on the yellow trench coat, and we rushed through the squad room, all eyes on him in apparent hero worship as we passed through the desks.

He nodded to the sentries. "Break in the case, gang. Be right back."

He led us down a corridor and out a side door to a parking lot where we jumped into his squad car, a real Jetsons-like flying car with jet engines hanging from gull wings. The vehicle was, of course, painted bright yellow with the word SENTRIES emblazoned on the side in blue.

Lights flashing, we skimmed over the buildings into a neighborhood I recognized from our on-foot investigation the night before. We dropped down to the street in front of a pumpkin-colored house. Sitting on the front step were Lucas, two Rhegedian boys, and an adult Rhegedian male with a pudgy face and a dad bod.

When Tracy opened the cockpit door, Sarah leaped from it. Lucas dashed from the step toward her.

"Mom!"

Sarah enveloped him in her arms, and the dam burst for both of them. She held him like she was clutching a life preserver. He clung to her, his body heaving. After more than a minute, they both calmed. Lucas wiped his eyes on Sarah's shoulder before pulling away. Sarah sat back on the ground, tears still streaming.

"What happened?" I asked.

Lucas started slowly, picking up speed and energy as he told the tale.

"This guy ... he grabbed me. He ... he carried me off and stuck me in an empty room and locked the door. And then some other guy came and looked at me, and they talked about finding some guy they wanted to kill, and they said something about getting rid of me. So I knew I had to get out, and this morning I crawled through an air vent and got out into the basement. Only the guy heard me and came down the stairs. I ran past him and out into the street, and he chased me. I ran through yards and jumped fences, but he kept after me. Then I went down into like a ravine and hid in a drainpipe. The guy found me in there, but he couldn't reach me. And when he went around to the other side, I crawled out and ran here, and these guys — that's Matty, and that's Ondy — they hid me and told the guy I had run off. And they let me use their bathroom and gave me something to eat. It was some kind of fruit and was crazy good."

At the end of this recitation, Tracy said, "Hi, Lucas. I'm Detective Tracy with the sentries. Can you go through all that again? And this time I'll probably interrupt with some questions." Tracy turned to the Rhegedian adult. "I'll need to talk to your boys too. Is there somewhere we can all sit?"

We spent the next hour in a family room inside the orange house. Sarah and I sat on a couch with Lucas, who Sarah wouldn't let out of arm's reach. Tracy and our host took chairs. The two boys sat on mats on the floor. Tracy had Lucas go over his story several times, looping back again and again to check for consistency and to probe for further details.

"This man who grabbed you, he was an augment?" Tracy asked.

Lucas stared at him. "I don't know what that means."

"He had cybernetic augmentations, implants."

The two Rhegedian boys nodded. One of them said, "Yeah. An eyepiece on one eye and three chips on the other side of his head."

"No, he only had two chips, Ondy," the other one said.

"You're nuts. There were three of them."

"Were not."

The boys started pushing each other until the dad yelled, "Hey!"

Tracy held up a hand. "I'll put down that he had a few chip implants. Let's leave it at that. Any idea what kind of chips?"

The boys unhanded each other and shook their heads no.

"And, Lucas, in the house where you were held, you say this person spoke with someone else?"

"Uh-huh."

"Did you see this other person?"

"No. It was dark."

"What did this other person sound like?"

Lucas shrugged

"Male or female?"

"Male … I think."

"Was his voice higher than mine, lower than mine? Did he have an accent?"

"I think higher than your voice. But do translator bots even do all that stuff?"

"Sure, they do. My voice sounds lower through translator bots than your two friends here, right? The bots translate tone and pitch as well as words. Even accents."

Lucas wrinkled his forehead as he took in the information. Oh, how this kid loved learning about science.

"So when these two people were talking, did either of them call the other by name?"

"I don't think so, Detective … um. What did you say your name was?"

"Tracy," Tracy said.

I made eye contact with Lucas and said, "Dak Tracy."

Lucas's face went blank for a second. Then he got the reference thanks to that time I showed him the old 1960s cartoon show. He snorted. "Seriously?"

Tracy furrowed his brow. "That's the second time you people have laughed about my name. What's wrong with it?"

I held up hands in surrender. "Nothing. Not a thing. It's just on Earth there's a fictional police detective with a similar name."

"Hmm. A fictional detective. Is he any good?"

"As I recall, he's one of the best."

Tracy's brows untwisted. His square chin jutted with pride.

Sarah said, "How about we get back to business?"

"Sure," I said. "Go on … Dak Tracy."

Lucas and I both snickered, and Tracy beamed.

"These people you overheard, Lucas," Tracy said, "What were they talking about?"

"Me, some. They were trying to figure out whether I could understand them and what they were going to do with me."

"What did they decide?"

Lucas answered in a small voice. "I think they were going to kill me."

Sarah gasped and hugged Lucas to her.

Tracy's bushy brows again drew together. "Did they talk about anything else?"

"They were trying to find a guy."

"A guy … as in male?"

"I think so."

"Did they mention the name?"

Lucas shook his head.

"Why were they trying to find this person?"

"It was confusing. Earlier in the park when the big guy was talking on the phone, he said he was looking for a guy and would make him disappear."

"Phone? Oh, you must mean the cubes … the netcom cubicles. The park has some. Did they say why they wanted to hurt this person?"

Lucas leaned his head on Sarah, making me think he was starting to wear out. He spoke in a monotone. "Something about recovering some merchandise."

"What kind of merchandise?"

Lucas shrugged. "Merchandise. That's all I know."

"You're doing an amazing job here, Lucas," Tracy said. "One more question. Can you remember anything they said about this person they were trying to find?"

"No … um … kind of. They said they were checking with people who fence."

"Fence as in buy and sell stolen property?"

Another shrug.

"All right. That's it. Thanks, Lucas. You did well. Your parents must be proud of you."

Lucas pitched a funny look in my direction but let it pass.

Sarah said, "Detective Tracy, can you catch the person who kidnapped him?"

Tracy waggled his head left and right. "I can't guarantee anything. But, as I said earlier, there can't be that many augments with criminal connections. Plus, now we have a better description of the perp's augmentations for cross-referencing. And we have three witnesses who can identify him. I think we'll nab him."

"Good," Sarah said. "I don't want him to ever do this to anybody else."

Tracy stood. "When are you folks heading back to Earth?"

I said, "We were supposed to have left last night. Then all this happened. Why do you ask?"

"Because when we catch this guy, it would be useful to have Lucas identify him."

Sarah started shaking her head. "That could take days. I just want to put this behind us and go home."

I said to Tracy, "You don't have to have Lucas, do you? These other two boys can identify him."

"Yeah," Tracy said. "They could. But Lucas's identification would carry more weight since he had more interaction. There's a chance Lucas could also identify the co-conspirator he heard. We're not only talking kidnapping here. Lucas stumbled into a murder plot. He literally could save a life."

Sarah said, "And put himself into more danger in the process. No, I don't want to have anything to do with murderers."

I had to smile at the irony of her statement. She had twice before been involved in murder cases with the Galactic Detective Agency.

Sarah eyed me. "What are you smiling about, Gabe?"

In one of those cases Lucas ended up in danger. On second thought, maybe that was precisely what was making her skittish now.

"Nothing," I said.

Lucas said, "Mom, I want to help save a life."

Sarah cast a silent frown at Tracy.

Tracy said, "Ms. Gallo, you have a child here who is both intelligent and brave. To escape that house and get away from the guy and tell me his story, that's something."

"It sure is," said one of the blue boys on the mat. "I want to save a life too. Can I help too, Papa?"

The Rhegedian adult gave the kid the universal parental look to hush.

Sarah's eyes went to me. I couldn't tell if she was asking for my opinion or looking for support for her position. I decided to test the waters with a statement of fact.

"Well, the chrono drive can take us back to Earth the same night we left in any case," I said.

"I know, but what do you think about all this?"

"I think … I think if we stay, then the Galactic Detective Agency can help the cops catch this guy, both these guys."

"Yay!" Lucas said.

I added, "Of course, I'm not the mom here."

"Aw," said Lucas.

"Then again, you and I and Zastra can all keep an eye on him. Or we can park him in the *Shaymus* with Jace. I don't think this guy would risk trying to grab Lucas again if any of us were around."

"Is it okay, Mom?" Lucas said, pleading with his eyes.

Sarah said, "Lucas, you should not get the impression you'll be part of this case. This is a job for the police … and Oren. Once these guys are caught and you identify them, then that's it. In the meantime, you are not leaving my sight."

"Okay. Yeah, Mom." It sounded like a kid agreeing to anything to get what they wanted, hopefully with details to be renegotiated later.

Tracy said, "Then it's settled. Under the circumstances I will welcome the participation of the Galactic Detective Agency. And to that end perhaps I should meet with your team to go over the facts and set some ground rules. Can I offer you folks a ride back to your ship?"

A *beep* came from Tracy's wrist. He pulled up the sleeve of his trench coat and tapped on his device. He gave it a moment's attention, then he looked up. "We need to make a stop along the way. One of my sentries has detained an augment near here who was acting suspiciously. Let's go see if this is the guy."

## Chapter 18

# Dak Tracy Meets Oren Vilkas

*Gabe*

Tracy opened the door to the back seat of his flying squad car, and Sarah and Lucas climbed in. I stared at the remaining few inches of seat uncertainly.

"I guess I'll ride up front with Detective Tracy," I said. "Unless you want to, Lucas."

"Can I?" Lucas asked with excitement.

"Sorry," Tracy said. "It's against regulations for civilians to sit in the front. Too many switches and buttons that do things we might not want done."

"Then don't let Gabe sit up there," Sarah said.

Yeah, I've been known to push a few random buttons in my time. Reluctantly I joined Sarah and Lucas in the back, finding a way to fit if I sat sideways using only half my caboose.

We winged up into the air, coming back down a few blocks away where another yellow flying car was parked. Green and orange flashers blinked on top. Beside it two sentries in yellow vests and peaked caps stood over someone seated on the ground, shielded from our view by the looming bodies of the cops. Jammed against Lucas, I could feel him tense as we landed.

Tracy said, "You all stay here. I'll have the guy stand up, and you can take a look. Stay low."

He got out and approached the other sentries.

"Mom," Lucas said.

Sarah took his hand. "I'm right beside you. Not to mention the three police officers here. This guy is in custody and can't hurt you."

Through the cockpit window we watched as the two sentries took a step back. The person they had arrested slowly worked out how to get to his feet while wearing handcuffs. The guy had a robotic arm, and one side of his head was capped by a piece of gun-metal gray headgear studded with computer chips. Both eyes, though, were natural.

Lucas relaxed back into the seat. "That's not him. He's way creepy enough, but not the guy."

I shook my head at Tracy. The sentries removed the cuffs and sent the man on his way.

"Sorry about that," Tracy said when he returned to the car. "Wrong implants. The headpiece was a hearing enhancement, and the robotic arm was for industrial work. Now that we have the boys' descriptions, we're circulating a better suspect bulletin. Hopefully, we won't have many more false detentions. It's bad for PR."

"It's not easy on us either," Sarah said.

We once more lifted into the sky, this time soaring over the city to the landing pad where the *Shaymus* was parked. Jace was at the ramp waiting for us. He tousled Lucas's hair in welcome as we boarded the ship.

Deploying the stairs in the central shaft, we climbed to the office where we found Zastra, Buad, Blan, and Oren. I showed Tracy to one of the red leather chairs in front of the view screen and sat Lucas and Sarah beside him. I took the seat at my desk. Tracy crossed his legs and took off his hat, perching it on one knee.

During the 1950s and 60s Hollywood put out a whole slew of cross-franchise meet-up movies — *Abbott and Costello Meet the Invisible Man, King Kong vs. Godzilla.* Even *Jesse James Meets Frankenstein's Daughter*, which made no sense either in theory or in the plot they cobbled together.

This get-together here on the *Shaymus* seemed almost like one of those. The yellow-trench-coated hero of the Rhegedian Sentry Service, Detective Dak Tracy, meeting the most famous private detective in the galaxy, Oren Vilkas. The conference started with several seconds of the two of them eyeing each other before either of them spoke.

"Good day, Detective Tracy. I am Oren Vilkas."

Tracy bobbed his head. "Yes. Of course, you are. It is a pleasure to meet you. Everyone in the service has heard of you and your exploits." There was a formality in Tracy's tone that was absent in our previous conversations.

"How may I be of assistance to the Rhegedian Sentry Service?" Oren asked. He was always formal, but this time he sounded downright stiff.

"Let me tell you what we have." Tracy tapped on his wrist device and scrolled through his notes as he discussed the kidnapping case. At certain points Lucas would nod or throw in comments, such as "Yeah, he was humongous," or "Actually, the drainpipe was really close to Matty and Ondy's house."

"So that's about it so far," Tracy said as he finished. "Thoughts?"

"Several," Oren said. "The first is that our Lucas here is both a resourceful and an extremely lucky young man. Never underestimate luck, Lucas. Some have it, others don't. You and Gabriel each seem to possess it in abundance. However, I would caution you against relying on it. Luck has been known to run out. You too, Detective Tracy, in this case have been lucky. Lucas essentially freed himself from his kidnapper."

Tracy's square jaw shifted left and right, taking the chiding like bad tasting medicine. "Oh, I'm sure we would have located him soon enough. We were canvassing that same neighborhood at the time Lucas managed to call in."

"No doubt." Oren wore a condescending smile. "As for my other thoughts, this murder scheme, which the kidnapper referred to, that is of interest."

"It is to us as well," Tracy said. "Though we should keep in mind the possibility that the child may have misinterpreted what the kidnapper said."

Lucas crossed his arms. "I know what I heard."

Oren said, "When you say the child, I presume you mean Lucas. He has a name."

"Sure. Lucas. Anyhow, speaking on behalf of the sentry service, and in the interest of putting this case to bed as soon as possible, we welcome any contribution you and your team can make in bringing the kidnappers to justice and in thwarting this possible murder they appear to be plotting. Of course, I'm acquainted with your eye watering fees. The sentries don't have budget to pay anything close to your normal rate."

Oren waved it away. "The Galactic Detective Agency is always gratified to assist any police force. In this particular case, we are not interested in collecting any fee. An affront has been made to one of our own, and we do not intend to let it go unanswered."

"That is good of you."

"I should point out," Oren said, "we are at the same time engaged in another case related to a piece of stolen artwork. Unlike the sentries, we do not have unlimited personnel."

Tracy straightened himself in his chair. "Our resources are far from unlimited as well. However, we are committed to obtaining justice for the ... for Lucas."

I piped up. "Sarah and I can stay and help on both cases. We've already agreed to keep Lucas here to help identify the kidnapper."

"That will be beneficial," Oren said. "Now, how to proceed? One could say we have three mysteries to unravel — recovering the stolen artwork, identifying the kidnapper, and discovering the person the kidnapper is trying to murder. How best to deploy our resources and those of the sentries?"

Tracy fiddled with his hat a moment before returning it to his knee. "I want to take Lucas back out to try to identify the house where he was held. If we can find the house, we can trace the owner, which could lead us to the kidnapper."

Sarah said, "You're not taking Lucas anywhere without me."

"I have no problem with you coming along," Tracy said.

"I'll go too," I said.

Oren cleared his throat. "I would prefer, Gabriel, having you and Zastra continue working on our art theft … in the interest of keeping all our investigations moving forward. I will be glad to send Jace along with Sarah and Lucas if it would make them feel more comfortable."

Sarah nodded. "It would."

"Satisfactory." Oren flipped up a palm in the direction of the habitat. "And I would like to deploy our Avanian associates, Buad and Blan, in reconnaissance for the kidnapper. Their eyesight is keen, and they can move quickly over the city."

Tracy said, "While my officers run down the records on augments."

Oren said, "What about the device the kidnapper used on Lucas to disable the translator bots?"

"Probably an electromagnetic pulse gun."

"Can it be tracked?"

"Unfortunately, there is no registry for them."

"That is unfortunate."

Tracy responded with an expression of what-are-you-going-to do.

Oren said, "Can you send officers to stores that sell such devices and inquire about purchases by augments?"

"That would not be allowed. Augments have civil rights like everyone else."

Oren's nostrils flared. "What about Lucas's civil rights? What about his right to not be abducted and terrorized?"

"I'm afraid, Mr. Vilkas, in your business you need only please one client at a time. The sentries must answer to many constituencies."

Oren glowered. "In other words, the only thing the sentries can do is computer work to cross-reference augmentation surgeries?"

Tracy's voice came out harsh. "No. I said I was taking Lucas back to search for the house. After that we'll stake out the place in case the kidnapper returns. We'll also continue canvassing the neighborhood. We are pursuing a number of lines of inquiry." He pulled his hat off his knee and put both feet on the floor as if he was ready to jump up and storm out.

Clearly, neither of these men were comfortable working with someone they couldn't command. Tracy was a hotshot in this city. For all I knew, he might be the superstar cop of Rheged Prime. He probably didn't kowtow to many people. But Oren Vilkas was a big deal across the galaxy, and he bowed to no one.

An awkward silence fell on the room as they glared at each other. Zastra stared down at her desk. Buad and Blan began quietly chirping in their habitat. Sarah became interested in something on her fingernails.

That left it to me to intervene. "Well, it sounds like between the two groups here we have a dynamite plan, and I'm excited to see it in action. I say we get to work. Go team!"

# Chapter 19

# Returning to the Scene of the Crime

*Lucas*

"Before we go anywhere, Lucas, we need to get you into some clean clothes."

"Oh, Mom!" I couldn't believe she was worried about clothes when we had a kidnapper to catch. "What's wrong with these clothes?"

"They're ripped and filthy, that's what."

I glanced down my front. "A little … I guess. But only because I was crawling around in air ducts and drainpipes."

She shot me a mom look. "Exactly."

"But I don't have any other clothes here. And, besides, we need to go back out there and find the house so they can arrest the guy."

"Not looking like that we don't. You're a sight." Mom turned to Zastra. "Jace said something about being able to replicate new clothes from old ones."

"Sure," Zastra said. "Have Lucas take those off, and I'll take care of it."

Mom made a gimme gesture with her hand. "Hand them over, baby."

"Mom!" I wasn't about to strip down to my underpants in the office of the *Shaymus* in front of Zastra and Detective Tracy and everybody. My cheeks grew warm — I mean the ones on my face.

Gabe came to my rescue. "Tell you what, Lucas and I will go to the galley and take care of it, just us guys."

Buad said, "If you want, I could stand lookout in the hall. Make sure nobody comes in."

So that's what we did. Alone with Gabe, I slipped out of my jeans and t-shirt. He had the replicator break them down to subatomic particles, which destroyed them. But then it made them over again fresh. It took a couple of tries because Gabe wasn't sure how to phrase the command. The first time, the replicator remade them with the exact same rips and dirty spots they had before. The second time, for some reason, it remade them in pink, which I wasn't going to go for even on an alien planet.

Finally, we got it worked out. When I climbed into Detective Tracy's flying car, I was wearing new duds. I crowded in the back seat with Jace and Mom, and we took off.

We flew to the neighborhood where Matty and Ondy lived. The flying car descended to house level, and we zipped up and down the streets.

"Now, Lucas," Tracy said. "Tell me what you remember."

I gazed all around. "Over there is the clump of trees where I hid in the pipe."

"So is the house where you were held somewhere on this street?"

"No. I crossed a couple of streets when I was running away."

"Which way then?"

I leaned forward in the seat and pointed. "Go that way, I think. Yeah. Yeah. That's the fence I jumped over. Can we take a closer look?"

"Hang on," Tracy said. "Everybody's seat belts are on, right?"

Tracy pulled a lever on the controls, and the flying car flipped upside down. Mom made a kind of high-pitched *erp* sound. At least she stayed in her seat. Jace, who wasn't belted in, fell out of his and banged his head on the dome roof.

We swerved into the yard and hovered near the fence. I spotted the red box. The top was all smashed in.

"Ha! He did crash through. That's awesome. He deserved it."

Tracy said. "Where do we go from here?"

"Go over another street or two."

The detective righted the car and flew on.

"This is the street," I said. "I recognize these houses. That neon green house was two or three down from the place I was kept."

Tracy landed the flying car. "Can you identify the house where you were held?"

I wasn't sure. I came to the place in the dark and left in a hurry.

Jace said, "This is only a guess, but how about the one with the front door standing wide open?"

The old house was nearly broken down. Paint was peeling. Windows were boarded up. I remembered the crumbling walkway running through the yard. The single step in the front looked like the one I had sailed over as I fled the house. "Yeah. Yeah. I think that's it."

We climbed out of the car. An old lady standing in the next yard over stared at us.

"Ma'am," Tracy said, "you should go back inside your house."

"Say, you're that Detective Tracy fellow, aren't you?" the lady said.

Tracy's face lit up. "Yes, ma'am."

"Finally coming to raid this place. Well, all I can say is it's about time."

"What do you know about the people who live here, ma'am?"

She laughed like Tracy had said something dumb. "Nobody lives here. But there's comings and goings all hours of the day and night. I never seen the like."

"Can you describe any of these people?"

"What?" She wrinkled up her face.

Tracy spoke louder. "The people. What do they look like?"

"What people?"

"The people who come to the house."

"Oh. Why didn't you say so? One of 'em was a hulking guy with chips in his head and a bot camera in his eye. For Zahn's sake, why do young people do these things nowadays, that's what I want to know? If you ask me, tech is tech, and people is people, and never the twain shall meet. But I guess I'm old and behind the times."

"Was that the only person you ever saw, the augment?"

"The what now?"

"The augment."

"What hog? I don't know what any hog meant. What could a hog mean by anything? They don't talk."

Tracy rubbed his eyes. "No, I ... Sorry. I said augment. An augment is a person with cyborg devices built into their bodies."

"I know it. I'm not completely out of touch. Why do young people do that these days? Stick all those things in their bodies? That's what I don't understand." She pointed a bony finger at me. "Or change the color of their skin. What's wrong with good old Rhegedian blue skin? Tell me that, why don't you?"

"Thank you, ma'am," Tracy said. "You should return to your home. We're going to breach the house."

"Why do you want to bleach the house? Just paint it if you don't like the color."

"Not bleach, ma'am. Breach. This is a sentry operation."

"Well, that's obvious. I saw your yellow coat, and I said to myself, 'Evelyn, that's a sentry for sure, and isn't it about time they came out and took care of this situation?' But there I go blabbering on. You should get on with your raid before the people see you and duck out the back."

"Right. If you would go on inside."

"I don't want to go in that place. I'm no good on a sentry raid. I'm an old woman, for Zahn's sake."

"I meant to go back into your own house."

"Oh, sure. I'm going, I'm going. It's about time for my stories to come on the vids anyway." She turned and headed back to her house in slow, tiny baby steps. Tracy, Mom, Jace, and I stood there watching her until she reached her door and closed it behind her.

Tracy stepped to the open door of the kidnap house. "Sentry service. Is anyone home?"

He paused a few moments before moving inside. The rest of us followed. In the front room two doors faced us along the back wall. One door stood open, dark inside. Tracy motioned for us to stay put while he checked it out. He disappeared through the doorway.

"This room has stairs leading to a basement," he said. His shoes clomped down steps, paused, and clomped back up. "The ceiling down there has a broken vent duct."

I pointed to the other door, and Detective Tracy opened it to reveal a small room, empty except for a few boxes open on the floor.

I stepped closer to Mom. "This is it."

Detective Tracy tapped his wrist thingy and held it to his mouth. "Tracy here. I need an ownership and rental check on one-seven-zero-one Crater Street. Step on it. This is a kidnapping and attempted murder investigation."

Tracy moved into the little room and tapped his watch. It started making a high-pitched *wah-wah-wah* sound as he slowly turned around in a circle. He stepped to the doorway and pointed the thing at me. He tapped the device again, and the sound stopped.

"There are residual air droplets here from four other individuals besides Lucas. I'm sending them to the lab for comparison with known criminals. But it's possible there were other kidnap victims."

"They kidnapped other people?" Mom asked. She put an arm around me. With Jace and Tracy around, I shook it off.

Tracy frowned. "We could be dealing with a kidnapping ring. We might have incorrectly interpreted what Lucas heard. Maybe the merchandise they were talking about was another victim."

Tracy's watch beeped. He looked at it. "Here's the ownership information. Hmm. This house is owned by the city. It's abandoned property. That's no help at all."

# Chapter 20

# The Gallery

*Gabe*

On Earth one night some forty-five thousand years ago, a hunter-gatherer finished dinner, a dinner I strongly suspect consisted of pork ribs or tasty bacon, maybe some ham. I can picture him — or her, as the case may be — leaning back against the wall of his — or her — Indonesian cave, savoring the memory of the tasty meal, our cave person feeling inspired to immortalize the moment and the animal who had given its life so deliciously. And though this had never before been done in the history of Earth, our paleolithic protagonist dipped fingers in a deposit of clay permeated with an ochre-colored iron oxide and proceeded to draw a picture of a pig on the cave wall. It was Earth's first art.

And if people then were anything like people now, the next day a fellow hunter-gatherer said in their rudimentary language, "Well, that doesn't look like a proper pig. The head is too small and the legs too thin."

To which a third hunter-gatherer said, "Ah, but don't you see? It captures the essence of a pig. One must delve beyond the literal to grasp true meaning."

Thus, within the span of a few short hours, Earth had its first artist, art critic, and art snob. Or so I imagine.

Such were my musings when Zastra broke into them. "Gabe! Gabe! Let's go already."

Our hover taxi had stopped in front of a storefront. In the window stood an easel with a painting of an old blue woman in a long black dress sitting in profile.

"Where was your head?" Zastra asked.

"Hmm? Oh, I was thinking about how art theft wouldn't be a problem if people still painted on cave walls."

She shot me a look I couldn't read. Believe me, it isn't always easy to pick up on facial cues with a lizard.

We stepped through the door to a bell ringing somewhere in the back. The flat white walls were covered with paintings of all sizes. Many of the works favored swirling geometric shapes done in vibrant colors. Imagine Van Gogh's *Starry Night* painted by Picasso.

Accent lights shone down from the ceiling onto each canvas. I say canvas, though few of the artworks had been done on cloth. Most were painted on metal or paper or glass. Some were holographic light shows. One appeared to be a kind of gelatinous material plopped down on top of a white pillar.

Zastra said, "Don't touch anything."

I threw her a look. "I already have a mother, thank you."

"You do? I'd like to meet her sometime to ask if she has any idea where she went wrong."

In the center of the room stood a sculpture of an octopus creature on the ramp of a flying saucer holding blasters in two of its tentacles. A small card in front of the artwork said: *We Come in Peace*. I couldn't tell if the art was supposed to be ironic kitsch or serious commentary or both.

As I stood there taking it in, a voice behind me said, "You have excellent taste. You are viewing an original Daygah."

I turned to find a stick thin Rhegedian woman with blueberry colored hair. "It's … um … nice," I said. "Though probably too large to fit in my bungalow."

She looked me over like a price scanner trying to read my bank balance. Her lip curl gave me the distinct impression I had come up short. "Welcome to the Nurke Collection. May I point you in any particular direction?"

Zastra said, "We want to talk to Trub Nurke."

The woman said, "Mr. Nurke is not often in the gallery. I am his assistant, Aras Rune."

Zastra said, "We need to talk to Nurke. We are investigating a stolen painting."

Aras Rune raised a haughty blue chin. "I assure you all our paintings have impeccable provenance."

"We're not saying you have stolen property. We want to talk to Nurke as an art expert. He was recommended to us by our client, Bella Balok."

"Ms. Balok is a customer of ours."

"Yes," I said. "Does that mean we can see Mr. Nurke?"

"As I said, Mr. Nurke is not often in the gallery."

"You certainly did. What you didn't say is whether he is in fact currently here."

Aras Rune's eyes flicked back and forth between the two of us. "What painting is this regarding?"

Zastra said, "A Cormabite."

The face didn't change. The gallery assistant swept her arm toward a painting hanging on another wall. "This is a Cormabite here. You may recognize it. It is called *Possibilities*."

The painting looked like a kid's watercolor done on paper, a turquoise circle dipping into a rose-colored rectangle. That was the extent of it. The use of light and shading was … well, frankly, nonexistent. I seem to remember Lucas drawing something like this when he was five.

"That's a Cormabite?" I asked. It didn't look at all like the *Self-Portrait*, not that anybody's portrait would look like an intersecting circle and rectangle.

"One of her best."

"What does something like this go far?"

"Are you interested in buying it?" she asked, as if quoting the price somehow cheapened the entire discussion.

"Put it this way," Zastra said to me, "we could probably trade the *Shaymus* for it." She turned to Rune. "This isn't the Cormabite we want to discuss. But what we do want to discuss, we want to do so with Mr. Nurke."

Rune huffed out an offended grunt. "All right. I'll go ask if he can see you. Would either of you care for a spritzer while you wait."

Zastra shook her lizard head.

I said, "I'm as spritzed as I care to be."

The assistant disappeared through a curtained doorway.

Zastra said in a whisper. "Our friend is back. Out the window."

"The Pardiun?" I gave the window a quick glance. In a café across the street a person with golden fur sat at a table drinking from a cup, a floppy, wide-brimmed hat pulled down over a brown mane of hair. "That's our boy."

"Kah-Rehn," Zastra said over the translator bot connection as she stepped to the window, "tie into my visual translator bots and record an image of this guy. Run it through facial recognition for Rheged Prime and Pardus and anywhere else you can think of until you find a match."

The Pardiun across the street must have caught Zastra's stare because he rose from the table and walked away.

Aras Rune slipped through the curtain. "You may come through."

We followed through to a small hallway with a kitchenette and an open office door at the end. Inside the office an older Rhegedian with a craggy face, short red hair, and scraggly beard sat behind a desk covered with papers. Across the room stood an easel holding a blank piece of metal. Nurke looked up with a furrow creasing his forehead.

"Excuse me. Who are you?"

"I'm Zastra, and this is Gabriel Lake. We're from the Galactic Detective Agency. Bella Balok has hired us to recover a painting that was stolen from her."

"Which painting?"

"Cormabite's *Self-Portrait*."

"No! For the love of Gort! Please, have a seat."

He waved us to two chairs in front of the desk, both filled with books and catalogs. We cleared the seats and sat.

"I take it you're familiar with the painting?" I asked.

"Familiar with it? Who doesn't know Cormabite's work?"

"You weren't aware of it being stolen?"

"No. Of course, not."

"Has anyone approached you about buying it?"

His face pinched up like a rubber mask. He answered me slowly, deliberately. "I do not deal in stolen artwork."

"The thief might not know that … or might be willing to give it a try anyway."

Nurke shook his head. "When was it taken?"

"A few nights ago," Zastra said. "It appears thieves stole the code for the security system and made off with the painting while Ms. Balok was away."

"What is this planet coming to? People stealing art. Crime on the rise. Seriously, we're becoming like Thomia."

"Surely not that bad," I said.

Zastra said, "Ms. Balok thought you might be able to suggest some people who could fence something like that."

Nurke's head jerked up. "She did, did she? I have no contact with criminal enterprises. I'm not even sure a Cormabite could be fenced. It's a masterpiece."

"Then why would it be stolen?"

One corner of his mouth rose. "Private sale."

"I suppose the sales commission on a painting like that would be substantial."

"If you are implying that I would participate—"

Zastra cut off his outraged response. "Merely an observation. Who might want to acquire the painting?"

"There is a handful of collectors who would be interested if a thief approached them discretely. Possibly, one of the collectors even commissioned the robbery."

"Such as?"

"I'm certainly not going to sit here and slander my own customers by accusing them of illegal activities."

"You wouldn't be. We only need the names of people to talk to. One of them may have heard something or been approached by the thief. Surely, they would like to help Ms. Balok recover her property."

"Well."

I tapped open the phone app where I kept notes. "Bella mentioned Udra Danril and Dun Luce."

"Yes, those are premier collectors. I suppose if a thief was trying to sell a work as culturally significant as Cormabite's *Self-Portrait*, those would be two people to contact."

"Who else?"

"If you want to include off-worlders, I have dealt with Holo Grenton of Pardus. Though he seems to collect only Pardiun art. Odd stuff, Pardiun art. Nearly every piece deals with death or dying. Thematically, they are quite limited."

So a Pardiun was in the mix. I glanced at Zastra. She responded with a single bob of her head.

"How much would the painting be worth?" I asked.

Nurke threw up his hands. "Millions."

"Millions?" I asked. "And yet they couldn't publicly display a stolen painting in their living room. What if Bella stopped by and saw it? I don't see the point."

"Mr. River."

"Lake," I corrected him. "Gabriel Lake."

"Mr. Lake, you underestimate the thrill of the illicit. Part of the allure of a stolen work of art is that it is stolen. Even if it cannot be displayed publicly, what can be enjoyed privately is both the art itself and the feeling of superiority of getting away with the crime, of having put one over on the entire galaxy."

"What you're saying is we're looking for a narcissist."

"True, but I'm afraid that won't narrow it down much in the art world."

Zastra pulled a card from a pocket of her duster coat. "If someone does contact you or you think of anything else, please let us know."

"I will." Nurke stood, his old body unfolding from the chair like a rusty hinge. We took his rising as an indication that we should as well.

I gestured toward the easel along the wall. "Do you paint?"

A smile flickered across his face for an instant. "I dabble. I doubt if any of the collectors we mentioned would be interested in my work."

We left the office, nodded at Aras Rune as we passed through the showroom, and exited to the street.

"Now what?" I asked.

Zastra said, "I'll stay here. You hustle around back."

"For what reason?"

"To find out what happens next."

A narrow, arched passageway ran beside the gallery. I darted through the arch and along a dark brick walkway down a few steps, emerging into an alley running behind all the shops on the street. I stood there a few moments wondering what Zastra thought was supposed to happen.

Then a door creaked open. I ducked behind a stone wall beside steps leading to one of the shops. Peeking over the wall, I saw Trub Nurke walking slowly through the alley. I waited until he was out of sight and followed. He shuffled to the next street and hailed a hover taxi. Now where was he off to?

I spotted another taxi and jumped in it. "Follow that cab." The driver had a basically human face fringed by dark fur all over his neck and hands. He looked like Bigfoot, but I wasn't about to inquire about his species.

We took off, winding through the streets.

"Zastra, I'm in a hover taxi following Nurke in another one."

She answered in my ear. "So there was someplace he had to go right after we interviewed him. Do you believe in coincidence?"

"No more than you do."

As we passed out of the city center into residential areas, the driver looked back at me. "Where are you from?"

"What?" My mind was on Nurke.

"I'm guessing you're not from around here with your funny colored skin."

"Oh. I'm from Earth."

"Does everybody on Irf look like you?"

"Earth. There's a 'th' sound at the end. Yeah, we all look about the same. Two arms, two legs, no fur or scales or anything. We have a smallish range of skin colors."

"So do Rhegedians — sapphire, indigo, cobalt, even some cerulean out east."

"Those are all shades of blue."

"Well, technically."

We climbed a familiar hill and ended up in front of a mansion of glass and gleaming white walls overlooking the city — the home of Bella Balok. The other taxi was speeding off as Nurke knocked on the door of the house.

"You getting out too?" the driver asked me.

"No. Take me back."

"Sure thing, mister. How'd you say that planet name again? Irf-tha? Ir-thth?"

# Chapter 21

# A Few Answers and a Lot More Questions

*Gabe*

"His name," said Oren, "is Krellan Kaktal."

A picture flashed on the view screen in the office aboard the *Shaymus* — a muscular Pardiun with fierce, yellow eyes and a rust-colored mane hanging down to his shoulders.

I said, "I assume this picture is a mug shot." The wall behind Kaktal was striped with regularly spaced lines marked with a series of dots. The Pardiun came up to the line with six dots, four of which were filled in, whatever that meant.

"Correct, Gabriel. This was when he was arrested for jaywalking."

"Jaywalking? The scoundrel!"

Oren flashed a sly smile. "Jaywalking along with burglary, theft, and interplanetary transport of stolen property. He was illegally crossing the street carrying a stolen statue of Zahn at the time of his arrest."

"So why is this cat burglar following us?" I asked. "Did you all see what I did there?"

Buad and Blan squawked annoyed chirps.

Zastra ignored the joke entirely. "Perhaps he's also looking for the stolen Cormabite, though probably not to return it to its owner like we are."

Buad said, "Or maybe he has it and is tailing us to find out if we're getting close."

"That sounds like a risky move," Blan said. "Why take the chance of drawing attention to himself?"

"Exactly," said Oren. "Of course, art theft is inherently a risky endeavor. There's more. According to his record Kaktal generally works with a team. His known associates include Mot Vagis and Carsta Rio."

"Mot Vagis," I said. "That sounds familiar."

"Ms. Balok mentioned him as a possible suspect, the former assistant to her art collector friend, Dun Luce."

"Who is this Rio?"

"Apparently, a Rhegedian woman. Her rap sheet goes back decades with scores of robberies of all kinds. Now that we're aware Kaktal is tailing us, we will return the favor. I want Gabriel and Zastra to interview Dun Luce and have Buad and Blan shadow them. If you pick up Kaktal, follow him and see where he goes."

"You mean give up on looking for Lucas's kidnapper?" Blan asked.

"For now. We will leave the search for the augment in the hands of the sentries for the time being."

I said, "And you want us to ask Dun Luce about his assistant."

"Correct. Also ask him what he knows of the robbery. The art collecting world is a small one. He may have heard something. We'll also need to talk to Udra Danril as soon as possible."

"Danril is the other collector Bella mentioned, right?"

"Correct. The sewer king."

"The who now?"

A smug smile played at Oren's lips. "You'll see. Now, what are we to make of Trub Nurke?"

Zastra said, "Interesting that he ran straight to Bella Balok."

"Yes. Why would a gallery owner leave to consult with her immediately after we told him about the stolen Cormabite? Tell me, did he appear surprised by the news of the robbery?"

"As far as I could tell," Zastra said.

"Maybe he wanted to console her on the loss," Blan said.

"Or try to sell her a replacement picture," Buad said.

Zastra said, "Or perhaps he has information about the theft, something he wanted to tell her but not us for some reason."

"Let's examine that idea," Oren said. "What might it be that he knew? And why wouldn't he tell us?"

"Probably because it incriminated him somehow," Zastra said.

I said, "Like maybe a scheme to recover the painting that involves underworld connections he didn't want to admit he had. But back to this sewer king—"

Oren ignored my attempt to steer the conversation. "Did you observe anything at the gallery suggestive of criminal activity?"

"Only the prices," Zastra said. "Nurke also mentioned another Pardiun as a potential buyer, Holo Grenton. Could be that tailing this Krellan Kaktal will lead to him."

I asked, "Did you learn anything from Bella's other staff, the chef and driver and assistant? What was that assistant's name?"

Zastra said, "Sciatica."

I chuckled. "Yeah. I just wanted to hear it again."

Everyone stared at me. Apparently, the Earth ailment wasn't known out here among the stars.

Blan said, "The chef and driver couldn't tell us much. The chef was in the kitchen during the entire dinner party and didn't see anything of the guests. The driver wasn't even on duty the night of the party. They both knew of the picture but claimed to have no knowledge of the security setup or codes."

Oren said, "And I had Kah-Rehn run the usual checks on them. Nothing popped up that would raise suspicion."

Zastra said, "The assistant has been with Bella for five years and handles the purchasing of everything other than what comes through the kitchen. She wasn't at the dinner party. But get this. When I asked if she had noticed anything unusual or suspicious, she said there had been a Pardiun hanging around."

"Ah hah!" I said. "When was that?"

"Yesterday. Before Bella came here to talk with us."

"You mean after the robbery? Not casing the place before the robbery?"

"Right. She said she also saw a Rhegedian watching the house."

"Male? Female? Young? Old? Large? Small?"

"Male. Hefty. Adult of undetermined age."

"What's this mean?" I asked.

Oren said, "Difficult to say at this point. Was the Rhegedian she saw Mot Vagis or someone else? We don't know. Were the Rhegedian and the Pardiun conducting surveillance together or working independently? We don't know. What were they looking for? Again, unknown to us."

I asked, "Any news on the kidnapping?"

"Nothing positive," Oren said. "The sentries are staking out the house, but so far, the augment has not returned. I doubt he will. They are canvassing the neighborhood, but the only people who witnessed anything saw Lucas running from the augment this morning, which doesn't help since we have all that information from Lucas. Hopefully the database cross-referencing will yield a lead on the augment."

I glanced out the dome to a view of fading daylight. "Do you want us to go visit this Dun Luce guy now?"

"I believe so. No time like the present."

"All right. Let me check in with Sarah and Lucas first."

I descended to the crew deck and moved to my cabin, stopping outside for the door to *ding*.

"Come in," Sarah called.

She was in the chair, Lucas on my bunk, watching some vid about Rhegedian wildlife where a blue guy in khaki shorts and shirt was holding a creature that resembled a cat-sized stegosaurus. He said, "Crikey! Isn't she a beauty!" while the mini dinosaur snapped at his finger.

Sarah paused the vid.

"How's it going?" I asked.

"I'm bored," Lucas said.

"Does anybody want to go out with Zastra and me on an interview?"

"Sure!" said Lucas.

"No way," Sarah said. "I'm not taking him back out there … or letting him out of my sight. Not while that cyborg psycho is on the loose."

"But Mom! I don't want to stay cooped up in here. It could be days before they catch the guy."

"I don't care, Lucas. If you hadn't stowed away, we'd all be home now. And when we do get home, you're going to be grounded, so get used to being bored."

Lucas threw himself back on the bunk and stared blankly at the ceiling with an aggrieved pout.

"Sorry I brought it up," I said.

"It's all right. I know what he means. I'm getting bored myself."

"*You* could come. Jace would stay with him."

"I'm not leaving him."

"As you wish," I said, quoting *The Princess Bride*. "How about I leave my phone?"

"For what purpose? I'm reasonably sure your provider's network doesn't extend to Rheged Prime."

I waved the handset in the air. "I have some excellent e-books downloaded. If you like mysteries, I have Dashiell Hammett's *The Thin Man*. It's a classic. Some Ray Bradbury short stories too if you prefer sci-fi."

She made a face. "I'm living the sci-fi right now … and the mystery. Do you have any literary fiction? Something with a woman protagonist?"

"Um …"

"We need to expand your reading list, Gabe."

"If you say so." I slid the phone back in my pocket.

"Wait. I'll take it. I can check your texts to see if you have other girlfriends."

I handed it over. "All you're going to find are memes sent between Adam and me. Content advisory, some of the humor you might find … um … juvenile … boogers and such."

I left the cabin and found Zastra, Buad, and Blan waiting for me at the ship's ramp.

"Took you long enough, knucklehead," Blan said.

I held up a hand. "There's kind of a situation going on in my cabin. I had to do my best to smooth things over."

"Still planning to ask about building a nest together?" Buad asked.

I shrugged. "Who knows when we'll get back to that?"

Zastra said, "Let's go, Gabe. You and I will leave first. Buad and Blan, give us a couple of minutes and then hit the skies."

As my lizard associate and I hailed a hover taxi, I caught a glimpse of a tawny mane inside a tea shop. I said through the translator bot connection, "Buad and Blan, the Pardiun should be coming out of a place called Fit to a Tea."

"We're on him," Blan said.

Zastra gave the address to the taxi driver, a tall doggy creature with the jowls of a mastiff. He shook his furry head, spewing slobber across the front seat. "I can't take you there."

"Why not?" asked Zastra.

The driver pointed a paw toward the sky.

"What's that mean?" I asked.

"It means this thing hovers. It doesn't fly."

I said, "Hover taxis fly. They go up and over people and other taxis."

"That's more of a hop, not real flying. This address is for a sky suite. You'll have to take a pod shuttle."

We climbed out of the taxi.

I said, "At least it wasn't me who got us kicked out this time."

That earned me a glare. We walked down the block to a shuttle pad. As we stood there waiting for a shuttle, we spotted our Pardiun shadow leave the tea shop, shoot us a glance, and hurriedly duck into another store.

A yellow pod landed on the pad. We sidestepped between the rotors and climbed in.

"Destination, please," the driverless pod said.

Zastra recited the address.

"Insert payment stick, please. Prepare for take-off."

The pod shot up like a rocket hundreds of feet into the air. At this height our destination could be only one of a handful of skyscrapers. The pod headed toward a huge silver cylinder of a building with a dome perched on top. Or not a cylinder exactly. As it rose and tapered, it also twisted in a helix shape.

We headed for the building at what seemed like crash velocity. I directed a concerned glance at Zastra, but she seemed untroubled by our impending doom. Reflexively my arms and legs tensed.

Then I noted cutouts in the side of the building. The pod slipped through one of them into a covered landing pad. Retro rockets ignited, throwing me against the front of the pod's canopy. The vehicle braked to a stop. Zastra, who had stayed in a more relaxed position, laughed at me.

I emerged from the pod, bracing my legs as gale force winds sweeping across the platform threatened to turn me into a skydiver without a parachute. Shuffle stepping, I moved carefully toward an inside doorway.

Buad spoke over the translator bot connection. "We picked up your boy."

"Did he follow us?" Zastra asked.

"Yeah. He took a pod up to the roof of the next building over. You can probably catch sight of him."

I looked out beyond the overhanging roof. A couple of blocks away was a gleaming green skyscraper. On a roof observation deck a gold head stared in our direction.

"Funny thing, though," Buad said. "I think there was somebody else who was following him."

# Chapter 22

# Lucas Helps Fix the Shaymus, For Real

*Lucas*

I rolled over in Gabe's bunk and stared at the wall. This was soooo boring!

Here I was, out in space on an alien planet, which should have been amazing. I mean, what kid doesn't want to visit another planet? Except I was confined to the *Shaymus*. Of course, the *Shaymus* was a spaceship, which should be awesome all by itself. But my mom wouldn't let me out of her sight. She made me stay in Gabe's cabin the whole time like a rat in a cage.

I couldn't believe it. This was so unfair. It wasn't my fault the guy kidnapped me. Okay, it *was* my fault I stowed away, but that was beside the point.

And who knew how long I was going to be stuck here? The Rhegedian police were looking for the kidnapper, but that could take days! Weeks!

The nature vids Kah-Rehn helped us find were interesting … for a while. You can't imagine all the strange alien things in them. Plants that walk around. Animals who evolved with wheels instead of feet. Real live flying dragons. But you can only take so much of that stuff, and I had had plenty.

I briefly thought about slipping off the ship to try to find the kidnapper myself just so I could get back to my real life. But, of course, sneaking out was what had gotten me into this mess in the first place and would only make things worse with Mom. So much worse. I would probably end up grounded until college.

Mom was in the chair reading from Gabe's phone. I rolled back to face her. "I'm hungry. Can I go to the galley and replicate something?"

She set the phone down and gave me the once-over. I expected her to say she had to come with me, but this time she didn't. "Okay. But only the galley, Lucas. Got it? Don't wander all over the ship." Apparently, she was easing up … a little.

I walked around the hallway to the galley and approached the food replicator. Now what to eat? I knew the thing could make donuts, bananas, pizza, hamburgers, tacos, and a bunch of alien food.

"Two tacos, please. No wait. Make it three tacos. No wait. Nobody's here to tell me no. Replicator, I want ten tacos."

A platter full of mouthwatering tacos appeared on the counter. I carried it to the table and started munching them down. I had gotten through one and a half of them when Jace walked in with a mug.

"Hi, Lucas." Jace placed the mug under the replicator. "Coffee refill, cream, one sugar."

He carried the coffee to the table and sat down on the other side. "How are you doing after your ordeal and all?"

"Okay, I guess. I'm glad I'm back with Mom, but ..." I trailed off.

"But what?"

"This is the first my mom has let me leave her side."

"That's to be expected. She had a quite a scare."

"She had a scare? What about me?"

"You too. But you should have seen her. She was beside herself."

"The trouble is now *I'm stuck* beside herself, and I'm bored to death. Do you want some of these tacos? I think I got carried away making them."

Jace reached for one. "Mmm. Thanks. I love these things. Say what you will about Earth, you guys have great food."

"I'm thirsty. Does the replicator make soda?" Mom usually doesn't let me have soda, but this was my chance.

"What's soda?"

I didn't know how to describe it. "It's sweet. Bubbly. Carbonated, whatever that means."

"Well, if you want something sweet to drink." Jace stood and walked over to the replicator. "One pumpas juice."

A glass of blue liquid appeared on the counter. Jace brought it to me, and I tried a sip. The flavor was fruity and sweet like honey. "Ooh. That's good."

"Glad you like it. I grew up on the stuff. All the kids on Rheged drink it. I think it's what makes our skin blue."

I stopped mid-sip. "Seriously?"

Jace grinned. "No. I'm kidding. We're born this way. But I've no idea what it might do to you?"

I checked my hands. No signs of turning blue yet.

Jace said, "If you're bored, I wonder if your mom would let you help me for a while. I have a job that could use smaller hands than my own. Do you want to learn something about spaceship maintenance?"

"Do feet stink? Yeah." Anything would be better than spending all day on Gabe's bunk. Working on a real spaceship would be unbelievable.

"Finish your tacos, and we'll ask her."

I was working on my third and starting to bog down. "I don't think I can eat all these."

"Well, the nice thing about a replicator is there's no waste. It can take what you don't eat and deconstruct it back to quarks and electrons to make something fresh next time. Even the plate."

"You mean this taco shell might have once been a coffee mug?"

"Or a banana peel or one of my old jumpsuits. But now it's a taco."

"Yeah, I'm done."

Jace showed me where to dump the remains of my meal. We returned to Gabe's cabin, and Jace explained the idea to my mom.

"Is it safe?" Mom asked.

"Sure," Jace said. "You remember helping me that time every circuit blew out. The job is mostly replacing parts and running tests on them."

"And it's all inside? I don't want him going outside the ship."

"We can do it all from engineering."

She twisted her lips to the side and fiddled with her necklace. "Um … sure." She pointed at me. "Be on your best behavior."

"I will, Mom. Thanks."

"Do whatever Jace says."

"I will, Mom. Bye-ee"

We walked down the stairs in the central shaft to engineering. A panel was pulled out from the wall showing a set of glowing circuit boards.

Jace said, "We need to resynchronize the ion drive cells."

"What's that mean?"

"You know we have two engines, right? The chrono drive for interstellar trips and the slower ion engine for trips inside a solar system."

"Um … yeah?" I remember Gabe one time trying to explain it all to Mom and me.

"Well, there's a thingumabob for burning the ions we have to tinker with. It's merely a matter of reaching in behind a panel and adjusting the thingy knob with this doohickey device."

Okay. Those weren't the actual words he said. He used a bunch of techno words, but I had no idea what they meant. The upshot was that he needed me to stick a space wrench into the opening and turn something.

Jace handed me a wrench with a bunch of lights running along the handle. "All you have to do is stick it back there on the bolt. The jaws of the wrench automatically size to fit any bolt or screw you touch and stick to it magnetically. The button there on the end releases the magnet when you're done."

I reached with the wrench. It connected with something, and the wrench sang out a series of notes.

Jace asked. "Was that *duh-dee-dah-dah*?"

"Um … I don't know. It sounded more like *duh-duh-dah-dee*."

"Hmm. Can you see the lights?"

I twisted my head around and squinted. "Two blues and a red."

"Ah. That's the what's-it-name contraption." Again, I don't remember the actual words. "Hit the button to release from it and move the wrench to your right."

I moved the wrench. This time it sounded *duh-dee-dah-dah*. "The lights are blue, yellow, red now."

"There it is!" Jace said. "Now hold there while I turn on the whatdoyoucallit gizmo." More technobabble.

A screen came on showing a blue line forming a wave. A jagged red line also appeared on the screen above the blue line.

Jace said, "Turn the wrench to bring the red line down to the blue line."

"Which way do I turn it?"

"Whichever way makes it align."

I pushed on the wrench, and the red line jumped off the screen entirely. "Oops. I guess I need to go the other way." I pulled back, and the line appeared again. After two more pulls and a tiny push, the red and blue lines became one purple line.

"Nailed it," I said.

"You did. Good job, Lucas."

As I released the wrench and pulled my arm from the opening, Jace reached into a bin on the floor and pulled out a clear plastic triangle with gold lines etched on the sides.

"As for your pay, how would you like to have a genuine spaceship part?"

"For real? What is it?"

"This, my friend, is a phased signal attenuator."

"Wow! Thanks. A phased signal what?" I wanted to remember this one.

"Attenuator. It's part of WALT. Or it was. I replaced it this morning. But this still works and everything."

"Phased signal attenuator. What's it do?"

"It changes the power of a signal. Like a volume control. See this screw on the side? That's what adjusts it."

"Are these the connectors?" I ran my thumb along two nubs sticking out of one side."

"Yup. You could plug it into any standard circuit."

"Wow! Thanks, Jace."

"And don't worry. Before we leave, I'll make sure you get out to see some of the sights of my home world. Even if Zastra and I have to break out the blasters and form an armed guard to protect you."

Steps clanged on the stairs. We turned and saw Mom.

"Mom! I helped fix the *Shaymus*. I aligned the ion engine. And Jace gave me this. It's a phased signal attenuator."

"Goodness," she said with the first smile I had seen on her since she discovered me on board. "That's great. Can you spare that part, Jace?"

"Sure. It was getting toward the end of its life cycle and needed to be replaced before it failed."

"I guess it's all right then," Mom said. "Did you thank him?"

"Of course, I did. Do I have to go back to the cabin now?"

"Eh. I'm getting bored in there myself. Maybe Jace has something else for us to do."

A grin spread across Jace's blue face. "There's always something to do on a spaceship."

# Chapter 23

# The Missing Assistant

*Gabe*

*Ding.*

Zastra rang the bell on the door to the sky suite of Dun Luce. While we waited for an answer, I experimentally eased nearer the edge of the covered landing pad to gaze out over the sweeping view hundreds of feet below. Feeling blood rush to my head, I pulled back and shuffled nearer the door.

*Ding.*

A rasping growl emitted from Zastra's throat as she rang again.

"I hear you. I hear you. On my way." The voice reached us from inside, muffled and high-pitched.

A minute later the door swooshed open to reveal a round Rhegedian with a soft, jowly face and thinning gray hair. With appropriate attire, this guy could have been a sumo wrestler. Not that I would want to see it. I wondered if he could even fit through the doorway I was currently viewing him through. The man leaned a hand against the doorframe, heaving breaths as if he had hiked up a mountainside rather than merely walked from another room.

"Sorry ... for the wait," he said in a nasally voice between heaving breaths. "I don't sprint ... to the door ... you understand."

No kidding. How could he?

"We're looking for Dun Luce," Zastra said. "We called earlier. From the Galactic Detective Agency."

"Yes. Yes. Of course." He thumbed his chest. "That's me. I'm Dun Luce. I have to open my own door these days ever since my assistant left me."

"Your assistant, Mot Vagis?"

"Yes." He stretched out the word as he said it and shot us a sideways glance. "Do you know him?"

"No, but he's one of the things we wanted to ask you about?"

His voice shot up an octave. "Well, if he gave my name as a reference, don't expect a glowing report. The man left me high and dry. One day he was here, the next he simply didn't show up. But come in. Come in."

As our corpulent host turned his back to us, I murmured, "Are you getting this, Oren?" He had wanted to tap in through our translator bots to see and hear Dun Luce himself.

"Loud and clear," the boss said in my ear.

Dun Luce ushered us in shambling steps down a hallway to an expansive window-lined room overlooking the city from high above. It was like stepping into the Jetsons' Skypad Apartments. The room was full of hyper-modernistic Jetsons-esque furniture on slender legs.

The walls were hung with landscape paintings of strange alien worlds. One depicted a huge blue planet above a still, eerie lake. Another was a scene of tall pink mushroom-like plants under a starry sky.

Dun Luce motioned us toward a group of built-in swivel chairs. "Sit. Sit. May I offer you something to drink? Some tea perhaps?" He plopped his paunch down on a shell-shaped couch, nearly filling it from side to side.

"Yes. Thank you," Zastra said.

Which surprised me. Zastra was generally all business. I wondered if she was trying to ingratiate herself with him. Obviously, this guy enjoyed his snacks. Why not have a little something with him?

Dun Luce reached out to press a button on the arm of the couch. The movement came across as unnatural somehow, as if his hand had started moving, but it took a second for the inertia of his plump arm to tag along after it.

A robot trundled out from another room, a pod brewer on wheels. It rolled up to Zastra. A cup popped out from the belly of the bot and filled with tea from a hidden spigot. As Zastra reached for the cup, a compartment opened in the side with packets of cream and sweetener. She waved them off and took hers plain. Another compartment slid open, and a tray emerged holding a plate of pale cookies.

"You must try the tea cakes," Dun Luce said. "They have a hint of prunce and spice. So yummy."

"No thank you," Zastra said.

"Prunce?" I asked.

"A delightful fruit," Luce said.

As the bot moved from Zastra to me, a door on its top clicked open. A pod, presumably containing the used tea grounds, shot up into the air like R2-D2 launching a lightsaber to Luke. The first door closed as another gaped open to catch the falling pod.

The bot then made me a cup. I added some sweetener, which poured out in green granules. I also sampled one of the tea cakes, which was delicious. Dun Luce took a cup for himself and three tea cakes before the bot rolled away.

"Mmm. Scrumptious," he murmured, digging into the cakes.

As we sipped and chewed, a thumping sound started up from somewhere as if someone was beating on a wall.

"What's that?" I asked.

"Oh, for the love of Zahn," Luce said. "The neighbors are it again."

"At what?"

"Renovation." He pronounced the word as if it had slithered out from under a rock. "Here." He pressed another button, and orchestral music blared through the room, drowning out the thumping and nearly our voices as well.

"Now what's this about Mot?" Dun Luce shouted.

"What?" I yelled.

"Not what. Mot."

"What about Mot?"

Luce squinted as if that would help him hear better. "That's what I asked you?"

Zastra held up a hand. "Would you mind turning the music down? I'd rather have the thumping."

"Well, I wouldn't," Luce said over the cacophony.

I tried again. "Mot's name has come up in regard to a case we're investigating."

"What case is that?"

"What?"

Luce raised his voice. "I said, what case is that?"

"Seriously," Zastra said, yellow eyes flashing. "Turn it down."

Making a face, Dun Luce pressed a button, which lowered the music.

"Thank you," Zastra said. "Our case concerns the Cormabite *Self-Portrait* stolen from Bella Balok."

Luce crossed his arms, which barely reached each other across his portly belly. "Yes, she told me. Good."

"Good? You endorse the theft of artwork?"

"I do in this case. That painting rightly belongs to me."

"It does?" I asked. Outside the panoramic window a pod shuttle flashed across the sky.

"Technically, it belonged to my grandfather. He was persuaded to loan the painting for a display at the Depository of Art for Tikal."

"That's a museum, I take it?"

"Yes. However, the DAFT—"

"Excuse me?"

Luce frowned at me like I was interrupting a movie to ask what was going on. "DAFT, the Depository of Art for Tikal."

"Oh. Right. DAFT. Wow. I mean … wow. Continue."

"Well, long story short," Luce said, "the painting was stolen. Suspiciously, only that one painting was taken from the display. We always assumed the crime was committed specifically against my grandfather. He … had many enemies. Years later it came to light that the Balok family possessed the painting. Bella's great-grandfather would have been one of those who disliked Grandpa. Old man Balok either bought it as stolen property or, more likely, hired the thieves himself."

"Why couldn't you recover the painting once all that came out?" I asked.

Luce flipped up a beefy palm. "Well … it turned out my grandfather had originally purchased it after a similar theft. The court declined to intervene."

"So if the *Self-Portrait* were to come on the market again, would you be interested in acquiring it?"

"Are you trying to trick me into confessing that I was in on the robbery?"

"We're investigating, asking questions."

"Do you think Mot Vagis had something to do with the robbery?" Luce asked.

"We don't know yet. It's one possibility."

"Have the sentries uncovered any leads on finding the Cormabite?"

"As I said, we're investigating, not them."

"Interesting. You mean Bella took the case to you instead of the authorities. Hmm. Almost as if she had something to hide from public scrutiny."

He had a point.

Luce asked, "Do you have any leads?"

I waggled my head back and forth. "This is only our second day on the case. But you know Oren Vilkas. We'll recover the painting."

"And will you recover Mot as well?"

"I wouldn't be surprised. Tell me, when did he disappear?"

"Now let me think, when was it? It must have been two days ago."

Zastra said, "That would be the day after the break-in. Are you familiar with Carsta Rio or a Pardiun named Krellan Kaktal?"

"No. Who are they?"

"According to police reports they are associates of Mot Vagis, criminal associates."

Luce pulled his mass up straighter on the couch. "I was not aware Mot had a criminal record."

"How long was he in your employ?"

"Hmm. I suppose about a year."

"And what were his responsibilities?"

"He did everything for me. He kept track of my appointments, my correspondence. He prepared my food. He accompanied me everywhere. As you can imagine, I require some assistance in getting in and out of pod shuttles and the like."

"How are you getting by without him?" I asked.

"Bots. Food delivery services. Why? Would you like to apply for the position?"

"No thanks. I have all the gigs I need right now."

Oren sounded in my ear. "Ask more about Mot Vagis."

I said, "Tell me more about Vagis."

"What can I say? He's very intelligent. Has a fine eye for art."

"How big is he?" I was thinking of the hefty Rhegedian that Sciatica said she had seen outside Bella's house.

"Thin. He keeps himself in good shape."

"Where is he from?" Zastra asked.

"Rheged Minor. A little town outside of New Dork ... I believe."

"New Dork?" I asked. "There's a place called New Dork?"

Luce leveled another idiot look at me. "It was named after the city of Dork here, if you remember your history."

Zastra said, "How did you miss Vagis's criminal background? Didn't you check him out before hiring him?"

"Of course, I did." Luce rubbed the back of his broad neck. "I ... um ... um ... hmm. Now that I think about it, I never saw the people he used as references. I made voice calls to them. I suppose it could have all been a con."

"Have you noticed anything of yours missing?"

"No. Nothing."

"So perhaps he took the job with you solely to gain access to and steal Ms. Balok's Cormabite."

"Oh, I can't imagine Mot being involved in anything like that. He may have had problems with the law in the past, but … no. I simply don't believe it."

"Bella Balok had a dinner party a few nights before the robbery. Were you and Vagis in attendance?"

"We were, though I wish I had skipped it. She served us cheap replicated food."

I said, "We heard her chef was on duty that night."

"Well, it smacked of replicated food to me."

"Do you have something against replicated food? I mean, if it's identical at the molecular level—"

"Dear boy, it is not simply about molecules. One needs a chef to add the love."

That hadn't been my experience with the grub I had programmed into the *Shaymus's* replicator. If you started with good source food, then the love, as he called it, seemed to be present there at the molecular level along with the other ingredients. But I'm not a foodie. Clearly from his girth, Dun Luce was.

Zastra asked, "The night of the dinner party did Mot act at all suspicious?"

Dun Luce tittered. "Was he casing the joint, do you mean? No. He barely left my side except once to go to the washroom."

"And where is the washroom at Bella's house?"

"Somewhere upstairs. I don't know exactly. I don't climb stairs myself."

Zastra scanned around at the artwork. "Is that a Natisse?" She didn't unusually stray from the case at hand, but I assumed she had her reasons.

"It is indeed. The famous *Landscape at Cunedda*. It is the prize of my collection."

"What about that one?" She pointed toward a painting of multi-colored polka dots on a white canvas. The frame was ornately carved and painted gold."

"That is a by a newer painter, a Snuul named … well, of course, Snuul names are unpronounceable by most of us."

"You have so many wonderful pieces, and such a lovely home. I'd love to see the rest of it."

Mystery solved. If I knew Zastra, she was more interested in searching for signs of the stolen artwork than in architecture and home decorating.

"Alas," Luce said, "I spent all my energy getting up to let you in. I'm stuck here for the foreseeable future."

Oren's voice sounded in my ear. "Zastra, Gabriel, something has come up. Can you talk?"

"Are we done here?" Luce asked.

"In a minute," Zastra said, answering both of them at once. "What about the others at the party? Did anyone else seem nervous or behave oddly?"

Dun Luce's eyes danced behind their thick lids. "Now that you mention it, one of the guests was Trub Nurke, the gallery owner. Have you met him?"

"We have. What about him?"

"He kept glancing at the Cormabite on the wall. At first, I thought there must something wrong with it. Perhaps it had been damaged. But the painting seemed fine."

Zastra bobbed her head. "Well, thank you for your time. If you hear from Mot Vagis, please contact us."

Luce waved a dismissive gesture. "Oh, I will. It was a pleasure meeting you both."

We exited to the landing pad outside the apartment. I leaned against the wall to prevent wind gusts from knocking me over.

Zastra said, "We can talk now, Oren. What is it?"

Oren answered. "A body."

# Chapter 24

# Cormabite Confab

*Gabe*

"What body?" I asked Oren over the translator bot connection.

"I had WALT monitor planetary communications for alerts related to any of the names connected to our investigation. He got a hit."

"On who?"

"On whom," Oren said. "The alert was for Krellan Kaktal."

"The Pardiun? He's the body?"

"Yes. He has been found dead, shot."

"Wait. Weren't Buad and Blan tailing him only minutes ago?"

Buad's voice cut in. "Yeah. We followed him to the roof of that other building. Then after Gabe and Zastra went into the apartment, he left the roof and went inside. He didn't come out."

"Was that the Cassiopeia Building?" Oren asked.

"Beats me what they call it. Huge thing. Green and shiny."

"That's the one," said Oren. "The body was discovered there in an elevator."

Zastra said, "Blan, you said you believed someone else was following him."

"Yeah, but we couldn't tell much about them. A Rhegedian, thin. He or she was covered head to toe."

I said, "Thin? We had a report of a hefty Rhegedian watching Bella's house. How many different people are in on this?"

Oren said, "Buad, Blan, scout around for the person."

"We'll try, Boss, but it's getting dark."

"Understood. Zastra and Gabe, return to the ship. Buad and Blan, join us after you complete a survey of the area. We have much to discuss."

Sometime later we assembled in the office of the *Shaymus*. Oren was on the view screen, the Avanians in their habitat. Zastra and I were at our desks.

"This murder opens up additional lines of inquiry for us," Oren said. "Who killed Krellan Kaktal, and how is it related to the robbery of the Cormabite?"

"Are you sure the murder is related to the theft?" I asked.

"Kaktal was following you as you investigated the robbery. It stands to reason they are connected."

Zastra said, "And how is this related to the disappearance of Mot Vagis? Was Vagis also killed? Is someone picking off the gang that stole the painting one-by-one?"

Blan said, "That's assuming Vagis and Kaktal stole the painting. It could be someone else stole it, and Kaktal was trailing you guys to try to steal it from them once you found them."

"Yeah," said Buad, "then the real thieves found out about it and bumped him off."

"Then why wouldn't they try to kill Zastra and me too?" I asked.

Blan made kind of a chirping *hmph* sound. "Give 'em time. You may be next."

That was a comforting thought.

"Or maybe Vagis knocked off Kaktal," Buad suggested.

Zastra asked, "In that scenario, is Vagis the thief or is Kaktal?"

Buad shrugged his wings. "Eh. It could go either way."

I said, "There are also questions about Trub Nurke, the guy from the gallery. What's going on between him and Bella to make him run to her right after we asked him about the robbery?"

Zastra said, "Plus, remember we also have a kidnapper to find."

Oren said, "Yes. Our plate is full. We are trying to find a thief, a murderer, and a kidnapper."

I said, "What if they're all the same person? The guy who kidnapped Lucas was talking about murdering someone and some merchandise."

"That is a possibility," Oren said. "Indeed, there are any number of possibilities."

Zastra said, "The main thing we need to do is recover the painting like our client hired us to do."

Oren flashed a cheeky smile. "That is correct, though I have an idea where our painting may be hiding."

"You do?" I asked. "Well, let's go pick it up."

"All in good time. We should first see how the other parts of this complicated case play out."

"So what's next?" Zastra asked.

"Several things." Oren cleared his throat, which I realized he must have done simply for the effect since a digital person doesn't have a physical throat to clear. He enumerated the tasks on his fingers. "First, Detective Tracy has agreed to allow us to view the body. Second, we still need to interview Udra Danril, the other collector Bella told us about. Third, I think we should return to Trub Nurke's gallery and ask him about his trip to Bella's house after your last visit. Finally, we need to remind Bella to provide us the list of her dinner party guests. One of them may have put a camera on the wall facing the security pad, and one of the others may have seen it happen."

I raised a hand. "What about that Holo Grenton guy that Nurke mentioned?"

"We will see. We may yet need to speak with him. There is also the question of Krellan Kaktal's other criminal associate, Carsta Rio. She could be the murderer … or the next victim. We need to find her. Hold on. We're being contacted."

The view screen split down the middle. Oren still appeared on one side. On the other the face of Dak Tracy, or most of it anyway, popped up as he loomed over his wrist device.

"Good evening, Detective Tracy," Oren said.

"Hello," Tracy said, his square jaw and bushy eyebrows dominating the screen. He nodded at our assembled team. "Um … I was hoping to speak with Ms. Gallo and her son."

"I'll fetch 'em," Buad said. He flew out of his habitat and disappeared down the central shaft.

"Has there been a development?" I asked.

He gave a one-word answer. "Perhaps." We were left staring at each other in awkward silence until Sarah and Lucas climbed the stairs. Tracy drew his thick eyebrows together and leaned forward. "Ah, Ms. Gallo, how is Lucas?"

"He's recovering. We both are. What do you have?"

"We have checked on all augments in the city and narrowed it down to six with eye implants. We are rounding them up tonight. I was wondering if you and Lucas could come to the sentry post in the morning for a lineup."

Sarah placed a hand on Lucas's shoulder. "They won't be able to see us, will they?"

"No. The identification will be completely anonymous."

Lucas looked up at her. "Let's do it, Mom. Let's nab the guy."

She patted her son on the back. "All right. Let's be done with this."

"I'll go with you," I said.

Oren said, "If you don't mind, Gabriel, I have other assignments for you."

"But …"

Sarah said, "It will be okay. Can Jace come with us, Oren? It's nice to have a local person to guide you around a strange planet."

"Certainly," Oren said.

She turned to Tracy. "All right, Detective. We'll stop by in the morning."

"Thank you," Tracy said. "We'll round up the suspects. Oh, and whenever your team wants to view the body of the Pardiun murder victim, come on by. He's chilling in the morgue. Once I have this kidnapping wrapped up, I can take the lead on the murder. Tracy out."

Tracy's side of the screen went blank, and Oren's side expanded to full screen.

Sarah said, "C'mon, Lucas. We'll go back to Gabe's cabin and finish the movie."

"I'll be down soon," I said.

As they left, Buad said, "What do you want us to do, Chief?"

"I want you two to hit the skies again tomorrow morning. You are looking for the person who was trailing Krellan Kaktal."

"Right," said Blan. "A thin Rhegedian. Which could be a lot of people."

"A thin Rhegedian who may still be covered head to toe. Zastra and Gabe, I want you to return to the gallery tomorrow to confront Nurke. Then call on Udra Danril, the sewer king. And pay a visit to our client to try to get the guest list."

The meeting broke up. I found Sarah and Gabe in my cabin watching a Rhegedian sci-fi vid about a group of interplanetary explorers who crash-land on quarantined Earth and have to try to blend in with the natives while repairing their ship. Fortunately, in this story the Earthlings also had blue skin, which, though not accurate, was convenient for blending in. The Earthlings were portrayed as little more than cave people, and most of their dialog was along the lines of "oog" and "gruh." That's movies for you.

I sat on the arm of the chair beside Sarah and searched for something encouraging to say. I ended up with the obvious. "So you're going in tomorrow for the lineup."

She nodded without taking her eyes off the screen. "That will be the end of it."

"I wish I could go with you."

"We'll be fine."

"Still, I want to be there for you."

She reached out and took my hand. "You are."

"My assignments shouldn't take all day. You can fill me in when I get back. How was your day today?"

"Slow. Except when we helped Jace, which Lucas loved. I'm ready to go home."

Which made the whole popping the question thing seem increasingly unlikely. As for myself, I was far from bored. I was getting immersed in the robbery and murder case and wanted to see it through to a conclusion, though I didn't want to say all that. Instead, I said, "Let's hope Lucas can pick the guy out from the lineup."

"Knock on wood. Is there any wood around here?"

"We could find a tree outside. Do you want to take a walk?" I was hoping a little moonlight stroll (or with two moons, should it be moonslight?) … well, it might set a mood to allow me to pledge my troth.

She made a face. "What about Lucas?"

"Zastra will hang with him. Jace would too. Or Buad and Blan."

"Not Buad and Blan." Clearly after losing Lucas the first time, Buad was still classified under the heading "unreliable," and Blan was guilty by association. "Not anyone in fact. I'm not ready to stray that far from him."

"We don't have to go far." Even if the time wasn't right for proposing, I craved a few minutes alone with her. To put my arms around her. To walk hand in hand or dance in the moonlight. Man, how did I get to this place where I had it so bad for her?

She shook her head. "Don't think so. Now shush. I need to see if these brave Rhegedian explorers can escape the clutches of the crazy, blue-skinned Earth cave dwellers. There's also a love angle to resolve. See the cave woman in the animal hide miniskirt who somehow or another has her prehistoric hair done perfectly?"

Another strike out. I hoped the Rhegedian hero fared better with the cave woman.

# Chapter 25

# The Lineup

*Lucas*

"Sarah … Sarah … Sarah." The voice of Kah-Rehn filtered in over the speaker in Gabe's cabin.

Mom mumbled something that wasn't words and ended with a snore.

"Sarah … Sarah … Sarah." Kah-Rehn kept saying the same thing over and over.

My eyes clicked open. The light was dim, but this time I knew where I was. I was on Gabe's bunk. Mom was curled up in the huge, comfy chair. Gabe had put us there last night and then gone off to another cabin so we could be alone. It wasn't home, but waking up here was gobs better than waking up in the kidnap house.

"Sarah … Sarah …"

"Be quiet, Kah-Rehn," I said.

"Good morning, Lucas. Your mother asked me to rouse her at this time."

"I'll wake her up." It was what I had to do every Saturday and Sunday morning. The other days, she woke me up.

"MOM!"

She sat straight up with a gasp. "What is it, Lucas? Are you okay, baby?"

"Mom, Kah-Rehn was calling you to wake up."

Mom stared at me blankly for a moment. "Oh. Oh! We're supposed to go to the police station this morning for the lineup. Kah-Rehn, what time is it?"

"The Rhegedian sun has completed fifty-nine percent of its rise toward the meridian."

"What?"

"Converting to Earth terms, the time is thirty-four minutes past nine in the morning."

"Oh my gosh. Get up, Lucas. We need to be moving."

Isn't that what I had just told her? Parents! They have to turn every conversation into an order.

I took a sonic shower, which I liked better than regular showers or baths because I didn't get wet. While Mom got ready, I headed for the galley to eat some breakfast.

I ran to the replicator and said, "One donut and one pumpas juice." The glazed goody and the blue drink appeared on the counter.

"Morning, Lucas." Gabe stood in the doorway rubbing his eyes.

"Hi, Gabe."

Gabe moved to the replicator. "Coffee black." He glanced at my plate. "And a donut."

We sat and dug into our breakfasts, not saying much. Grownups are like that until they get enough coffee in them.

Mom came in and frowned at us. "Donuts? Doesn't that thing have any nutritious breakfast options?"

"It can make bananas," Gabe said.

Mom made a banana and a cup of coffee and sat down with us.

Gabe said "You're off to the sentry post?"

"Uh-huh," Mom said.

"Wish I could go with you. Oren wants me to go back to the gallery and then visit the sewer king."

"The who?" I asked.

He leaned in toward me. "My question exactly. The sewer king. I think that job is going to stink."

I snorted and almost spit my juice.

Jace came in. "You guys ready?"

Mom said, "As soon as we finish here. Hurry up, Lucas."

I jammed the rest of the donut into my mouth. "Ah'm rerry."

"Lucas!"

What? She wanted me to hurry.

We left the *Shaymus* and walked along the street. The blue sun rose in our faces, and the morning was warm. Jace flagged a passing hover taxi. The guy driving was pale green and had a lot more forehead than humans do.

I leaned forward in the seat and said, "Hi."

The driver turned toward me. "Hi, kid."

"My name is Lucas. I'm from Earth."

"Pleased to meet you. I'm Stweet. I'm from Diere."

Mom said, "Let the man drive, Lucas."

Jace said, "Gabe has been to Diere. He met the queen."

"You guys have a queen?" I asked. "Cool!"

Stweet said, "Yes, it is quite cool on Diere. Everyone wears sweaters. And we do have a queen. However, I find that representative democracy in most cases better reflects the political wishes of a citizenry. That is, of course, unless moneyed interests gain too much influence over the legislative process."

"Uh-huh." I didn't know what any of that meant. I decided to sit back and watch the city go by.

The police station was full of blue people in uniform. Yellow vests, yellow hats, and some, like Detective Tracy, in yellow coats. Tracy ushered us into a small room. One whole wall was covered by a view screen showing another small room with bright lights.

Detective Tracy said. "Now the room you're seeing is on the other side of the building and another floor. The suspects will be taken back to the cells until you leave the building. There is no way the people you see will ever see you. If you identify one of them, we will hold the person for trial. Do you have any questions?"

I shook my head.

Tracy said something into his wristwatch. A door opened in the other room and six Rhegedians walked in. They each wore a different colored jumpsuit, blue, green, yellow, red, purple, orange. They looked like a box of crayons standing there.

Tracy said, "If you spot the kidnapper, Lucas, shout out the color."

All the suspects had eye implants. And they all looked creepy and scary and like people I would want to avoid. None of the implants were right, though.

One wore a silver half-helmet with a glowing purple eye. One wore a black face mask with a red light shining out from the side like Captain Picard when he was a Borg. Another wore dark goggles with two glowing yellow eyes. One had two telescoping eyes, which kept extending and contracting the whole time — super spooky. One had the right kind of camera lens implant, but his whole head was covered by a helmet like Magneto. I ran my eyes over them down the line, back up the line, down the line again.

"What do you think, Lucas?" Tracy asked.

I shook my head.

Tracy spoke into his wrist. "Have them all turn to the side."

When the suspect guys turned, they didn't all turn the same way, which meant some ended up facing each other. They sneered and started yelling and shoving. Sentries rushed in and broke it up and turned them all to face in same direction.

I said, "The guy who took me was bigger than any of these. And his eye implant sat right on his eye like a camera lens. He didn't have helmets or masks or stuff. And he had those circuit chips stuck on the other side of his head."

"You're sure?" Tracy asked. A muscle in his jaw poked out.

"Detective," Mom said, "he said none of these guys are the one."

"All right." Tracy muttered something into his wrist, and the guys marched out.

Mom said, "Can you round up some more that match Lucas's description?"

"Honestly, Ms. Gallo, these were the ones who came up the closest from the implant database. I don't know where we go from here."

Jace asked, "Is it a database of the whole galaxy?"

"No, nothing like that exists. It covers the Rheged system, here and Rheged Minor."

"So it sounds like this guy had his implants done in a different system."

"Or on the black market."

"Back alley cybernetic implants?" Mom said. "That doesn't sound like a good idea."

"It isn't," Tracy said.

"What do we do now?" I asked.

Tracy smiled at me in the way grownups smile at kids, like we're funny or stupid or something. "All the sentries on patrol have the description you gave. If a sentry spots him, we'll arrest him."

Mom said, "We can't wait around on this planet forever."

"I understand. If you need to return to Earth, you may do so."

Jace said, "We can always bring you back when they find the guy."

"If they find the guy," Mom said.

"Sorry," Tracy said. "That's about all we can do for now."

Mom sighed. "Thank you, Detective. I guess we'll head back to our ship."

# Chapter 26

# The Question of the Carafozzio

*Gabe*

I certainly wouldn't call myself an art connoisseur, but I managed to pick up a few things in my fine arts class in college. I can comment on Rembrandt's use of light, Van Gogh's skill with color, Monet's mastery of texture. Though seriously, it doesn't take much to appreciate those guys. I can also appreciate First Fridays in Indy when galleries throw open their doors to the huddled masses like me, which makes for a date night both classy and cheap … unless you buy something. Returning to Trub Nurke's gallery with a First Friday mindset, I walked in like I knew what I was doing.

"Gabriel Lake and Zastra, is it not?" Aras Rune said as we entered. "Welcome back to the Nurke Collection. Would you like to revisit the Daygah?" A smile flitted across her face, giving me the distinct impression that she knew I couldn't afford it and was making fun of me.

I decided to play the game back at her. "Actually, I'm more taken with this abstract." I pointed at a canvass of odd shapes in greens and oranges.

The condescending smile flickered across her face once more. "This is not an abstract. It is a quite realistic painting of a bomber beetle from Arsawa painted by the renowned nature artist Pole Sayzan."

I twisted my head one way then the other, trying to make the weird shapes come together in my mind as a bug. "Bomber beetle?"

"It drops onto your head and delivers a toxic bite."

"Remind me not to visit Arsawa."

Zastra said, "We'd like to see Trub Nurke again."

Rune stared at us for a second before turning on her heals and disappearing through the curtained doorway. She returned a minute later. "Mr. Nurke will be with you momentarily. May I offer you something to drink while you wait?"

"No thanks," Zastra said.

"He may require a few moments to finish what he is doing. Why don't you sit?" She swept her hand toward a grouping of chairs. Until that moment I hadn't been sure whether they were for sitting or were part of an art installation.

I sat. As I expected, Zastra hmphed and continued standing. Rune sat beside me, which I didn't expect at all.

She crossed her long legs and clasped her hands around one knee. "How is your investigation progressing? The case must be terribly exciting!"

Zastra didn't respond. I felt it only polite to say something. "Well, I wouldn't say exciting. We mainly go around asking people questions."

"And what have you learned in asking all your questions?"

"It's early days. We're still trying to form a picture, no pun intended."

Rune leaned in and conspiratorially asked, "Who do you think stole it?"

"We don't know … yet." I was thinking about the thin Rhegedian, who had followed and possibly killed Krellan Kaktal. Aras Rune, who now seemed fascinated by the robbery, was plenty thin.

"You don't think Mr. Nurke is involved, do you? Surely that isn't why you visited again."

Zastra shot her a grim look. "We simply have a few more questions for him. But since you're here, let me run a few names past you. Mot Vagis. Carsta Rio. Udra Danril. Have you heard of any of them?"

"Mr. Danril is a client. And the first person you said — Vargis or whatever. I think he is the assistant to Dun Luce."

"The name is Vagis, not Vargis," I said. "And he's a former assistant. He seems to have disappeared about the time of the robbery."

"Oh dear. I hope nothing has happened to him. He seemed like a nice person. Well, the one time I met him."

Zastra said, "When was that? The time you met him?"

"I don't … remember exactly. I think he came in here once on an errand. Dun Luce doesn't go out much himself."

"Understandable given his girth," I said. "Do you recall what the errand was?"

"Oh. No." She rose. "Excuse me. I'll see if Mr. Nurke is ready for you now."

She disappeared through the curtain once more. Zastra and I threw each other knowing glances concerning Rune's inquisitiveness and hesitancy to answer questions.

A few moments later the craggy-faced Nurke burst through the curtain. "All right. What do you need now?"

"We need to ask you a question," Zastra said as I stood.

"Then ask it already."

"You might prefer we ask it in a more private setting."

Nurke leaned to peer around the partitions of the gallery. "We're all alone here. I sent the girl out for tea."

I said, "All right. After we left yesterday, you went straight to Bella Balok's house. Why?"

He glared at us. "You followed me? Am I a suspect in the robbery?"

Zastra said, "We're investigating a crime. This is how we work. Also, this investigation now includes a murder. Are you acquainted with a Pardiun named Krellan Kaktal?"

"No."

"Yesterday he was sitting in the café right across the street from here."

"It's a busy street." Nurke rubbed a thumb against a spot of something on his other hand. It appeared to be umber-colored paint.

"So why did you visit Bella Balok?"

Nurke sniffed. "As I understand it, she's your client. Why don't you ask her?"

"We will. At the moment we're asking you."

"I merely wanted to offer my condolences for the theft and tell her that if she needed anything, she had only to ask."

"You could have done that with a vid call."

He straightened his wiry frame and smirked. "Perhaps I'm old-fashioned, young lady, but I believe in the personal touch."

I said, "If you want to help Bella, you could start by being more forthcoming with us."

"I already told you everything I know. I have no knowledge of the robbery … or this Pardiun."

He was hiding something. I would bet anything on it. But what he was hiding and how to pry it out of him was another matter. I paced a few steps, which took me to the other side of a partition running through the room. I took another step, drawn in by a painting hanging there.

"Excuse me," I said. "This painting with the humongous pink mushroom things."

Nurke scoffed. "That's hardly a fitting description for a Carafozzio, one of the preeminent Antarean artists of the realism period."

"Whatever. My point is this picture was hanging in Dun Luce's apartment. Same indigo sky. Same weird plants and cracked lava-filled ground."

He tsked. "Weird plants! This piece of art happens to be an extremely realistic rendering of the Anterean barren region."

Zastra stepped to my side. "Gabe's right, though. Same painting."

Nurke waved a dismissive hand. "What Dun Luce has is probably a print or a reproduction. The work is quite famous and popular. It adorns a hundred thousand college dorm rooms."

I said, "Dun Luce doesn't live in a dorm. Far from it. And he doesn't seem like a print kind of guy. He seems more like an original artwork kind of guy."

"I wouldn't know. I haven't seen his … copy."

"You're sure this is the original?"

"Of course, I am sure. I authenticated it myself. This painting is worth more than the house you live in."

I said, "Hey, you don't know my house. Granted, it's no mansion. But the housing market in my neighborhood is hot right now."

Zastra asked, "How long has your assistant worked for you?"

"Aras? Let me think. She came to me nearly a year ago. Why do you ask?"

"Do you know Mot Vagis?"

"Vagis. Is he the person who always comes in representing Dun Luce?"

"Always? He comes often?"

"Often enough. Dun Luce is a collector, and Vagis keeps an eye out for art he might like."

"Kept," I said. "Vagis quit coming to work. Do you know anything about that?"

"Why would I? Now are we done here?"

"One more question. What were you doing in the back that we had to wait so long?"

"What are you talking about? I came right out."

"You weren't busy with something?"

"Listen, what I do in my gallery is my business and not yours."

"Painting perhaps?" I considered pulling a Sherlock Holmes and pointing out the telltale paint smudge, but I didn't.

"As I told you yesterday, I dabble."

"I would love to see your work?"

"I assure you I have no intention of displaying my work to someone who views Carafozzio's *Morning in the Barren* and sees 'weird plants.' Good day." He turned on his heels and disappeared through the curtain.

As we stepped out on the street, Zastra put out a hand to stop me. "Take a peek at the clientele in the café this morning. But be subtle about it."

"You know me. I'm the essence of subtlety."

"Yeah. Generally, about as subtle as a tsunami."

I stretched and rolled my neck, catching a glimpse in the shop window of a Rhegedian in sunglasses wearing an unseasonably warm coat zipped up all the way with the hood covering the head. The only reason I knew the person was Rhegedian was the blue nose.

I said, "Do you think that's the person who was following Kaktal?"

"Seems likely. And possibly his murderer. I feel like a cup of tea myself. While I do that, why don't you slip around back again and see if Nurke puts on a repeat performance from yesterday?"

I strolled down the alley to the back of the gallery and took a seat on the steps. I waited five minutes in which absolutely nothing happened and then contacted Zastra over the translator bot connection.

"I don't think he's bolting this time. How are you getting along?"

"I hate to say it, but I lost the mark. They went into the washroom and never came out. I checked, and it has an outside window. It's small, but a thin person could squeeze through."

"Do you think it was Aras Rune? Nurke said she went for tea."

"Who could tell in that getup? She has the body type, but so do a lot of other people, including our client. I guess we're done here."

I started back down the alley. "What about the other painting with the pink mushrooms, the Caravaggio."

"Carafozzio. Who's Caravaggio?"

"Oh … um … Italian artist of the Rococo … no, the Baroque period. I do know a thing or two about art."

"Earth art maybe. You're a blank canvas when it comes to the galactic masters."

"I used to watch *Masters of the Universe* when I was a kid."

"What?"

"Anyway, Carafozzio sounds like a character in a Muppets movie about the Renaissance."

"What?"

"Which would be amazing. I wonder what they would call it. *The Muppet of Venice. A Muppet for All Seasons. Muppedeus.* Man, I would so watch that."

"Why is it I never understand what you're talking about?"

"Don't worry. Not everyone can keep up with a mind like mine. So which one of the Carafozzios do you think is the original?"

"Good question. Oren can pull images from our translator bots and have Kah-Rehn do an analysis."

"What do you think it means?"

"It means one of them, Nurke or Dun Luce, has either been duped or is trying to dupe someone else into buying art forgeries."

## Chapter 27

# The Sewer King in the Study with the Cane

*Gabe*

Zastra and I hailed a hover taxi. As we climbed in, the driver extended a bright orange tentacle above the front seat. The tentacle swiveled back and forth in our direction. I couldn't tell if the appendage was scanning us or waving howdy. I wiggled my fingers to wave back, but Zastra grabbed my arm and jerked it down.

This wasn't any species I had encountered before. The cabbie was like a mutant starfish with about a dozen arms but no discernible eyes, ears, or mouth. How was this guy going to pilot this thing?

The driver raised one of its many arms to a keyboard and tapped while another arm hung over the attached screen as if watching. A computer voice sounded from a speaker. "Where to?" The arm that had been hanging over the screen now swung in our direction. Apparently, there was an eye in there somewhere.

Zastra said, "The home of Udra Danril. Do you have the address?"

While the arm looking at us held its position like a cobra preparing to strike, a third tentacle swung into the "seeing" position in front of the screen. Maybe several of these arms contained eyes — or all of them for all I knew. In any case, with all the tentacles swinging this way and that, the effect was starting to resemble a solitaire game of Twister.

The typing arm tapped some more, and the speaker said, "Looking it up. Seven-four-six-five-six Delta level minus K."

"What's minus K?" I asked.

I didn't get an answer. The arms swept to the steering wheel, taking positions at ten and two … and also nine and three. With another arm jauntily propped up at twelve and another resting leisurely at six. A couple of other arms poked straight up, I suppose, as eyes.

The taxi took off through the streets at a breakneck pace, bounding over pedestrians and other hover vehicles. Rounding a corner, we flew into a parking structure and sped down a ramp. At the bottom, we turned and took another ramp down, then another ramp. We looped around going deeper and deeper.

Daylight was now several floors above us. The only lighting came from eerie green floodlights built into the ceiling. A few more levels down, there weren't even parking spots, only the ramp, which seemed to be descending into the bowels of the planet. Finally, the hover taxi pulled to a stop beside a black door, and we climbed out.

I glanced around at our gloomy surroundings and the weird green glow from the lights. "This doesn't look like a great spot to hail another taxi. Should we have him wait?"

"Yeah. Good idea." But as Zastra turned back to the vehicle, it sped off. "I guess we'll worry about that after we talk to the sewer king."

"Yeah. About that sewer king name …"

She didn't answer. She found a button beside the door and pressed it. Nothing happened. She pressed the button again, then several more times in quick succession, which made me wonder if she disliked the creepy ambiance of this place as much as I did.

The door at last slid open. Behind it stood a gleaming white metal bot. Two vent pipe arms extended from a wide cone-shaped base, perched on top of which was a head the size and shape of a toaster turned sideways. Two blue dots of light scanned us from inside the flat, black face.

Zastra said, "We're here to see Udra Danril."

The robot answered in a soft, fawning voice. "Names, please?" A half-moon of blue light appeared on the lower part of the toaster face as an imitation electronic smile.

"We're Zastra and Gabriel Lake from the Galactic Detective Agency."

"Yes," the robot said, pronouncing the word slowly and with deference. The blue light smile continued to shine.

"We would like Mr. Danril's advice on a case we are investigating, one involving stolen artwork."

"Yes."

This was about the time one would expect the automaton to wheel back and let us pass. It did not.

Zastra said, "Mr. Danril should be expecting us."

"Yes." The robot continued to stand in the doorway blocking us. "And what specific questions did you want to ask Mr. Danril?"

Zastra's answer was curt. "We'll ask him ourselves."

"Mr. Danril would prefer for me to relay the questions to him."

"That's not how this works."

"Yes." The smile might as well have been painted on.

I said, "Yes what?"

"Yes … sir."

Zastra blinked yellow eyes at the robot. She placed a hand on one of its arms. "Do you have a name? A designation?"

The half-moon smile widened. "I am CAF."

I said, "CAF? C-A-F? Is that an acronym for something? Let me guess. Cyborg Automaton Footman. Computerized Android Flunky. Companion And Friend."

Zastra held up a hand. "CAF, are you familiar with Srathans?"

The blue lights in the toaster head blinked off and on. "Srathans are an intelligent reptilian species who originated on the planet Sratha in the Fesarius system."

"That's correct." She patted the robotic arm. "And does your record on Srathans note that I could snap these arms of yours like a breadstick?"

The blue lights blinked faster. CAF backed up and turned to let us pass. "Please enter. Mr. Danril is in his study. Follow me."

The bot led us to the room, parking itself near the door. Personally, I wouldn't call the space a study. A study implies bookshelves filled with leather-bound volumes, rich carpets, armchairs, chandeliers. These walls were gray concrete, the ceiling low. A massive desk filled the room surrounded by a few chairs. Vivid landscape and still life paintings hung on the walls. This was more like somebody had set up an office in the basement of an art museum.

Behind the desk sat a man, straight and thin as a pole with intense eyes and slicked back hair the color of mud. Over his shoulders hung a scarlet cape. You don't see many capes nowadays on any planet. Bold style choice.

As we entered, he looked up from a tablet device with a scowl. Setting down the device, he grabbed a cane from the side of the desk and stood. "Who are you? What's the meaning of letting them in here, CAF?"

"My name is Zastra," my partner said before CAF could answer. "This is Gabriel Lake. We work with Oren Vilkas. I believe our ship contacted you. We want to talk to you about a stolen Cormabite."

"You think I possess a stolen Cormabite?"

"I didn't say that. But since you mention it, do you? One was recently robbed from the home of Bella Balok."

"Which Cormabite?" He stepped around the desk, dragging one foot as he leaned on the cane.

"The *Self-Portrait*."

He stopped and leaned against the desk. "That painting was once mine … before it was stolen from me. All I have now is one of Cormabite's more minor works." Our host pointed his cane at a sign on the wall with hand-painted red letters that spelled out: *Eat at Joe's*.

"That's a Cormabite?" I asked.

"Yes," Danril said with a defensive bite in his tone. "She painted this early in her career … when she struggled to make ends meet."

"Well, we all have to start somewhere," I said. "When was the *Self-Portrait* supposedly stolen from you?"

"Not supposedly. It was. About a year ago."

"How long did you have it?"

"I bought it perhaps five years before."

Zastra said, "That's interesting since Bella Balok maintains the painting has been in her family for generations."

"That's a lie. The *Self-Portrait* hung in this very room. There." He pointed with his cane toward a painting of binary suns shining down over a red, Martian-like landscape. It looked like a matte painting background for a low-budget sci-fi movie.

"Who sold it to you?" I asked. "The *Self-Portrait*, I mean."

"I acquired the work in a private sale through the Nurke Collection. I never learned who the seller was. It was my first great art purchase after I gained my fortune."

"Did you alert the authorities when it was stolen?"

"Yes, of course. For all the good it did. Bunch of incompetents."

"How did someone ever sneak way down here and break in to rob the place?"

"I don't know. I have a top-notch security system, which somehow was switched off."

"That sounds like how the robbery at Bella's house went down. It happened following a dinner party."

"Well, I do not host dinner parties. The robbery occurred while I was off planet on business."

"Who else lives here with you?"

"No one. I have bots to take care of my needs — bots from my own company, Danril Robotics, I might mention. Our cybernetic designs are revolutionizing the industry across the galaxy. On Fornax you can hardly enter a home without finding one of our bots."

I said, "Oh, you make bots? I thought you were known as the sewer king."

Danril rapped the cane across the desk. "Who called me that? I do not appreciate that name."

"Who would? How did you come by it?"

"I didn't come by it." He scowled. "True, I made my fortune building the sewers of Tikal and other cities. However, my company has since diversified into mining, robotics, many other fields. I am a patron of the symphony. I have built up an enviable art collection. Yet some people refer to me as," he made a face, "the sewer king."

"Well, you do live way underground. And apparently you don't socialize." And wear a cape, I thought. For crying out loud, what did he expect?

Zastra asked, "Do you have any suspicions about who was behind the robbery — your robbery?"

"Why, Bella Balok, of course. Shortly after the theft I heard she had the Cormabite. Obviously, she hired someone to steal it from me and then made up the story about it being in her family for generations."

I said, "So — and I'm just brainstorming here — in retaliation you sent a gang of thieves to her house to steal it back."

Danril showed his teeth. "No! I am a successful businessperson. I am astounded, I am stupefied that you would accuse me." He closed his eyes and took a breath. Then in a gentler tone, "I could buy the painting from her many times over if I wanted."

"If it were for sale."

"I'm telling you, the painting is mine."

"Where were you four nights ago?"

"Was that the night of the robbery? I was here, as I almost always am."

"Was anyone with you?"

"No. I value my privacy. Should I have CAF run through the logs for you?"

Zastra said, "I don't see the point. Bot logs can be altered, especially by a robotics expert."

One of the paintings on the wall grabbed my attention, a still life of yellow and red poppies in a vase, the colors so vibrant the flowers nearly jumped off the canvas.

I said, "That resembles the work of an Earth artist named Van Gogh."

Danril beamed. "It is."

"You mean it's a real Van Gogh? How did you get it?"

He cocked his head. "Earth security systems are primitive."

The nerve of this guy stealing art treasures from Earth. I wanted to grab the Van Gogh right then and make a run for it, but it seemed unlikely I could escape up so many underground levels.

I asked, "Why do you live all the way down here anyway?"

The lips twisted into an odd shape that he probably considered a smile. "I moved down here while the sewers were being built to be close to the work. I stayed down here because I find people tiresome."

"But to never look out a window …" I let the question finish itself.

He waved his cane at the paintings. "These are my windows. Through these I can view any world I choose."

"If that's the case, why would you want a self-portrait? It would be like having a peeping tom."

He took a step toward us, working the cane with a step and shuffle gait. "I have a proposal for you."

"What?" Zastra asked.

"Simply this. Continue your investigation but work for me. Recover the painting and return it to me. Whatever Bella Balok is paying you I'll double."

"We'll inform Oren Vilkas, but he doesn't abandon clients."

"What about clients who are criminals, who, in hiring you, drag you into a criminal enterprise? You should consider my offer."

I said, "Oh, we will. Are you acquainted with Krellan Kaktal?"

"No. Who is that?"

"Mot Vagis?"

"No."

"Carsta Rio?"

He shook his head. "Who are these people?"

"Those names have come up in our investigation."

Zastra said, "You said you bought the Cormabite through Trub Nurke. Did you work personally with him?"

"Yes. More recently I have worked with his assistant, Aras Rune. Charming young lady." It sounded creepy when he said it.

"Do you know Dune Luce?"

"Everyone in the art scene knows Dun Luce. I find him annoying. Now, is there anything else? I have business to attend to."

"Oh, one other thing," I said, "I don't suppose you own a Carafozzio, do you? *Morning in the Barren* is the one we're interested in."

# Chapter 28

# A Long Shot

*Gabe*

Turns out Udra Danril did not own a copy of the Carafozzio. But we had found out he was a thief, of Earth artworks if nothing else, not to mention misanthropic and more than a bit weird.

As we left the underground lair and stepped back into the endless ramps of the parking structure, Zastra said, "I want to get back to the *Shaymus* and talk to Oren about all these conflicting claims on who owned the Cormabite when. You go visit Bella."

"By myself?" In this job I had faced off in firefights against aliens, battled robots, been beaten up, arrested, everything. Being alone with Bella, though, was I risk I didn't want to take, especially with Sarah on the same planet.

Zastra glowered at me. "Do I have to do everything around here?"

"No. No. But if this comes up in conversation later, remember this was your idea, not mine. How do we even get out of this place? I don't want to walk all the way back to the surface."

Not bothering to answer me, she spoke through the translator connection. "WALT, can you send two hover taxis, please?"

WALT's drawl sounded in our ears. "Of course, I can."

Zastra pulled out her tablet and tapped. "I'm sending the location."

"Whoa! Are you guys down a mine or something?"

I said, "We're about a dozen levels below a parking garage, WALT."

"Unbelievable. I'm making the call right now."

A few minutes later I was speeding along on the proper side of ground level toward Bella Balok's house in a taxi driven by a Srathan. It was too bad Zastra didn't take that one. She and the cabbie would have had so much to growl about together.

Koval met me at the door as bent and prickly as ever. "Good morning." She said it like a threat.

"Hi. Is Bella home? I have some follow-up questions."

Without a word Koval stepped back for me to enter. I followed her to the white-tiled room we had been in before. Bella was again lounging on the couch. When she saw me, she swung her blue legs around to a sitting position and patted the seat beside her.

"Gabriel! What a pleasure to see you again! And this time you came alone. Come sit."

I opted for a seat on one of the other couches. "I won't take much of your time. I only wanted to follow up on getting that list of dinner party guests."

"Oh, I completely forgot." She picked up an electronic device from a side table. "I did get it prepared. I can send this to your device right now, Gabriel."

I pulled my phone out of a pocket and held it up. "Well, I am on the latest version of Android, but I doubt it will interface with your space phone. Earth quarantine and all that. How about you send it to our ship?"

"Anything for you, Gabriel." She tapped on the device. "Done."

"Excuse me," I told her. "WALT, you should be receiving a list of names from Bella Balok."

"Yeah, it's coming in now," WALT said in my ear.

"Thanks." I turned back to Bella. "We got it."

She fixed her eyes on mine. "Is there anything else you want, Gabriel?"

"Um … well, have you ever heard of someone named Krellan Kaktal?"

"No, should I?"

"He was outside your house yesterday morning when we were here."

"Perhaps you should interrogate him, sweat it out of him as you detectives do."

"That would be difficult. Someone has since killed him."

"Oh my."

"This is now bigger than art theft."

"Nothing is bigger than art theft."

"Not somebody's life?"

"Well, of course. But you should see the art auctions I attend. Absolutely cutthroat. Would you like tea?"

"I can't stay long. I should check in with Sarah. You remember Sarah, the Earth woman with us. With me. We're dating. Almost engaged."

"Koval," she called. "Bring tea." Then to me, "Tell me how the investigation is proceeding. Your client requests a briefing."

It appeared I was staying for tea. "We've interviewed Trub Nurke, Dun Luce, Udra Danril."

Her eyes twinkled. "Ah, Danril. What did you think of the sewer king?"

"Turns out he doesn't like the name."

"I'm sure he doesn't, and yet here we are."

"Along the way we've picked up a few other leads. Are you familiar with Holo Grenton?"

She shook her head.

"He's a Pardiun art collector."

"Another Pardiun? Are you trying to pin the crime on Pardiuns for some reason?"

"We don't pin crimes on anyone. We follow the evidence. I don't suppose you ever owned a Carafozzio did you? *Morning in the something.*"

"I used to have *Morning in the Barren*. I sold it to Trub Nurke."

"It's still in his gallery ... or not. Interesting piece. Why did you sell it?"

She waved it away. "Cash flow."

Koval entered with a tray. While she was pouring the tea, Bella stood and walked to the huge picture windows. "Lovely morning."

A blue light flashed through the air, and the window beside her exploded into smithereens. Koval cried out and dropped to the floor, a scorch mark across the shoulder of her black uniform. She stared at me wide-eyed.

I glanced toward Bella, who still stood frozen in front of the broken window, her jaw gaping. I sprang from my seat, grabbed her, and took her to the floor as another laser blast pierced the air above us. Still exposed in front of the floor-to-ceiling window, I rolled across the floor with her in my arms until we reached the windowless corner of the room.

She looked at me, eyeball to eyeball. "My hero! What was that?"

I rolled off her and motioned for her to stay down. "It appears someone wants *you* dead as well."

I belly crawled to the corner of the window and peeked out, catching sight of another blast of blue. A table beside me exploded into shards, and a dagger-like fragment flew toward my head. I ducked back down beside Bella.

She raised one eyebrow. "Maybe they want you dead. No one took a shot at me until you came to visit."

"Nah. Everybody loves me."

I glanced over to where the maid was still lying on the floor. "Are you hit bad, Koval?"

"I'll live. Don't let me interrupt the witty repartee you two have going on."

Bella asked, "Do you think this is the same person who killed that Pardiun?"

"It stands to reason. Oren, come in."

Oren's voice sounded in my ear. "What is it, Gabriel."

"I'm with Bella at her house. A sniper started shooting up the place."

"Is everyone all right."

"The maid was hit but not badly."

"Like you would know," Koval said. "You haven't checked on me."

Oren said, "Is the shooter still around?"

"Search me. I took a peep a few seconds ago and was shot at."

"Well, peep again."

"With all due respect, Oren, blaster beams move at the speed of light, and I don't."

"How long has it been since the last shot?"

"I'm guessing … twenty seconds."

"Hazard a glance. But be careful."

I muttered, "Well, there's a mixed message."

I scooted up into a sitting position against the wall, then leaned forward slowly until I could see out the window. Everything on the grounds looked peaceful and deserted. I scanned the grounds trying to imagine where a sniper might set up shop. I spotted a clump of trees on a hill that looked likely, but no one was there.

Away in the sky a flock of what I first thought were birds soared toward us. Something about their movement seemed unnatural. I gazed at them and realized they weren't birds but rather yellow painted drones.

"Oren, do you see these things flying in?"

"Yes. Those are sentry drones. They must have picked up the blaster fire and are coming to investigate. With them on the way, you can bet your assailant is fleeing the scene. I'll contact Detective Tracy. Sit tight."

"Oh, I intend to sit tight."

I glanced at Bella. A line of pink blood trickled down one cheek, and there were cuts on her arms.

"You need to get cleaned up," I said. I stood and edged toward the window. When that didn't draw fire, I helped Bella to her feet. "Go on. I'll tend to Koval and welcome the sentries when they arrive."

She did, but not before folding herself into me and murmuring, "Thank you." I let my arms hang awkwardly at my sides.

Minutes later, Dak Tracy was sitting with me in the kitchen, our hands wrapped around cups of tea from a food replicator.

"I have to say," I had to say, "I'm pleased to see the boys in yellow show up. I finally feel safe enough to raise my head."

"So you never saw the shooter?"

"All I saw were the flashes. Are your people searching the clump of trees I mentioned?"

"They are. I don't expect to find much. I don't know what kind of weapons you have on Earth, but blasters don't leave much of a trace. They don't eject cartridges like the old projectile weapons did."

"It sure left a trace on the table it blew up … and on Koval's shoulder."

"Fortunately, she'll be fine. She'll be carrying trays one-handed for a while, though."

"Any leads on the kidnapping?"

He shook his head. "Not much yet. We're talking to all our regular informants. You would think somebody would know something."

"Maybe this guy doesn't move in the typical criminal circles.

"In what other circles would a kidnapper move?"

I grinned. "Answer that, and you'll find him."

"How about your investigation into the stolen painting?"

"As you can tell, we've gotten somebody's attention. Can I bounce some names off you?"

"Fire away. Oh, sorry. Too soon?" A smirk swept across Tracy's face.

"Ha. Udra Danril."

"Powerful person. You don't want to get on his bad side, and I don't think he has a good side. Have you been to his home?"

I nodded. "More like a lair, I'd say. What about Dun Luce?"

"He's harmless. Big man in the art world."

"You're all jokes today, Tracy. Yeah, Luce is a huge man. What about Trub Nurke?"

The cop blinked. "I'm not acquainted with him. Who is he?"

"He owns an art gallery."

"So is one of those the person behind the robbery?"

"Search me. That's Oren's job. I merely ask questions and get shot at."

"You think this shooting is connected? In my experience, art theft rarely turns violent."

I shrugged. "Violence is standard issue for our cases. I've been shot at and beat up on more worlds than I can count. I thought Rheged Prime was supposed to be a peaceful place."

Tracy removed the tall fedora and ran a hand through his hair. "Normally it is. Perhaps it will be again once you go home."

"Hey, it isn't me. I haven't shot at anybody. But, believe me, we're going to catch whoever is behind this."

Bella entered the room dressed in fresh clothes and sporting a bandage or two. Tracy stood as she entered. I followed suit.

"How are you doing, Ms. Balok?" Tracy asked. "Do you feel up to answering a few questions?"

"I suppose. How is Koval?"

"She's on the mend and on her way to the hospital. They expect a full recovery."

"Good. Good." Bella sat. She closed her eyes and rubbed her forehead with a hand.

"Tea?" Tracy said.

"Yes, please. I could use it."

The detective nodded at me. Apparently, I was his assistant now. I stepped to the counter and had the replicator make a third cup.

Tracy said, "I understand you were at the window when the first shot was fired. Did you see anything?"

"No. I was merely looking out at the weather."

"Do you know of anyone who would want to harm you?"

"No ... I ..." She trailed off without answering.

"What?"

"Nothing." She fixed her eyes on the detective. "I can't think of anyone who would take a shot at me."

I said, "This has to be related to the robbery."

Tracy looked at me side eyed. "How exactly? Why would someone try to kill a robbery victim?"

"Maybe Bella knows something about the thieves."

"I don't," Bella said.

"Something she doesn't know she knows." I turned to her. "Can you think of anything odd in the days leading up to the robbery? Someone unusual who was here? Something somebody said or did at the dinner party?"

She shook her head, eyes glued to the table. Then she looked up, biting her lower lip, gazing off with a thousand-yard stare. "What should I do? I can't stay here … alone." Her eyes flicked to me. "Gabriel, do you have any extra cabins on your ship?"

"Um … probably. Let me check." Hotel Shaymus was starting to fill up with me taking an extra cabin. I stood and stepped away from the table. "Oren, can we put Bella into a spare cabin? She seems shaken.

"Under the circumstances, certainly," Oren said. "Besides, it would be a good idea to have her where we can keep an eye on her."

I turned back to Bella. "It's all fixed up." I wondered what Sarah was going to say.

# Chapter 29

# The Body in the Morgue

*Lucas*

"What do *you* think, Lucas?" Gabe asked.

"Oh no, you don't," Mom said. "Don't pull him into this."

Believe me, I had no intention of getting in the middle of something between Mom and Gabe. Not that I didn't have an opinion. We were in Gabe's cabin. I was sitting on the bunk while Gabe was trying to talk Mom into the three of us walking around the city to look for the kidnapper ourselves. Which sounded good to me. I wanted to get out.

But Mom had other ideas. "I don't think we should put Lucas in any more danger. Especially not with people getting shot at around here."

Gabe said, "One person got shot, the Pardiun, and he was a criminal. Okay, Bella's maid got shot too but not badly."

"What? When was this?"

"I'll tell you about it later. Like I said, she wasn't hit badly."

"And that makes it all okay?"

"My point is that thousands of people are at this moment walking down the street outside and *not* getting shot."

Mom cocked her head to one side and raised her eyebrows, which is her way of saying something is stupid without having to explain why.

Gabe said, "All I'm saying is it's worth a shot. Poor word choice. I mean, an attempt, a try. The sentries are getting nowhere. We should take a crack at it."

"Where would we go?" Mom asked, which surprised me. For her to even ask meant she was thinking about saying yes. "Where would we look for this augment guy where the police haven't already looked."

"Sentries," Gabe said, correcting her, something that usually isn't a good idea. Mom rolled her eyes at him, and Gabe started blinking. "Sorry. Look, Lucas is our secret weapon. He actually saw the guy."

"And the guy has seen Lucas. What if he grabs him again?"

I pulled my knees up to my face. Mom was talking about me like I was a baby. Like I was a purse some thief might snatch.

"I won't let him," Gabe said. "Look, we can bring Jace if you want. We can bring Zastra."

"I don't know."

"How about this? Oren wanted somebody to take a peek at the body of the Pardiun in the morgue. We could do that. I know how much you like that sort of thing."

Which was the truth. Mom was always watching murder shows on TV. And turning them off as soon as I walked into the room. Some of them had some real gory stuff in them.

Mom didn't answer. On her face were all the signs that she was thinking about it. This was my chance.

"Yeah, Mom. I want to watch an alien autopsy."

They both shot me looks that told me I wasn't helping my cause. Rats! But I was dying to go out. I was on an alien planet for crying out loud and stuck inside.

Gabe said, "The autopsy is already done. We'll only look at him and talk to the coroner. And we'll walk around a little on the way there and back. We might get lucky and spot the guy."

Mom gazed up at the cabin ceiling. "All right. Let's go."

We left the *Shaymus* and walked through the streets along with other pedestrians, hover cars, and lots of different vehicles.

A big truck with clear, bubble-like wheels as tall as an elephant rumbled toward us. I guess it couldn't fly over people like the hover cars. Instead, it just rolled those huge wheels right over them. For a moment the people appeared inside the bubble as if they were in a snow globe. Then the truck rolled on, and the people popped out the other side as if nothing had happened. I wanted to have the truck run over me, and so did Gabe, but Mom said no.

All the time I was keeping an eye on all the people, looking for the big honking guy with the camera eye who kidnapped me. Mom kept her eyes on me.

Gabe mostly stared at an electronic gadget Jace gave him to direct us to the police station since this was the first time any of us had walked there on our own.

Even using the thing, we ended up getting lost and had to backtrack several blocks. Gabe said it was because it had a weird interface.

We stopped at a corner to gaze at a park. Rain dripped out of the sky onto the grass and umbrella trees. But only inside the park. No rain fell in the street where we stood.

"How do they control the weather like that, Gabe?" I asked.

"Hmm. Probably a force field. Or artificial air currents to direct the rain."

Mom gave Gabe the look she gives me when I annoy her. "You don't know that. You're just making it up."

Gabe said, "Well, it's possible."

Mom said, "If you want a real answer, Lucas, you can ask Jace when we go back."

Gabe said, "I bet it's a force field."

A block later we were passing a store, and I was looking in the window to see if they sold snacks, when Mom gasped. She stopped in her tracks and yanked me close to her. "Lucas, over there."

I looked in the direction she was looking. A Rhegedian with a cyborg thing in his eye was coming toward us. I said, "Not him. The thing in his eye is right. But he's not big enough."

I started to walk on, but Mom was still frozen to the spot. She stood there until the guy passed us and walked on down the street.

We finally reached the police station. At the desk in the lobby, Mom asked for Detective Tracy. Meanwhile, Gabe and I looked at pictures on the walls of famous arrests and shootouts.

Tracy met us and led us to an elevator. It was one of those super stretch elevators like they have in hospitals, the ones big enough for a bed on wheels to fit in. The elevator took us to a lower level and opened into a huge room full of shelving units and cold enough to be a refrigerator. Each shelf held a figure covered with a sheet. There were rows and rows of shelves, which made the place look like a Target store for dead bodies.

My breath clouded out in front of me, and I leaned against Mom for warmth. Which she took for fear and said, "It's okay, Lucas. Don't be scared." I didn't even try to explain it.

A Rhegedian woman in a green lab coat met us and said, "Detective."

Tracy said, "Dr. Aisles, this is Gabriel Lake and Sarah and Lucas Gallo. I'll leave you all in her hands. I need to return to the squad room."

"Yes. Hello," the woman said. "You want to view the Pardiun."

"Please," Gabe said.

The lady pulled out a tablet and tapped on it. With a nod, she tucked it under her arm and turned. "Right this way."

We followed her down a row of shelves, turned at a gap halfway down, crossed several more aisles, and then stopped. Dr. Aisles used the tablet to scan a tag on a shelf at about the level of my head and said, "This is it."

She pulled back the sheet to show the head and shoulders. I stood on my tiptoes to try to see better. The dead guy was like a lion. A brown mane flowed down his head. His furry catlike nose made him appear almost gentle.

"How did he die?" Gabe asked.

"Blaster shot." The morgue lady folded the sheet down to reveal a gaping purple hole in the guy's chest.

Gabe and I took a step back. Mom took a step forward.

"Wow! Can you tell anything from the wound?" Mom asked. "Was he shot from close range or from a distance?"

"Blaster beams are narrowly focused. Still, they do spread out over distance. From the size of this hole, I estimate the shooter was one hundred meters or more away."

Mom said, "Like a sniper shot."

My eyes darted back and forth between all the grownups, trying to follow the conversation.

"What about the type of weapon?" Gabe asked.

"Do you know a lot about blasters, Mr. Lake?"

"I mean, I've fired a few … and been fired at by a few. I'm no expert."

"We can't tell much. All blasters produce a similar type of wound. However, given the distance, the weapon was most likely a blaster rifle fired by a skilled shooter."

"Or a lucky shot," Mom said. "Do you have any other clues?"

"Not from the body," the morgue lady said. "Well, not directly from the body. Besides a payment stick and his ID, only one thing was in his pocket." She scrolled through the notes on her tablet. "This, a card. Here's an image of it."

She turned the screen toward us. The image was square with something like a QR code in the middle and words at the top. They said: *Holo Grenton.*

# Chapter 30

# Dial P for Pardiun

*Gabe*

"Who's Holo Grenton?" Sarah asked.

I stared at the screen in the coroner's hands. "You're saying you found that card in the pocket of our dead Pardiun?"

"That is correct, Mr. Lake. Do you think it's significant?"

"I do." I turned to Sarah. "Grenton is a possible buyer for the stolen painting."

Sarah said, "Something is handwritten across the card. A number, I think — two-one-eight-seven."

"Yeah. Dr. Aisles, has anything been done with this information?"

"I sent a report to Detective Tracy this morning. I don't know what he has done. It would be standard procedure to inform this person of the death."

"Sarah, Lucas," I said, "we need to get up to Tracy's office right away. Thanks, Doc."

We raced to the elevator and pressed the button for the ground floor.

As the car rose, I contacted Oren. "Hey, guess whose name was in Krellan Kaktal's pocket."

"All right," Oren said. "I will. Holo Grenton."

"What? Yeah. How did you know?"

"I didn't. However, your question implied that it was a name already associated with the case, which limited it to only a few people. Your tone implied it was someone surprising. I thought the Pardus connection most likely."

"If you say so. Anyway, we're going to talk to Tracy. I'd like to sit in on the conversation when he informs Grenton of the body … if we're not too late."

"Excellent idea, Gabriel. Did you learn anything else of interest from the body?"

"He was shot from a distance, probably with a blaster rifle."

"In which case, it may or may not have been someone he knew."

"It could be the same person who took potshots at me. The elevator is stopping. Go ahead and stay connected. We'll be talking to Tracy about this in a minute."

The door opened, and we shot through the busy squad room. I knocked on Tracy's glass-walled office, and he waved us in.

I said, "Have you contacted Holo Grenton yet?"

He stared at me blankly a moment. "Oh. The card. No, not yet. That was going to be one of my next jobs."

"Then I have a favor to ask. May I sit in on the call?"

He paused before answering then spoke the words slowly. "I suppose so. But let's get this straight. I will be in charge of the conversation. There are certain protocols we need to follow on death notifications. I won't appreciate you elbowing in and trying to turn it into an interrogation."

I held up both hands. "I'm fine with that."

"All right. What will you two be doing?" he asked Sarah and Lucas.

Sarah said, "We're not heading back to the ship without Gabe, if that's what you mean."

"I understand. You can sit in too … as long as you're quiet. We'll go to one of the conference rooms."

Tracy led us out of his office down a hallway to a room with a long table with chairs. A view screen hung on the wall.

"Have you ever used WoTCom systems?" Tracy asked as we took seats.

"What who now?" I asked.

"WoTCom, Wormhole Telecommunications. It's how we can do a video conference hundreds of light years away."

"We have WALT on the *Shaymus*. Is it a system like him?"

"Similar. Two-way video requires a somewhat larger wormhole. Even so, there's a bit of a lag. It won't be too bad for Pardus, which is in a nearby system, nearby being a relative term on an inter-stellar level." Tracy pressed a button in the center of the table. "Initiate call to Holo Grenton on Pardus."

The view screen flashed on, displaying one of those circle graphics that spin and spin while you wait for the computer to do something. Tracy drummed his blue fingers on the table. Lucas flopped back in his chair and stared at the ceiling. If technology has taught us anything, it's to be impatient.

Finally, the screen flashed on to show a Pardiun staring at us. The fur and mane were much like Krellan Kaktal, but this Pardiun was wearing a tailored jacket in a colorful print. He appeared to be sitting behind a desk in front of built-in shelves holding a variety of awards and knickknacks. In an inset window we could see ourselves like in a Zoom call.

"Hello," Tracy said.

The Pardiun continued to stare.

Tracy said, "Hello," again at the same moment the Pardiun mouthed something we couldn't hear.

Tracy spoke loudly. "I don't think your microphone is on."

The Pardiun continued to move his mouth for another second. Then he shook his head and tapped a button on the desk in front of him. A crackle sounded through the speakers, and a deep voice said, "Hello. Sorry."

Yeah, this was exactly like a Zoom call.

Tracy said, "My name is Detective Dak Tracy of the Rheged Prime Sentry Service. Is this Holo Grenton?"

The Pardiun blinked for a second or two before answering. "I am Holo Grenton. And who are the other people there with you?"

"This is Gabriel Lake and Sarah and Lucas Gallo. They're with the Galactic Detective Agency."

Another pause. "What is this concerning?"

"Mr. Grenton, I am calling to notify you of a Pardiun named Krellan Kaktal, who was found dead on our planet. He had a card with your name in his pocket."

Grenton, with a grim face, inclined his head. "What did you say the name was?"

"Krellan Kaktal. Did you know him?"

"I can't say that I did."

"Do you have any idea why he would have your business card?"

"I go through hundreds of those cards. I deal in real estate. Anyone wanting to either buy or sell might have my card."

"What about someone wanting to sell art?" Tracy asked.

"I do collect art pieces. Was this Kaktal an art dealer?"

"We don't believe so. He may have been a thief."

The Pardiun shook his head with vigor. "Then I would not have spoken—"

The screen froze and the circle graphic started spinning again.

Tracy pounded the table with a fist. "Connect. Connect. Come on, wormhole."

As if on Tracy's command, Grenton unfroze. "… market."

Tracy said, "Sorry. We missed some of what you said. Would you repeat it?"

"I said, I wouldn't be speaking to a thief. I buy my art only from reputable dealers. Nothing from the black market."

I raised a hand to cover my mouth and whispered to Tracy, "Ask about the number."

"Oh, yes." Tracy said. "Mr. Grenton, there was a number handwritten on the card." He turned to me. "What was the number?"

"Twenty-one eighty-seven."

"The number was a twenty-one followed by an eighty-seven, Mr. Grenton. Does that mean anything to you?"

"Not offhand, no. I'm sorry."

"Don't worry about it. We'll run it through our databases. By the way, when was the last time you visited our fair planet?"

"Rheged Prime? I don't believe I have ever had the pleasure. My business keeps me close to home. What are you implying?"

"We're only trying to piece together the facts."

"How is the Galactic Detective Agency involved in this?"

Tracy said, "Are you familiar with Cormabite's *Self-Portrait*?"

"Every collector knows the *Self-Portrait*. Why?"

"It has been stolen."

"Stolen from Rheged Prime?"

"Yes."

"It shouldn't be on Rheged Prime anyway."

"It shouldn't?"

"The painting should be returned to Axan, to Cormabite's home planet, as part of their cultural heritage."

"Then you wouldn't be interested in adding it to your collection there on Pardus?"

"No, I would not. I would welcome a good copy to my collection. But I am convinced that art originals should stay on their home worlds."

"To answer your earlier question," Tracy said, "the Galactic Detective Agency is investigating the theft."

"And how exactly is the robbery related to this death?" Grenton asked.

I took that as my cue to finally speak out, in the process catching a glimpse out the corner of my eye of Tracy scowling. "We're not sure yet, but we believe they are related. Mr. Grenton, do the names Mot Vagis and Carsta Rio mean anything to you?"

"No. Who are they?"

"Possible accomplices in the theft."

"I'm telling you, I know nothing of this stolen artwork, and I have no interest in it."

"All right," Tracy said, "Thank you for your time. If you think of anything, call back on this connection and ask for me. Oh. One other thing. I still need to contact Krellan Kaktal's family to inform them of the death. What resources can I use on Pardus to track them down?"

Grenton passed on the information, and the call ended.

Tracy sat back in his chair. "I don't know about you, but I believe him. I don't think he had anything to do with this."

"I agree. But the dead guy had his business card for some reason. If we could figure out that reason, it might be the key to solving this case. Oren, what do you think?"

I heard his voice in my ear. "I concur. I'm disconnecting now. Return to the *Shaymus* at your earliest convenience. Now that we finally have the guest list from Ms. Balok's party, we need to interview those people."

I told Tracy, "Oren agrees. Thanks for letting us sit in on this."

We left the sentry post, heading toward the ship. As we walked along, Sarah seemed lost in thought. Finally, she said, "So you think the guy in the morgue was one of the robbers?"

"Probably. Along with those other names I mentioned on the call."

'But he was following you instead of making a getaway with the stolen painting."

"Yeah. It doesn't make sense."

"And who killed him?"

"That's the question."

"Maybe the killer was trying to steal the painting from the robbers."

Lucas said, "Maybe the owner of the painting found out who stole it and is hunting them down."

I laughed. "I don't think that's the case. The owner is our client, and somebody took a shot at her this morning."

Sarah said, "What?"

"Yeah. That's when her maid got hit. She's going to be all right, though."

Sarah stopped in her tracks and scrunched up her nose.

"What are you thinking?" I asked.

"I'm thinking I can't imagine a motive for anyone other than Bella to go after the thieves."

"So you think I'm right, Mom?" Lucas asked.

"We'll see, baby."

"Mom, could you quit calling me baby? I'm not a baby."

"I know you're not, baby. I mean ... We'll see about that too."

"How about shorty?" I said. "Though at the rate he's growing, you may not be able to use that for much longer either."

Sarah said, "This guy we talked to on the other planet, he's a potential buyer of the painting, right?"

"His name was mentioned as one along with some others. Apparently, he's not interested."

"Who else do you have?"

"Well, there's an art collector named Dun Luce who is the size of a boat. And another collector named Udra Danril, a weird guy who lives underground all by himself. There's a gallery owner, Trub Nurke, who is acting suspiciously. And so is his assistant, a woman named Aras Rune."

Sarah walked on with her brow furrowed.

I said, "It looks like you're becoming interested in the case."

"Well, until they catch the kidnapper, I need something to occupy my mind."

"Glad to hear it. Because there's another job I would like to take you on."

# Chapter 31

# The Daffy Dumonts

*Gabe*

The job in question — the one I wanted Sarah to help me with — was interviewing the guest list from Bella's party. When we returned to the ship, we found Oren, Zastra, and the Avanians in the office getting down to work on that very subject. Sarah and I joined the meeting while Lucas went off to the galley to replicate something to eat.

"It was a party of eight," Oren said. "Four of them we know — Bella Balok, Dun Luce, Mot Vagis, and Trub Nurke from the gallery. We have already interviewed all of them except for the missing assistant. The other four guests were Julius and Teragram Dumont, Atherton Froona, and Cabott Niska. I suggest you split up the list among yourselves."

Zastra said, "Do we know anything about these people?"

"Not much. They are all Rhegedian. The Dumonts are an older couple. The other two are younger and came as individuals. All are what one might call high society."

"Great!" Blan said with a sarcastic tone. "Rich people. Last time I was in a rich alien person's house, they put papers down for us … like we were birds or something."

I said, "Sarah has agreed to go with me, and we'll take Lucas along. We can handle the couple."

Blan said, "They'll probably put papers down for Lucas. I tell you, rich people."

"Satisfactory," Oren said. "You taking the Dumonts, I mean. Not the papers."

I said, "Where do we find these people?"

The address flashed up on the screen. I made a note of it on my phone.

Oren said, "I will have WALT contact them to expect you."

We left while the other assignments were being worked out and helped Lucas polish off the last two pieces of a pizza he had replicated. We flagged a hover taxi passing by the ship and climbed in.

The driver turned and said, "Where do you folks …" He stopped in mid-sentence, eyes glaring. "You again." Our cabbie was the Fornaxi, the one who had kicked Zastra and me out because I had called him Donovian by mistake.

I said, "Again, I am extremely sorry."

He opened his mouth as if he was going to tell me off some more, but his eyes moved to Lucas, and his face softened. "Where to?"

We told him, and he took off, though he eyed me with a dirty look in the rear view mirror.

As we pulled up in front of the place, Lucas asked, "Can I help with the detecting?"

Sarah said, "You should let the grownups talk, kiddo."

I said, "However, if you pick up on something, let me know." I could use all the help I could find.

The person who answered the door at the Dumont's spacious residence was a slip of a man with a bushy black mustache and huge eyebrows that dominated his face. He held a stubby brown stick between two fingers.

"You must be the detectives. You don't look like detectives." His eyes darted between us. "Shouldn't you be wearing trench coats and carrying magnifying glasses? Say, I could use a magnifying glass myself. The old eyes aren't what they used to be. I'm Julius, by the way. Come along. I'll take you to my wife. Are you two married? Ah, marriage. We were married by a judge. I should have asked for a jury." At the punchline he turned to us and waggled those eyebrows. "Teragram is in a room down here. It's a fantastic room. We got it from room service."

By the time he finished the monologue, we found ourselves stepping into a fussy sitting room. The stiff chairs and couches were lined with pillows, the tables littered with little blue figurines in a variety of schmaltzy poses each wearing short pants. An impeccably dressed matronly woman, as rigid as a ladder, regarded us with an aristocratic countenance from one of the chairs.

Julius said, "May I present my wife, Teragram. Tera, these are the detectives."

She spoke. "Did you get their names, Julius?"

"I wasn't sure they had names. I didn't want to embarrass them by quizzing them about names if they didn't have any. Do you folks have names? I'm sorry to ask, but I must insist. My wife's idea." He jabbed the brown stick between his lips and made a sucking motion with his mouth.

"What's that?" Lucas asked.

Sarah said, "Don't pry, Lucas."

Julius removed the thing from his mouth and examined it as if he had never seen it before. "No, it's a fair question. This, son, is a garro root."

"Do you eat it?"

"Eat it? No, it would taste terrible. You put it in your mouth and let the flavor seep out."

Teragram breathed out a haughty snort. "It is a filthy habit. Those objectionable sucking sounds. And at the end, you have a soggy mess."

Julius grinned. "Well, after all these years I'm something of a mess myself, though generally not soggy."

I said, "I'm Gabriel Lake. This is Sarah and Lucas Gallo."

Teragram said, "Please sit down. I must say, this is much more pleasant than I anticipated. Investigations always seem tawdry and distressing. But here we are — merely two families visiting together."

"Well, we aren't exactly a fam—"

Teragram cut me off. "May I offer you refreshments?"

Sarah started to decline, but Lucas nodded enthusiastically.

Teragram waved a hand. "Julius, fetch the tea and sandwiches."

Her husband stood and shuffled out. He returned carrying a silver platter with cups, a pot of tea, and a plate of finger sandwiches made with a green paste. Julius poured the tea then held out the plate.

Lucas reached to take a sandwich. I headed him off and took one first, knowing how alien food can sometimes taste odd or even downright awful. I needn't have worried. The bread was poosha, a Rhegedian favorite of mine, and the green paste had a flavor like apple.

I said, "Try one, Lucas. You'll like it."

Sarah whispered, "Take a small bite first. And if you don't like it, don't say anything."

Lucas took a small bite, then a larger bite, then another bite.

"Do you like the finger sandwiches?" Julius asked, his eyebrows dancing up and down. "They're made with the finest fingers we could find."

"Julius! My word!" said Teragram.

But Lucas had giggled at the joke, which made Julius's eyes twinkle and turn impishly toward the ceiling. There would be no stopping him now.

I said, "We understand you attended a dinner party recently at the home of Bella Balok."

Teragram said, "Ah yes, it was a delightful party. You remember the party, don't you, Julius? Last Zahnsday if I recall."

"Oh, I remember it. But I believe, dear, it was Moonsday."

She gave him a patronizing glance. "Oh, I think you'll find the night was Zahnsday."

"Can't be. I recollect making a joke about not wearing pants for Moonsday." A roguish smile crossed his face.

Lucas giggled. "Moonsday."

Teragram gave her husband a cold stare. "You *would* make a joke like that. Well, whichever day it was, we attended the party."

Julius leaned over to nudge me. "That Bella is quite the looker, don't you think?"

I said, "Oh … um."

"Julius!" Teragram's mouth was an open circle of shock.

He titled his head toward Sarah, "You know, you're something of an eyeful yourself."

"Julius! They are married. So are we as it happens!"

I said, "Well, actually—" Sarah patted my knee, apparently seeing no need to correct the misconception. Likely the pat was to stop Julius from getting any more forward with her.

Out of the momentary silence came a soft *meep* followed by a furry face peeking from underneath Julius's chair. He leaned over and lifted the creature to his lap. The critter was as tiny as a chipmunk but had long floppy ears and sad eyes like a basset hound.

"Aw," said Lucas. "Can I pet him? Please?"

Julius drew the garro root from his mouth and wiggled it with his fingers. "You just said the secret word — please" He held the pet out toward Lucas. "This is Duke."

"Will he get bigger?" Lucas asked.

"No, he's fully grown now. You should have seen him as a pup. If fact, I should have seen him better myself. One time I almost sat on him."

The tiny animal rubbed against Lucas's finger and *meeped*.

"So how did you find the party?" I asked.

"Took a taxi," Julius said with a grin. Lucas snickered.

Teragram rolled her eyes, though I noted in them a tiny spark of appreciation. "The party was marvelous. I was seated next to that charming young assistant of Dun Luce."

"Mot Vagis," I said.

"Yes. That was his name. He was interested in art and quite knowledgeable. He asked about all our pieces. Of course, we don't have nearly the collection that Dun Luce or Bella Balok have, but we have managed to secure some interesting works over the years." Her eyes rose to gaze at a compact frame on the wall holding a small feather, each tuft painted a different vivid color.

"That's charming," Sarah said.

A smile twitched across Teragram's face. "We adore it. It is by the Avanian artist Birdichelli. That was his own feather."

"Wait," I said. "Did you say—"

Sarah stopped me with another pat on the knee. "And Mot Vagis wanted to hear all about your art?" she asked.

"He did."

"And possibly where they were located in your home?" I asked.

"Now that you mention it, he did ask about that. He said setting was essential."

"Did he also ask about your security systems?"

"He didn't ask me. But that's Julius's department."

Julius said, "He asked me for a recommendation on a security system. He said Dun Luce wanted to upgrade."

I glanced at Sarah.

Teragram cast a disapproving glare at her husband. "I'm surprised you had time to talk to him. You spent all evening cooing with Bella and Cabott Niska."

"Cooing? What am I, an Avanian? I was set between them and felt it my duty to entertain."

"Believe me, you were entertaining the entire table. Perhaps not in the way you intended, you old fool."

Julius said, "You were doing a bit of flirting yourself. But Mot Vagis was far more interested in that manager of Trub Nurke's gallery."

"Nonsense. I didn't flirt. Mot was merely being charming. Of course, he was more interested in her. She's his own age."

"Wait a minute," I said. "The gallery manager? You mean Aras Rune? She was at the shindig?"

Julius said, "She came toward the end to confer with Nurke about something, but she spent a lot more time conferring with this Vagis. They even slipped off together."

"That's interesting," I said. Rune had claimed to barely know Vagis. "I have to ask, though, did you tell Mot Vagis about your security system? We think he may be an art thief, and he might have been asking those questions to make you his next target."

Teragram's eyebrows shot up. "Well, I never! Are you telling me Dun Luce employs a thief?"

"Not anymore. Vagis has disappeared. Have either of you seen him since the party?"

They shook their heads.

Julius leaned back and sucked on the root. "Why are you interested in the party?"

"Didn't you hear? Bella's Cormabite was stolen shortly after."

Teragram said, "Stolen! Whatever is the world coming to?"

Julius said, "And you think Vagis stole it?"

"That's our theory."

"Well, I'll tell you this. He was eyeing that painting the whole time."

"Not the entire time," Teragram said. "You exaggerate, dear."

"Well, he was eyeing it … some of the time."

Sarah asked, "Did anyone at the party say or do anything suspicious?"

Julius said, "That maid of Bella's did."

"Koval?" I asked.

"Koval. Yes, that might be her name. She was tottering around like an old lady, but I don't think she's nearly as old and infirm as she lets on. Nurke spilled a drink while reaching for something, and you should have seen her jump back out of the way."

Teragram tsked. "Isn't it precisely like help to pretend to be unwell to avoid work. My mother would have had a thing or two to say about that."

"Your mother had a thing or two to say about everything," Julius said, "including me."

"She was a woman of deeply held beliefs."

"I'll say she was. Now that I think of it, that foreigner who helped serve was acting suspiciously too."

"Foreigner?" Sarah asked.

"Well, alien. Pardiun, if I'm not mistaken."

Teragram said, "You mean the one who was like a person-sized cat? I thought he was Srathan."

"Srathans? No. Srathans are lizard-like, aren't they?" Julius looked at me.

"Yes. Srathans are green, have scales. One is a friend of mine. She works with the agency."

"You don't say?" asked Julius. "I always wanted to meet one. What do they eat?"

"Julius! That is *not* an appropriate question."

# Chapter 32

# Rendezvous with Rumble

*Gabe*

We had arranged for the taxi driver to wait for us outside the Dumonts' house, but maybe he was still steamed about me calling him a Donovian because he didn't. We had WALT fetch us another ride and soon were hovering back toward the *Shaymus*, discussing what we had learned.

"So there was a Pardiun server at the party," I said.

"Is that what the dead guy was … is?" Lucas asked.

"Exactly. What are the odds?"

Sarah said, "You think it was the same one? You think one of the thieves got themselves installed on the serving detail?"

I said, "It would be a perfect way to check out where the Cormabite and the security panel were located and to plant the spy camera."

"I wonder how he landed the gig. Do you think he bribed somebody with the caterers?"

"Probably. It would be too much of a coincidence to assume he was merely in the right place at the right time."

"Hmm. Or did Bella hire him on purpose?"

"You think Bella was involved in robbing her own artwork?"

Sarah flipped up a palm. "That sort of thing has been done before. The whole deal might be an insurance scam. She has it stolen and sold to someone else. She collects both the sale proceeds and the insurance settlement."

"I suppose it's possible."

Lucas asked, "Is Bella that blue lady on the ship?"

"Um … yes," I said.

"She's on the *Shaymus*?" Sarah asked.

"Yeah. Didn't I mention that? When Bella's maid was shot, it kind of tore up her house too. She needed a safe place to stay."

Lucas said, "Yeah. She came into the galley while I was eating. She was talking on her phone to somebody and told them all about it. She said Gabe was awesome!"

"Do you know who she was talking to?" I asked, trying to change the subject.

"Awesome?" Sarah asked.

Lucas bounced in the seat. "Yeah. She said this blaster shot burst through the window right beside her. She froze and would have been killed by the next blast, but Gabe swept her up in his arms and took her to the floor!"

"Swept her up, did he?"

I cleared my throat, which had gone dry. "I ... I wouldn't ... put it quite like that. More like I knocked her to the floor."

"Uh-huh."

"Nothing I wouldn't do for anyone."

"So you say."

Lucas said, "Then Gabe stayed and talked to the sentries and took care of the maid who got shot. The lady said he was her hero."

"Hmm."

The hover taxi came to my rescue by stopping. We stepped out near the *Shaymus's* landing pad and began walking toward the ship, my mind still reeling from the conversation.

Lucas stopped. "Mom."

"What, baby ... I mean, kiddo?"

"He's over there on the corner."

Still lost in thought, I said, "Who's over there?"

I cast a quick glance. He was standing in front of a diner, pretending to be preoccupied with something on a tablet device in his hand but keeping an eye on the ship. Twilight was setting in, but I could clearly make out the cybernetic eyepiece and computer chips on the side of his head.

"You two go on inside," I said. "Tell Zastra if she's there."

"What are you going to do?" Sarah asked.

"I'm going to try to play it cool and talk to him. And then Zastra will come out, and together we'll capture him."

"Gabe, don't. It's too dangerous."

"That's why you're telling Zastra. Look, I'll be fine. I've been in fights before … if it comes to that … which it probably won't."

They hurried up the ramp while I leaned against the ship's hull, casually taking in the view of the city. If this had been an old black-and-white detective movie, I would have lit a cigarette as if I didn't have a care in the world. But it wasn't, and I didn't smoke. Even if I had a cigarette, lighting it would only have ended up with me in a coughing fit. What I needed was one of Julius's garro roots.

With a surreptitious gaze across the street, I determined the augment was still standing there, though he had now stashed the tablet and was eyeing me. I decided it was time to take a leisurely evening stroll. I set off toward the corner, not looking at anything in particular. The augment, appearing every bit as casual, turned and began walking away.

I crossed the street and called. "Excuse me."

The augment ignored me. I picked up the pace, hoping he wouldn't notice. He did and accelerated as well.

"If I could have a word."

Still no response other than him hurrying more. There was nothing for it now but to launch myself into a flat out run and try to chase him down. I'm not exactly the Flash. But he was stockier than me, and with a nearly empty street I was gaining on him.

At the next intersection a hover taxi sped across in front of him forcing him to stop short. I was on him. I reached out an arm and grabbed his shoulder, turning him around.

"Hey!" I said. "We need to talk."

Apparently, he didn't agree because his response was an uppercut to my chin. I stumbled back, then launched myself at him, pulling him to the ground. He shoved me off and struggled to his feet. I jumped up and hit him in the face. Unfortunately, my hand connected with the eyepiece, and it hurt like blazes. It must have hurt him too because he grabbed the lens with both hands. A trickle of pink blood ran down his face.

"Who are you?" I said with ferocity. "Why did you snatch Lucas?"

He answered with a shout. "Why are you attacking me? Help, anybody! This off-worlder is attacking me!"

I grabbed him around the neck. "You kidnapped a kid I care about. What are you up to? Who are you working for?"

"I don't know what you're talking about." His hand dropped to his side. My eyes followed and spotted him pulling a blaster from his belt.

I slapped at his hand once, twice. The weapon skittered across the street. He responded with an elbow to my gut.

I slugged him again. "You're going to pay for what you did to Lucas."

He threw a punch, connecting with my jaw, and said contradictorily, "I didn't kidnap anybody. I wasn't going to hurt him."

By now a small crowd had formed, staring at us, recording us with devices. The augment sprang at me, taking me to the pavement. He rolled off in the direction of the blaster. I grabbed a leg and pulled him back. He turned and punched me in the face. I tasted something wet, metallic on my lips. I touched it, and the back of my hand came away red.

The augment stood and lifted a leg to kick me, but at that moment a truck with bubble tires rolled over us, freezing us in place until the bubble uncovered us once more. I was ready and snatched at his upraised leg, pulling him down on his back. Somewhere in the distance sirens were screaming. I jumped to sit on his chest and tried to smack him, but he caught my arms in his hands and threw me off. I landed face first on the pavement.

He rolled away from me, rose to one knee, and set off at a run. I struggled to scramble to my feet as a blue flash of light erupted from behind me and struck a lamp post beside his retreating form.

He was gone, but Zastra and Sarah were at my side.

"Not smart, Gabriel," Zastra said, holstering her blaster. "You should have waited for me."

That's just what I needed right then — criticism along with contusions.

They helped me to my feet and supported me until I felt steady.

"Are you all right?" Sarah asked.

"I'll live. Where's Lucas?" I rubbed my jaw, shifting it back and forth. There was something going on with it that hurt with every word I spoke.

"He's with Jace on the ship."

"Sorry. The kidnapper got away."

"Buad and Blan are on his tail," Zastra said. "They may spot him."

A voice sounded from behind me. "Now what was this fight all about?"

I turned to see two sentries in yellow vests and peaked caps. "Hi. I was trying to apprehend a kidnapper."

"What made you think the person was a kidnapper?" one of the sentries asked with a scowl. "And what made you think you had the right to apprehend him in the first place? You're not from around here, are you, son?"

The other sentry said, "Same old story, Sarge. These aliens come in here. They drink too much, and they start fights. They make life difficult for peaceful citizens."

The first sentry said, "How much have you had to drink? Follow my finger with your eyes."

"I'm from Earth, and I'm not drunk. That guy kidnapped a kid and may be involved in a murder."

Someone from the crowd yelled out, "He started the fight, that beige guy there. He chased after the Rhegedian and knocked him down and started hitting him."

Several others in the crowd voiced agreement.

"Is this so?" the sergeant asked.

"For the record, he hit me first. But there's more to it than that." I rubbed the back of my head where it had banged the pavement. "Ow!"

"Well, let's say we start at the beginning. But first …" The sergeant stepped up to me with his head tilted back, eyeing me along the edge of his nose. He pulled out a bar with cuffs at each end. "Stick out your hands, Earth person."

I did, and he cuffed me. "Be careful with the hand," I said, wincing in pain. "Zastra, do you think you could help me out a little?"

"What?" She asked. "You mean you finally find yourself in a situation you can't talk your way out of?"

"Are all three of you together?" the sergeant asked.

Zastra said, "We're with the Galactic Detective Agency. We were pursuing the Rhegedian in connection with a case."

"Is that supposed to impress me?" the second sentry said.

Zastra's yellow eyes narrowed. "It should."

Sarah said, "We've been working with Detective Dak Tracy of the sentry service. He'll vouch for us."

"Oh, sure. You're working with Detective Tracy. Likely story."

"He's telling the truth," a voice said. A familiar yellow trench coat and super tall fedora slipped through the crowd. The sentries froze.

"These off-worlders are working for you, Detective?" the sergeant asked.

"Not *for* me specifically. I'm working a kidnapping case that involves them."

"You mean all that malarky about the kidnapper was true?"

"You bet it's true," I said, "and if you hadn't detained me, I might have caught him."

"You weren't catching anybody," the sergeant said. "By the time we arrived, the guy was in the wind, and I don't think you could run a hundred paces without dropping over." He was probably right.

Tracy said, "So you spotted the augment?"

I nodded.

"What can you tell me about him … other than he's a better fighter than you?"

"Hey, I held my own," I said. "You ought to see the other guy."

Tracy shared a smirk with Zastra.

"Hey, it's true!" I said. "Now can somebody get me out of these handcuffs?"

# Chapter 33

# The Galley Infirmary

*Lucas*

When we entered the *Shaymus* after spotting the kidnapper guy, Mom had sort of just dropped me in the galley and told me to eat something. She dashed out to find Zastra and tell her what was going on. I had the replicator make me a hamburger.

I was eating it when they returned with Gabe. His face was all red and scraped up and starting to swell. A line of dried blood streaked through dirt on his cheek.

"What happened?" I asked.

"Not now, Lucas," Mom said. "We have to take care of Gabe."

Like they couldn't talk and do stuff at the same time.

"Sit down." Zastra said it to Gabe like it was an order. Gabe sat.

"I'm fine." He winced as he said it.

"Not from where I'm standing," Mom said.

"I've had worse."

"That's not the point."

Zastra went to the replicator. "Cleansing cloth moistened with water and disinfectant, warmed to mammal body temperature."

A wet washcloth appeared on the counter. Mom held out her hand, and Zastra passed it to her. Mom used it to dab at Gabe's face.

I tried again. "What happened?"

Gabe said, "I confronted the augment. It turned into a fight." He held up a hand. His knuckles were scratched and red.

"What happened to your hand?"

Gabe made a fist a few times, grimacing with each squeeze. "Those eye implants are hard."

Mom snatched the hand and inspected it.

Gabe said, "Nothing's broken. Look." He wiggled his fingers while biting a lip.

I said, "You punched him in his cyborg eye? Whoa! Cool!"

Mom made a face. "Gabe didn't start the fight, Lucas. Did you, Gabe?"

"Well, I grabbed him from behind. He was running—"

"You didn't start the fight, did you, Gabe?" Mom repeated.

"Um … Well, to tell the truth, everything is kind of a blur."

I said, "But you caught him, right? Do the cops have the guy now?"

"Sorry, Lucas. He got away."

My stomach dropped like in one of those dreams where you're falling. The guy was still out there — hopefully punched up a little, but still running loose, maybe still after me. And now Gabe was hurt from going after the guy. And all because I had stowed away on the *Shaymus*. I set my hamburger down on the plate. I wasn't so hungry anymore.

The blue lady swept into the galley and rushed to Gabe's side. "Oh, Gabriel, more heroics? Aren't you the man of action!" She stroked Gabe's hair. He winced and pulled away. "Oh no, you have a nasty bump back there as well."

Mom said, "I'm fixing him up." She moved to block the blue lady. "If you don't mind, you're in my light."

The lady stepped back, glanced at Gabe, and glanced at Mom. "Well, I'll leave you to it. Try to be careful, Gabriel." She reached out to pat Gabe on the arm and left."

Mom gave Gabe a dirty look. He said, "What?"

Mom studied a cut on Gabe's cheek. "Zastra, I think this cut needs to be covered. On Earth we have adhesive bandages."

Zastra checked the cut herself, then returned to the replicator. "One stickyband, square, size five … no six."

She brought it to Mom, who stuck it on Gabe's face and smoothed it out with her finger. The band-aid was skin colored … or it would have been if Gabe had blue skin.

"There," Mom said. "Now try not to get into any more fights."

"I can't promise anything," Gabe said, "We still have a thief and a murderer to catch. And generally, they object to that sort of thing."

Mom leaned in and kissed Gabe on the forehead. She paused, pulled back, and raised his chin with her hand. Then she swept her hair back and ducked her head to give him a quick peck on the lips.

Zastra made a sound that was somewhere between a growl and clearing her throat. "Why do you Earth people do that?"

Gabe frowned at her. "It's a sign of affection."

"It's unsanitary is what it is."

I couldn't have agreed more. Mom and Gabe don't kiss around me much. Which is good 'cause I never know what to do when they do it. I mean, I like to see Mom happy. And having Gabe around makes her happy. And I know adults kiss people they like. And it kind of makes me feel like I have a dad. But kissing? Ugh.

Me, I don't kiss anybody except Mom and Gram. And definitely not in a lovey-dovey way. Who wants to watch their mom get all romantic? Not me. It's icky.

Jace walked in followed by Blan and Buad, who landed on the counter. "Sorry," Blan said, "we couldn't find the guy. One Rhegedian on a planet of billions of them … at night no less."

Zastra said, "At the least we scared him off. Maybe that will keep Lucas out of danger."

Mom patted Gabe on the head. "Well, you're patched up the best I can manage. I'm not a nurse."

Gabe said in a cranky voice, "Dammit, Jim, I'm a web designer, not a doctor."

"And still with the TV and movie quotes," Mom said. "Along with a word I don't like said around Lucas."

"Sorry. I needed it for the joke to work."

The talk about sheltering me from bad words was almost as embarrassing as the kissing. I put my head down on the table, wishing I was anywhere else. Well, not anywhere. Not back at that creepy hideout."

Mom said, "Stand up."

I looked up to make sure she was talking to Gabe and not me. Gabe stood, using the table to pull himself up.

Mom asked, "Are you dizzy? Lightheaded?"

"No, I think I'm fine."

"Are you having any confusion? Any difficulty thinking?"

Buad said, "More than usual, she means."

Blan cackled. "Good one, brother."

"Thanks," Buad said.

Mom shot the Avanians some side-eye, then turned back to Gabe. "Do you have a headache?"

Gabe said, "My face hurts. My hand hurts. My gut hurts. I don't think the pain in my head is any worse than all that."

"Did you lose consciousness at any time?"

"No. I'm fine. Seriously."

"All right. You're probably safe to go to sleep. But I think you should stay in your own cabin tonight with Lucas and me where we can keep an eye on you. Lucas can sleep in the chair with me."

I wasn't so sure about that. More than once when I crawled into her bed, I ended up pinned to the mattress, her arm flopped across me like a sandbag. But I said, "Sure" because I was worried about Gabe like everyone else.

Jace stared at me like he could read my mind. "I have an idea." He stood and approached the replicator. "One cot cushion."

A gray cushion the size of Gabe's bunk slid out from the counter like a paper tape shooting out of a cash register. When it fully appeared, it flopped on the floor. Wow! The replicator could make anything.

"There you go," Jace said, "Now Lucas can have his own cushion on the floor."

I flashed Jace a thumbs up.

Then the adults — I guess you count Buad and Blan as adults even though they're tiny — talked some more. The conversation was all stuff about the case, which I didn't follow, and jokes I didn't get. They replicated pumpas juice for everyone. I sipped mine while I listened. After a while I put my head down on the table, closed my eyes, and let the sounds roll over me. Finally, everybody but us Earthlings left. Mom sat beside me and stroked my head.

She said, "Lucas, go on into the cabin, and get ready for bed. I want to talk to Gabe alone a minute."

She looked at Gabe with a twinkle in her eye. I knew what that meant. More kissing.

# Chapter 34

# Oren Acts All Smug

*Gabe*

I woke up in my bunk with somebody playing kettledrum inside my head. Squinting from the pain, I pulled myself to a sitting position. Which turned out to hurt less, despite discovering, in the process, some aches in places I didn't even remember getting hurt. I guess that's what being hurled onto pavement will do to you.

Across the darkened cabin Sarah and Lucas were still in dreamland and looking all peaceful and homey in the chair and on the cushion. With my feet on the floor, elbows on knees, and forehead in my hands, I decided to focus on the case in a bid to take my mind off my aching everything.

By now I had worked enough jobs with the Galactic Detective Agency to figure out a thing or two, though, of course, never nearly as much as Oren. So here's where we stood ... at least as far as I could make out.

Somebody had stolen Bella's Cormabite *Self-Portrait*. Well, she claimed it was hers, but there seemed to be conflicting opinions on that score. The theft was most likely committed by a gang consisting of Mot Vagis, Carsta Rio, and Krellan Kaktal, although we didn't have any proof of it. Mot Vagis, who had been Dun Luce's assistant, was now missing, quite possibly dead. Krellan Kaktal was certainly dead, though not before he had followed us around on our interviews. Nobody knew anything about Carsta Rio, or so they claimed. Finally, somebody had taken a shot at Bella and wounded her maid.

Who was doing all this shooting, and why? Were any of the three thieves still alive? Where was the Cormabite now? Were any of our art collectors involved in this — the immense Dun Luce, Udra Danril (aka the sewer king), or the rich and still alive Pardiun named Holo Grenton? How did Trub Nurke and his assistant, Aras Rune fit into the story? And what about the augment who kidnapped Lucas

181

and had last night engaged me in fisticuffs? Was he mixed up in the robbery, or was that whole thing a totally separate crime?

So many questions. I hoped Oren was genius enough to figure out which string to pull to unravel the knot. It was all a jumble to me. I stood, letting out an involuntary grunt from more twinges of pain. Sarah murmured something and rolled over in the chair. Lucas didn't move a muscle. I stepped over him to get to the bathroom, washed my face in the dark, and made my way to the galley for coffee. Zastra was there with a mug herself.

"Oren wants to talk about the case," she said.

"Good. I hope he has some ideas. This is our fourth day here and as far as I know we still have no clue as to what happened." I replicated a cup of joe and leaned against the counter sipping it.

"I have my theories," she said.

I extended a hand toward her. "Share. Please."

"I think it's Nurke."

"The gallery owner."

"Yeah. He was at the dinner party. He has a way to sell the painting. And he's been acting suspiciously all along."

"Could be. I can't seem to make anything work inside my head."

"That's not a huge surprise. As I said, Oren wants to talk. I've been here waiting on you long enough. Let's go."

I trailed along behind my lizard companion to the office where Buad and Blan were breakfasting in their habitat.

"Ah, Gabriel," Oren said from the view screen, "feeling better after your derring-do?"

Blan cackled. "More like derring-didn't. Gabe got beat up, and the guy got away."

I dropped into my desk chair, too tired to give a retort.

"By the way, Gabe," Buad said, "have you looked at yourself today?"

"Yeah, kind of." I pulled out my phone and pointed the camera toward my face. A sickly shade of purple stretched from one cheek to under my eye. Not wanting to see any more, I stashed the phone.

Oren said, "Did you learn anything from the Dumonts?"

I nodded before grabbing my head to stop the pain sloshing around inside. "Aras Rune showed up at the dinner party. She said something to Nurke but spent most of her time with Mot Vagis."

"Interesting."

"I thought so, especially since she told us she barely knew the guy. Also, Vagis chatted up the Dumonts, asking about what art they owned and what kind of security system they used."

"Thieves gonna thieve," Buad said.

"And according to them, Vagis was eyeing the Cormabite."

"Excellent. That helps," Oren said. "Zastra, did you learn anything from Cabott Niska?"

Zastra emitted a deep growl. "I'm not sure anybody could learn anything from that woman. There wasn't a single fact in her head other than what everyone wore and who talked to whom."

"That could be helpful," Oren said.

"She talked to Bella about clothes. She talked to Mot Vagis. Small talk, jokes and such. And she was annoyed when Aras Rune showed up and took Vagis's attention away from her. She didn't talk to Dun Luce or the Dumonts at all. Evidently, they weren't young or fashionable enough for her. She didn't talk to Trub Nurke either, but she did note how he was eyeballing the Cormabite. I think she took that personally. She seemed to be of the opinion that everyone should have their eyes on her."

"Interesting."

I wondered what Oren found interesting about that.

"Buad and Blan, what about Atherton Froona?" Oren asked.

Blan said, "The guy's a real stuffed shirt, full of himself. Mostly what he talked about was how much Bella and Cabott fawned over him."

Zastra said, "That isn't what Cabott said. She thought Froona was rude."

"Doesn't surprise me," Buad said, "I didn't believe anything he said."

Oren leaned back in the digitally projected chair in which he digitally sat, closing his eyes and nodding.

"I don't get it," I said.

His eyes snapped open. "What don't you understand?"

"Any of it. We think Kaktal was one of the thieves. But if so, why was he following us? Why would someone who pulled off a robbery tail the investigators? And why was he killed?"

Oren flipped up a palm. "Ask yourself why someone would kill a thief?"

"Well, I suppose someone he stole from might want to kill him. But that would mean Bella, which doesn't fit because somebody took a shot at her too. What is this, a gang war?"

Buad said, "Somebody might want to kill a thief if the thief double-crossed him."

Oren said, "Ah."

I said, "But if Kaktal double-crossed somebody, you'd think he'd be hiding out or making a getaway. Instead, he was following us around. And another thing. How come everybody says they owned this crazy painting? And at overlapping times? Like I said, I don't get it."

Oren grinned and made a little sideways flip of his head. "We may be closer to a solution than you think?"

"How's that?"

The smile on his face told me he was most pleased with himself.

"You're not going to tell us, are you?"

"Forgive me. I don't want to say something that turns out to be wrong, and I need a few more pieces of information to be sure I'm right. I'll say this much. There is a clump of trees growing outside the city not far from here. It is of particular interest to me because I planted the first of them with my grandfather when I was a boy. Blan brought me this picture yesterday."

His face disappeared from the screen and was replaced by a stand of trees large enough to have filled two or three backyards in my neighborhood of postage stamp lots. "The one I planted is in the center somewhere. It grew to maturity and put out seeds, which planted several others. They, in turn, grew and spread seeds further, leading to more and more trees."

His face came back on the screen. I waited for him to continue. When he didn't, I said, "Wow! Nice story. What's the point?"

"The point, Gabriel, is that crimes, like trees, have generations. One crime can lead to another crime, which is the cause of yet another."

"Like dominoes," I said.

He blinked, probably taking the time to check the database of Earth information he had collected in violation of the quarantine. "Precisely."

"And that's what we're dealing with here?"

"I believe so. You will see in time. But first, we are going to have to execute some stakeouts. I want surveillance placed on Dun Luce, Udra Danril, and Trub Nurke."

Zastra said, "What are we watching for?"

"The brief answer is anything suspicious. But to elucidate, there is a painting missing as well as a couple of thieves. And somewhere is a collector who is eager to acquire the Cormabite. I'm hoping someone will make a move. Buad and Blan, you monitor Dun Luce. You can fly up to his apartment unseen. Zastra, you take Udra Danril. Gabriel, that leaves Trub Nurke's gallery for you."

"Back to the gallery again," I said. "If Jace can keep an eye on Lucas, I'll take Sarah along. I'm still trying to find a good time to pop the question."

"Yeah. Good idea," Blan said. "Ask her while you're all beat up. Maybe she'll say yes out of pity."

Oren said, "Certainly. Take Sarah. Propose if you can. As long as you keep one eye on the gallery."

Buad said, "Looks like one good eye is all he has."

"Good one," Blan said.

I left the office and descended the central shaft to engineering. I found Jace reaching behind a panel, a glowing tool in hand, no doubt realigning the proton fusion array or reconfiguring the harmonic torsional assembly or performing some other spaceship technobabble task that I didn't understand.

"Hi, Gabe, are you feeling better?"

"I'm a bit sore. Moving around is helping. Say, Oren wants me to go on a stakeout, and I'd like to take Sarah along. Could you hang out with Lucas?"

"Love to. I might take the *Shaymus* up into orbit and teach him how to move around in weightlessness."

"He'd love that. Thanks."

I headed back to the crew deck to spring the plan on Sarah. But before reaching my cabin, another door slid open, and Bella stepped out.

She moved to me and touched my face with a soft hand. "Poor baby. How are you feeling today, Gabriel?"

I took a step back from the caress. "Better, thanks. I'm on the mend. Speaking of which, have you heard anything about how Koval is doing?"

"They have her all patched up. She's at her home now resting. As soon as my window gets repaired and I feel safe enough to go home myself, everything can return to normal."

"There's nothing like the comfortable routines. I suppose Koval has been with you for years, and you both have your established patterns."

She tilted her head. "That's where you're wrong, Gabriel. Koval has been with me less than a year."

"Oh. I guess I assumed because of her age that you inherited her with the house or something."

"No, and, believe me, it took a little getting used to her moods. But she's quiet and minds her own business, which I like."

"Right. Well … um." I flipped my head toward my cabin door. "I should move on." I didn't want Sarah to come out of my cabin and catch us talking, not after Bella's little performance last night.

She made a murmuring sound and stepped aside.

I entered my cabin and found Sarah and Lucas awake and watching some nature vid. I said, "Hey, guess what?"

# Chapter 35

# The Stakeout

*Gabe*

"All I'm saying, Gabe, is somebody ought to keep tabs on the backdoor. You told me this guy sneaked out the other day to visit your blue girlfriend. It probably should be watched."

Sarah had a good point, not the blue girlfriend thing, but about watching the back. However, I was enjoying our time together doing surveillance in the café across the street from the gallery. The open-ended stakeout was an oasis of tranquility in what had definitely not been a relaxing few days.

It was anybody's guess whether the right moment to ask for her hand in marriage would arise, but I knew for sure that moment wouldn't happen with her here and me back in the alley.

I tried to pass it off with, "Maybe later. Right now, I'm enjoying my meal." I took another bite of the noodly dish smothered in blue sauce.

"I still think those white things in your sauce there look like larvae." She had a point about that too.

"Nah. I'm guessing they're berries of some kind. They're sweet enough."

"Long white berries? Keep telling yourself that."

"In any case, they were replicated, right? It's not like somebody dug this out of a rotting log. When in Rome …"

She raised an eyebrow and took a bite of her leafy salad. "I'll stick with this."

"Plus, I couldn't ask for better company." Sarah had changed back out of the jumpsuit into her re-replicated sundress, looking fresh and pretty.

She smiled at the complement and took a sip of tea, closing her eyes and exhaling.

"Releasing some of the tension of the last few days?" I asked.

She open one eye. "I could release a lot more if they caught the guy who's going around kidnapping my son and beating up my boyfriend."

"Hey, I gave as good as I got." I took another bite, wincing as my bruised jaw opened and shut.

"Um ... Gabe." She jerked her head toward the door.

I whirled around expecting to find the augment or Trub Nurke or somebody related to the case. Instead, walking into the café was a short, mustard yellow alien with eyes like saucers, a long nose, and no mouth. At least, no mouth on the front of their face. We alternated taking surreptitious glances as the alien filled a cup from the self-serve tea pot, took a seat, and then began pouring dribbles of tea into the top of their head.

Sarah asked, "Ever met his kind before?"

"Nope. Remind me to ask Jace if there's a bucket-head planet. I tell you what, kissing would be awkward for those guys."

"Based on what Zastra said last night, I'm thinking other species don't kiss."

"You may be right. I listened to a podcast once that said only a few other Earth species kiss, and not all human cultures kiss romantically."

"I know Lucas isn't a fan."

"Well, he's gonna have to get used to it."

"Does that mean you're planning on sticking around?"

Was this the moment? "As a matter of fact, I was thinking—"

"Look!" Sarah pointed out the window.

A hover taxi had pulled up in front of the gallery. Julius Dumont emerged with a painting-shaped parcel clutched in his hand. He entered the gallery.

Sarah said, "That was about the size of the feather painting on their wall."

"You're right. Normally people take paintings out of galleries. Why would he be taking one in there?"

"Repair?"

"When we saw it yesterday it looked fine."

"You should report it."

I agreed. I called Oren through the translator bot connection and relayed the news.

"Ah, yes," was all he said. Either nothing surprised his super mind or else he liked to pretend it didn't.

Julius Dumont came out empty-handed and walked down the street where he caught another taxi.

"Dessert?" I asked. "They had a cake up there."

"I'm game." She raised her mug. "Also, I could use a refill on my tea."

I went off to fetch the goodies. When I returned, we tucked in, enjoying the treats and companionship. I dropped my hand to my jacket pocket to pat the ring nestled inside.

"This is terrific," I said.

"Mmm. Yeah. Delicious."

"I wasn't talking about the cake, though you're right about it. I was thinking about us … here … like this. This is terrific."

"Uh-huh." There was a definite tone of hesitancy in her voice.

"I was thinking—"

I was cut off by Blan calling through the translator bots. "Hey, guys, somebody is visiting Dun Luce."

Once more interrupted mid-proposal.

"Who is it?" Now Zastra's voice was in our ears.

"Beats me. Tap into my optic bots. See if you recognize her."

We could do that sort of thing with translator bots. I blinked and said Blan's name. A bluish monochromatic overlay appeared superimposed over my own field of vision showing me what Blan was seeing. He was looking at Aras Rune ringing the bell to the door of the sky suite.

Zastra said, "That's the gallery assistant. What's she doing there?"

Blan said, "No idea, but maybe we can find out. Buad is hopping over to the door."

Oren said, "I'm connecting you to Buad's auditory channel."

The next thing I heard was the voice of Aras Rune. "Sweetie, I'm here."

"Hi, baby. Come on in." The voice was tinny, coming through the speaker from inside the apartment.

Dun Luce? Boy, I never would have put those two together — the age difference, the weight difference. Despite being annoyed at the interruption, I couldn't help jumping in. "Those two? What is it she sees in that butterball? He makes about ten of her."

Zastra said. "It does beggar the imagination."

Buad said, "She went inside. We'll take a few passes by the windows to check it out and get back with you."

The voices in our heads stopped, and Sarah and I were alone again. I tried to find a way to turn the conversation back to popping the question. I said, "Of course, you and I are much more compatible."

"Well, neither of us is a butterball" — she said it with air quotes — "if that's what you mean. Really, Gabriel. Body shaming? If I heard Lucas using that word, he'd be grounded. If you said it around him, I would ground you too."

"Sorry. See, right there, that's one of the ways you make me a better person. I go for the flashy phrase, the joke, while you consider whether the comment is helpful or hurtful."

She gave me a dead stare. I was losing my way here.

I asked, "Where do you want to be in five years?"

She scrunched her face. "What is this, a job interview?"

"No ... I mean ... Um ..." I took a breath. "Sarah, you are the light—"

"May I take those plates out of your way?" Someone in an apron was standing beside the table — someone who looked like a living, breathing self-portrait of Pollock Cormabite, which is to say, like Marvin the Martian.

"Um ... yeah, I guess ... Thanks."

"Oh, goody. I love to help." The server even sounded like Marvin the Martian. "Where are you folks from?"

Sarah shot me a wry grin. "Earth."

The server made a face with the little bit of face they had, essentially only huge eyes. "Mmm. I'm not familiar with that one."

I said, "I'm not surprised. It's off the beaten path. You're from — let me take a guess, and please don't be upset if I get it wrong — is it Axan?"

The round, black head bobbed as if on a string. "Yes. You are right. Axan. How did you know?"

"I'm familiar with the Cormabite *Self-Portrait*. Well, a photo of it. Cormabite was Axan."

"Correct again. Tell me, what is Irt like?"

I was hesitant to say. In the cartoons, Marvin the Martian was always trying to blow Earth up. I told myself this wasn't Marvin and gestured toward the window. "Earth is a lot like Rheged Prime in some ways. About the same gravity. Beautiful natural places. Less technology, though. Nothing hovers much except for hummingbirds."

"Sounds wonderful! Mmm. I do enjoy getting out in nature. Disconnecting and getting away from it all."

Which, I thought, was what our date the other night was supposed to be … until Lucas was kidnapped.

The server winked one enormous eye. "May I say you make a lovely couple."

As the server left with our used dishes, our eyes met, and we broke out in a laugh.

"There you go," I said. "The server thinks we belong together."

She smiled but said nothing.

I said, "I agree. In fact—"

I was cut off once again, this time by Zastra. "The augment is approaching the entrance to Danril's bunker."

Sarah jumped in her seat. "What? Are you sure it's the same one, the kidnapper?"

"Yeah, I grabbed a picture of him from Gabe's visual feed from last night during the fight."

"Wait. You can do that?" I asked. "Without my permission?"

She ignored the question. "By the way, he's limping, so good job, Gabe."

I glanced at Sarah. "Told you I gave as good as I got."

Zastra said, "Oren, should I grab him or just keep an eye on him?"

Oren said, "Watch him. Find out where he goes."

"Right. I'm stepping back into the shadows. He's still heading this way. Now he's pressing an elevator button beside the ramp to Danril's place. He's definitely visiting the sewer king."

"So this is all connected," I said, "the kidnapping and the robbery."

"We can't yet be positive of that," Oren said. "We don't know if Udra Danril has anything to do with either. We only know the kidnapper has some connection with him. Zastra, stay where you are. When the augment comes out, try to grab him."

"Check."

Oren said, "Sarah, I would like you to go into the gallery by yourself. Ask to speak to Trub Nurke. Tell him you would like to acquire a painting to take back to your home world. Don't say Earth. Tell him you come from … you decide. Make up a place."

"How about Romulus?" I said.

"Sounds made up," Oren said, "but it would do. I'm guessing if he doesn't know the planet, he will pretend he does. Tell him you don't have a lot of money to spend, but you want something to impress your friends."

"This isn't dangerous, it is?" I asked.

"It shouldn't be."

"What should I do while she's in there?" I asked.

"Wait for her … outside where Nurke can't see you."

So I waited. I ordered another tea and sipped it, keeping my eyes peeled on the gallery's front door. I decided if I finished the tea without hearing from her, I would do something. What I would do, I hadn't decided. I didn't want to mess up Oren's plan, but I wasn't about to let Sarah be in danger. I would at least talk to Oren and try to get his permission to barge into the shop to check on her.

As I was sipping the dregs, Sarah breezed out the gallery door and crossed the street to the café.

"How did it go?"

"Fine, I think. That's for Oren to decide. Oren?"

His voice sounded in our ears. "Yes, Sarah. Tell me what happened."

"I did what you said. I told him my name was Sarah Moon, and I was from off planet, and I wanted to bring home some fine art without spending a lot."

"Sarah Moon," I said. "Sweet."

"Nurke showed me some pieces on the gallery walls. They were all approaching millions of bills. I kept saying I couldn't afford such things. He said, 'Of course, top-notch works come at top-notch prices.' Finally, he asked me what planet I was from."

"Did you say Romulus?" I asked.

"I said Alderaan."

"I am so proud of you."

Oren said, "How did he react?"

"He said he had never heard of it. I said most people hadn't. Then he showed me a painting. It was of a girl with green skin wearing a headdress and looking over her shoulder."

"Ah," said Oren," that sounds like *Girl* by the Dieren painter Jessy."

"Right. He kept calling it Jessy's *Girl*."

I laughed. "Ah, the eighties. Rick Springfield."

Oren said, "What?"

"Never mind," Sarah said. "Earth joke. Anyway, the price tag on the painting was in the millions. Trub — he said to call him Trub — told me he knew where he could obtain one that would look exactly like it and fool everyone on Alderaan, and it would only cost me five hundred bills. I figured that was what you wanted, so I told him I would think about it and left."

"Excellent work, Sarah," Oren said. "Thanks to these stakeouts plus what Lucas told me a few moments ago, the pieces are falling into place. Now I only need a way to prove what I believe I know."

Sarah asked, "What did Lucas tell you?"

Oren said, "You can ask him yourself. Come back to the ship. We have plans to formulate."

Meanwhile, the engagement ring was burning a hole in my pocket, seeming to grow heavier by the hour. This must have been how Frodo Baggins felt. Well, except for being tempted by evil and hunted by orcs and having to hike two thousand miles.

# Chapter 36

# Nobody Pays Any Attention to Kids

*Lucas*

"Okay, Lucas," Jace said, "we're ready. Would you run up to Ms. Balok's cabin and tell her we're taking off?"

"Do I have to?" Here I was ready for a fantastic experience, and he was making me go talk to some grownup I didn't even know.

Jace was going to launch the *Shaymus* into orbit and teach me how to propel myself around in zero-G. Of course, I had already felt weightlessness on the trip from Earth when I stowed away in the docking chute. Without straps, I had started floating around, which was terrifying. I was afraid if I hit the top of the chute, it might open and dump me out into space. For the whole trip, I pressed my legs against the sides of the tube and hung on like crazy.

So I was looking forward to this adventure where I could have fun with weightlessness. What I wasn't looking forward to was having to go up and talk to that Rhegedian lady. She had never once made eye contact with me. Plus, I knew Mom didn't like her, and Mom must have a good reason for that.

I said, "Can't you talk to her over the ship's intercom?" Grownups are always sending kids on errands they could easily do themselves.

"I could," Jace said, "but she wasn't too happy earlier when I told her we would be spending time in weightlessness."

"So you're sending me because you're afraid of her?"

"I'm not afraid of her. I only thought she might take the news better from you. People like kids."

"Do they?" That sure wasn't my experience. Sometimes I had to go with Mom to business meetings. I always had to wait around in a boring lobby, and people walking by would stare at me like I was someplace I didn't belong.

Jace said, "I like kids. Who doesn't like kids? Go on. Cabin five."

I huffed so Jace would realize I didn't want to do this and trudged up the spiral staircase out of engineering. I made my way to cabin five but hesitated before stepping in front of it. My gut was tight the way it gets before a test. I didn't want to talk to this lady, but I really did want to go up in orbit. Finally, I stepped to the door, which made it *ding*. I called out, "Ms. Balok?"

The door slid open. She was in the chair in the middle of the cabin looking at something on the view screen. She turned to me with narrow eyes. "Yes, child, what do you want?"

Child? Nobody wants to be called a child. Clearly, she didn't like kids. "Um … Jace says we're ready to blast off."

"All right." She turned back to the screen and waved a hand to dismiss me.

I peered at the view screen just for the fun of watching the alien letters swim around to become English. As the door was shutting, I read: *Trub, I need your skills again.* The door closed, cutting me off from reading anything else. I returned to engineering.

"You gave her the heads up?" Jace asked.

"Uh-huh."

"Thanks. I've got only the one jump seat down here. We need a place where we can both strap in together. How about we go up to the office?"

"Is it okay to use Oren's office."

"If he's not on the screen, then it's like he's not even there."

"Where does he … go when he's not on a screen?"

"Off into his circuits. He reads. He watches vids, views art. Not like you or I do those things, of course. It's more like a download."

We climbed the stairs all the way to the top of the *Shaymus*, me thinking the whole time that if we waited until we got in orbit, we could just float up there, which would be a lot more fun. We sat in two of the red chairs in the front.

Jace said, "Whenever you're ready, Kah-Rehn."

Kah-Rehn's voice came over the speakers, "Prepare for launch."

Straps popped out of the chairs and clicked in place around us, and we blasted off. The view screen showed the scene outside as buildings, then the entire city, then the whole countryside grew smaller beneath us. The sky darkened as we rose. And all the time, the g-force of the launch was pressing me back into my seat so much I could barely breathe. Then, as if somebody had thrown a switch, the force stopped. My arm floated up off the chair arm. My legs started floating away from the floor. I turned to Jace. He was grinning at me.

Kah-Rehn's voice came over the speakers. "We are now in orbit. You are free to move about the ship."

Jace said, "Kah-Rehn, please release the harnesses for Lucas and me."

The straps around me slipped away and I began hovering above my chair.

"Do you want to do a somersault?" Jace asked.

"Yeah! How?"

"Lean your head forward and pull with your legs."

I tried it, but I got stuck while stretched out sideways. I flailed around with my arms and legs but couldn't unstick myself.

"Curl up," Jace said. "Grab your knees."

I curled into a ball. Jace locked his feet into the arm of the chair and spun me round and around.

"Now stretch out and push off the chair with your legs."

I spun twice more trying to time the kick. I extended my body, tapped the chair, and shot off toward the ceiling. With the dome coming at me, I extended my arms to catch myself. I hung there in the dome, gazing at all the stars and the green planet below us.

"Beautiful, isn't it?" Jace said, bounding up to join me.

"How come I don't see stars like this back home?"

"City lights drown them out. Admire the view all you want. When you're ready I'll show you some other tricks."

I wanted to learn tricks, so I tore myself away from the view. Jace taught me how to spin like a top and use my arms to speed up and slow down. He showed me how to bounce like a pinball from floor to ceiling. I know about pinball because one of my friends has a game in his basement. It was awesome — the weightlessness, I mean. Pinball is probably awesome too, but my friend's dad won't let kids play on the machine. After a couple of orbits, we strapped in and landed again.

Later back in Gabe's cabin, I watched some vids about the stars while I waited for Mom and Gabe to return. One of the vids showed a star map with words identifying different stars — Sarga, Ilanga, Rheged. Earth didn't rate a mention.

Then I remembered something — something I thought I ought to tell Oren. I almost ignored the idea because sometimes grownups don't like it when you tell them things. One time I told my teacher she had a science fact wrong. She scowled at me and made some excuse that didn't make any sense. But this might be important. I left the cabin and climbed back to the office. The lights were dim, and no one was there.

"Oren? Mr. Vilkas?"

The screen flashed on with Oren's face.

"Hello, Lucas."

"Hi. Um … I wanted to tell you something. I don't know if this is important or not, but I thought I should report it."

"Certainly," Oren said, "What do you want to tell me?"

I took a breath. "See, before we took off … um … Did you know we took the *Shaymus* into orbit?"

"I did. I approved the plan."

"Well, thanks. Anyway, Jace sent me to Ms. Balok's cabin to tell her. And … um … something was on her screen. And I read it. I mean, she didn't hide it or anything. It was like I didn't matter. Nobody pays any attention to kids."

Oren raised one eyebrow. "Was this something personal?"

"No. I don't think so, but it might be important … to the case, I mean."

"What did it say?"

"It said, 'Trub, I need your skills again.' It said more than that, but the door closed before I could read anything else."

"You are sure those were the words? 'Trub, I need your skills again.'"

"Uh-huh."

A smile spread across Oren's face. "Well done, Lucas."

# Chapter 37

# The Setup

Oren tented his fingers in front of him. "The last pieces have fallen into place. I believe I now understand everything."

We were gathered in the office of the *Shaymus* — Buad, Blan, Sarah, me, and, at Oren's insistence, Lucas. Zastra was the last to arrive after hanging around Udra Danril's bunker for hours waiting for the augment to emerge. He never did, at least not the way he went in.

I said, "So do we contact Dak Tracy to make the arrest?" I again chuckled at the name and tried to cover it with a cough. Seriously, Dak Tracy. Lucas giggled too. Sarah buried her head in a hand.

"No, Gabriel, I do not yet have the kind of proof the sentries require for prosecution. What we need is a ruse, a gambit, a maneuver. Something to coax the criminals into revealing themselves."

"What do you have in mind?" Zastra asked.

A dinner party," Oren said. "Blan, would you fly down and invite Ms. Balok to join us?"

"Sure, Chief," Blan said.

He winged out of the habitat and disappeared down the central shaft. A couple of minutes later he flew back followed by a light tapping of footsteps echoing up the stairs. Bella Balok emerged into the office, glancing around the assembled group with an expression of concern on her face.

"What is all this?"

"Ms. Balok," Oren said, "please have a seat."

She took a red leather chair beside Lucas, who immediately wiggled over to the other side where his mom was seated.

Oren said, "I was wondering if we could impose upon you to throw another dinner party."

"I suppose so. If it will help. When?"

"Tonight. It is short notice I realize, but I believe we can wrap up this entire case this evening."

"The window will be repaired today, so I don't see why not. What's the occasion?"

"You will tell the guests that the Galactic Detective Agency has recovered your stolen Cormabite, and you want to celebrate."

She leaned forward in her chair. "You've found it?"

"It is not in hand yet. However, I believe I know where it is."

"You believe. You mean don't know for sure?"

"The true purpose of the party is draw out that information along with the identity of the thieves."

"I see. Who am I supposed to invite?"

"Dun Luce, Trub Nurke, Aras Rune, and Udra Danril."

Her lip curled. "I despise Danril, and he wouldn't come no matter what. He's a recluse."

"I dare say he *will* come. Leave that to us. Also, the guest list will include Dak Tracy, Zastra, Gabriel, and Ms. Gallo." His eyes went to us. "Sarah and Gabriel, let me be clear, for the evening you will not be a couple. Trub Nurke knows Sarah as Sarah Moon, an art collector from the planet … What planet was that again, Sarah?"

"Alderaan." She gave me a wink.

I said, "I hear the art scene there is really blowing up."

Another giggle from Lucas.

Oren continued. "Except for Ms. Balok and Mr. Tracy, the others do not know Sarah at all. It will work best if she maintains that identity. Someone may say something to her that they wouldn't if they knew she was connected with us. Ms. Balok, can you treat her as such? We could say you two met at a club during her current visit to Rheged Prime."

Bella nodded, running her eyes over me in my blue jeans and Sarah in her sun dress. "They will need appropriate attire for a dinner party."

"Agreed," said Oren. "And since we don't have anything from which to replicate dinner attire, Sarah and Gabriel, you are authorized to go shopping."

Bella jerked her head toward Zastra. "The Srathan will need dinner attire as well."

Zastra said, "I'm wearing Srathan dinner attire."

"She's right," I said. "Srathans have a one-style-fits-all-occasions philosophy."

Bella frowned and shook her head. "Fine. You mentioned another person also. Did you say Dak Tracy? The sentry?"

"Yes. Also, I will come myself in holographic form, though I will not require sustenance."

"May I add two more guests? It is my dinner party after all."

"Certainly. Whom do you want to invite?"

"Julius and Teragram Dumont."

Oren propped up an eyebrow. "Why them?"

"I find them amusing. Especially Julius. The party could use some frivolity with stuffed shirts like Udra Danril and a sentry for Zahn's sake."

Oren glanced around the room. "Any objections to the Dumonts?"

Sarah raised a hand. "They also know me as Sarah Gallo."

"The problem is not insurmountable. When we invite them, we will tell them the fake name is part of our investigation, which it is. Ms. Balok, please make sure Koval is on hand to help with the serving. Buad, Blan, and young Lucas here will assist her."

Bella's jaw dropped. "You can't be serious. You want me to use a child and two birds to serve the food?"

Buad said, "Hey. We ain't no birds, lady."

Bella rolled her eyes.

Oren said, "Along with Koval, yes. You are free to hire others as you think best."

"Wait. Wait. Wait," Sarah said. "Not Lucas. He's staying here out of harm's way."

Lucas visibly shrank as she spoke.

Oren said, "Sarah, I understand your instinct is to protect—"

She cut him off. "I don't think you understand at all. How could you have any idea?" She swept her arm out toward the rest of us. "You put these people in danger all the time."

"The risk to him will be minimal," Oren said.

"He's seven years old."

"He brought me a vital piece of evidence, recognizing its importance. "

Zastra said, "He did?"

"Indeed."

Lucas's chin came up.

Oren said, "Let me tell you what I have observed about our Lucas. He is as bright as a supernova and as brave as a Srathan. His presence at this dinner may be crucial to our success."

Sarah sat there with lips pursed, brow furrowed.

After a few seconds I said, "We'll all be there in case anything happens."

Zastra said, "Lucas has proven he's highly resourceful."

Sarah said nothing.

Buad said, "You know how Avanian kids learn to fly? Our parents push us out of the nest."

I said, "You know, that explains a lot."

"Watch it, wise guy," Buad said. "I'm making a point here. You know what I learned when my mom did that to me?"

"I hope it was how to fly," Sarah said.

"Wrong. What I learned was I already knew how to fly. Only I didn't know I knew it … if you know what I mean. Leastwise, that's what I learned. Blan just hopped down to another branch, so I ain't got a clue about him."

Blan said, "What I learned was that Buad could fly. And I figured if he could do it, I could too."

Lucas gazed up at her. "Mom, please. I want to be part of it. You know what it's like to get involved in a case."

She shut her eyes and took a breath. Finally, she nodded. "All right. But stay close to one of us at all times. At least one of us."

"I will, Mom."

Oren said, "That's settles everything. Do you agree, Ms. Balok?"

"It sounds as if you're calling all the shots for my party."

"A fair assessment. However, if all goes well, by the end of the evening you will have your painting."

"All right then."

"Thank you," Oren said. "You may return to your cabin for the time being. The rest of us have plans to execute."

Bella left the office. Oren turned to the Avanian habitat and flicked a head toward the central shaft. Buad flew down the shaft before returning. "She's gone."

Oren said, "The first task will be to invite the guests. Zastra, I would like you to visit the gallery to ask Trub Nurke and Aras Rune. Buad and Blan, call on Dun Luce and the Dumonts. Gabriel, you can invite Udra Danril. I will contact Detective Tracy."

I said, "What if they don't want to come, or they have other plans?"

"Tell them what I told Ms. Balok, namely that the Cormabite has been recovered. They will all want to see it, though for different reasons. I'm sure that will be of more interest to them than anything else they may have planned."

Sarah asked, "Won't the thief know we haven't recovered it?"

"Yes. However, they will still want to come to find out what we are up to."

"What do you expect to happen at this party?" I asked.

"I expect the dinner guests to act in their own self-interest, and, in doing so, reveal their crimes."

"Including the murderer?"

"Yes, with some goading."

"How about you give us a heads up as to who it is … so we can be ready and all."

Oren's eyes twinkled. "Oh, I have complete confidence in you all. When the time comes, you'll know what to do. Until then, indulge me and my penchant for showmanship. Well, I believe that is all for now. We will need everyone on their toes tonight. We have four crimes to expose."

"Four?" I asked. I held up fingers to count them. "Robbery, murder, kidnapping. I take it the kidnapping is part of it?"

"It is. Indirectly."

"What's the fourth?"

Oren started to speak but instead burst into a self-satisfied grin. "I would prefer to save it for tonight. All will be revealed at the proper time."

I let it go. There's no arguing with a genius. I had a hunch of what the fourth crime might be anyway. Maybe you do too.

An hour later I was standing in Udra Danril's underground chamber beside CAF, waiting for the sewer king to grace me with his presence. He limped in on his cane and greeted me with, "More questions, I suppose?"

"Nope," I said, returning his scowl with a broad smile. "We have it all wrapped up. We have the Cormabite, and Ms. Balok is hosting a dinner party in celebration of the recovery."

He scowled again. "And?"

"And you're invited."

"Poppycock. She would never invite me, and I would never come."

"C'mon. Stretch your wings a little. Come up to the surface for an evening. It will be fun."

His eyes narrowed. "What are you trying to pull?"

"Pull? Nothing … except a fun evening at the conclusion of yet another successful case for the Galactic Detective Agency. The Cormabite will be there. I know you would like to see it again."

His jaw was set. "She stole it from me."

"You could bring that up. I mean, it might be awkward, but there's nothing like clearing the air, am I right?"

He tsked. "I suppose …"

"Then come. What do you have to lose?" I assumed Oren wanted him invited because he did have something to lose, but I had no clue what that might be.

"All right. You talked me into it. I will attend."

"Wonderful! See you there."

The rest of the day was a blur of activity. Sarah, Lucas, and I hit the shops for clothes, bopping in and out of stores, trying on piece after piece like in a 1980s movie montage. We picked up pants and a vest, both black, along with a white shirt for Lucas to wear in his guise as a server. I went with the Rhegedian equivalent of a suit — a charcoal tunic with matching jacket and pants that would look good with my fedora. Sarah chose an olive-green wrap dress for her role as Sarah Moon, socialite and collector of art works on the cheap. It was a classy dress, and she was a knockout in it.

Then we headed out to Casa Balok to set everything up. Bella's chef began meal prep with the enthusiasm of a bee finding a flower garden. Koval, negative as ever, grumbled about having to serve with one arm in a sling. She was also aghast at her serving help, though she started to come around when she saw how quickly Buad and Blan could move. They couldn't carry heavy trays, but they could make multiple trips in less time than most people could make one. Lucas was a trooper and seemed to take to the role. At the least, he appreciated being included in the enterprise.

My only regret was that Bella's assistant, Sciatica, did not make an appearance. I would have loved to meet the person and crack a few jokes about back pain. I guess I can only say that Sciatica had a lot of nerve not showing up.

Zastra came in rolling a large metal box which she sat in the corner underneath a chair. She flipped a switch and a holographic image of Oren appeared seated in the chair, looking for all the world like a regular corporeal person except for being shimmery around the edges.

Oren launched into giving directions on seating arrangements and other details. One of the props for our performance was a canvas about the size of the Cormabite, which Zastra had replicated aboard the *Shaymus*. We hung it between the windows where the Cormabite previously hung and covered it with a cloth.

We finished all the setup with time enough to take real water showers at Bella's house and change into our dinner clothes. Now all we needed was for whatever was supposed to happen to happen.

Chapter 38

# I Love it When a Plan Comes Together

*Gabe*

To me there's nothing like a movie about a caper, a heist, a con job. *The Sting, National Treasure, Ocean's Eleven.* The scheme, the obstacles to overcome, the play acting, the psychology — it's all so fun.

Oren's maneuver, as he called it, had many of those same elements, though it seemed simple enough. Like a mad scientist playing with chemicals, his plan was to mix the suspects together, counting on an explosion to happen.

The guests were beginning to arrive as I descended the staircase feeling cool in my new charcoal suit. The first to arrive were Trub Nurke and his assistant, Aras Rune. Koval opened the door. I went over to say hello and usher them into the room where I had been shot at only the day before, the window now repaired, and the room set with a table and places for twelve.

Nurke's eye immediately went to the covered canvas on the wall. "Is that it there — the Cormabite?"

I shook a warning finger. "No peeking. We're going to have an official unveiling later."

Dun Luce wobbled in next, eyeballing Nurke before engaging Aras Rune in a quiet conversation.

The door dinged again. Koval opened it to Dak Tracy, who for the occasion had abandoned his trademark hat and trench coat for a canary yellow tunic and jacket. I'll say this for the guy, he knew how to commit to a color scheme. Tracy was followed by Sarah, who had apparently sneaked down the back stairs and gone outside to make her entrance as a guest. I tried and failed to wipe the smile off my face as we nodded to each other from a distance and moved off to make small talk with the other partygoers.

Next came Julius and Teragram Dumont. Julius scanned the room before making a beeline for Sarah. Who could blame him? Teragram glided across the room to speak with Dun Luce.

A minute later Trub Nurke joined Sarah and Julius. "Ah, Ms. Moon, so good to see you here. Have you thought any more about Jessy's *Girl?*"

Julius jumped in with an impish grin. "I've been thinking about her all day. But now with you here, Ms. Gallo … I mean, Ms. Moon, all other girls are gone completely from my mind."

"Excuse me, Dumont," Nurke said curtly. "We're discussing business here."

"Well, why don't you go discuss it over there and leave the two of us alone?"

Sarah glanced at me standing close enough to eavesdrop on them and said, "I wish that I had Jessy's *Girl.*"

Julius and Nurke both turned to stare as I chortled myself into a coughing fit.

The door dinged, but this time Koval was nowhere to be found. After two more dings, I answered it myself, and Udra Danril limped into the room. He had changed capes for the occasion, this one a shimmery satin kind of material, black on the outside, red on the inside. I supposed this was his good cape, which made me wonder how many he owned. Unlike the sewer king, I owned exactly zero capes.

When he caught sight of Dun Luce, Danril's eyes narrowed. "Hello, Luce. Still fat, I see."

"Good evening, Danril," Dun Luce said, his nose in the air. "Still unpleasant, I see."

Julius said, "Now this is what I call a party!"

They might have continued this witty banter, but all eyes turned to the staircase where Bella was making her entrance, descending the stairs in a long glittering gold gown that could have come straight out of the golden age of Hollywood.

"Welcome, everyone," Bella said with outstretched arms. "Please, come sit at the table. Your places are marked."

The announcement was followed by a fair amount of side comments and fluttering about as everyone shuffled to their places. The holographic projector had been moved to a chair at the end of the table. Zastra flipped it on, and Oren appeared sitting there.

Unlike at fancy meals on Earth where a complex lineup of silverware flanks the plate like armies on a battlefield map, our table settings had only two pieces of cutlery, a knife and a spork. You remember the spork, a spoon with fork tines on the end. As a survivor of past dinner missteps, I have to say I approved. We all sat except for Bella, who stood at her place at the opposite end of the table from Oren.

"Thank you all for coming this evening to help me celebrate the return of Cormabite's *Self-Portrait*. I believe not everyone has met, so allow me to make introductions. To my right is my friend and fellow collector, Dun Luce. Beside him is a new friend of mine, Sarah Moon, who is visiting us from the planet Alderaan. Next to Ms. Moon is my dear friend Julius Dumont."

Julius said, "What? Sorry, I wasn't paying attention."

Bella grinned and continued. "Next we have someone you all know, Trub Nurke of the fabulous Nurke Collection, followed by Detective Dak Tracy of the sentries, who helped recover my painting."

Tracy held up a hand. "I played only a minor role. Most of the credit goes to the Galactic Detective Agency."

"You are too modest, Detective Tracy," Bella said. "Speaking of the Galactic Detective Agency, its brilliant leader, Oren Vilkas, is at the end of the table in holographic form. As you may know he is digital and older than most of us put together."

Julius's eyes darted around the table. "If I'm doing the math right, that's saying something."

"Julius, please," Teragram said.

Bella said, "Coming up the other side of the table is Aras Rune, sales assistant at the Nurke Collection."

"Manager," Rune said with a forced smile.

"Are you now? I stand corrected. Beside Manager Rune," Bella emphasized the job title, "we have Zastra of the Galactic Detective Agency from the planet Sratha. Beside her is our friend Teragram Dumont. Next, we have Udra Danril, another important collector. And let me say, Mr. Danril, I am touched that you chose to join us. Finally, on my left is Mr. Vilkas's charming operative Gabriel Lake from the mysterious quarantined planet Earth."

Bella rang a bell beside her plate. "Dinner will now commence. I would like to propose a toast." She raised her glass. "To the Cormabite."

We all echoed the toast and sipped from our glasses.

Lucas marched in carrying two salad plates heaped with greens and topped with a purple fruit. With his head down, focused on the plates the whole time, he served one plate to Bella and the other to Dun Luce.

Buad and Blan flew in carrying a single plate between them and placed it in front of me.

Blan muttered, "Eat up, bonehead ... I mean, sir." They flew off cackling.

I looked across the table to Sarah. "So, Ms. Moon, is it?"

"Yes, it is. And I understand you are Mr. Lake? Tell me, it must be exciting being a detective."

I flashed a flirtatious smile. "Oh, you know. Dashing from planet to planet, chasing criminals, dodging laser blasts. Living dangerously suits me. Tell me about your life on Alderaan."

"Well, compared to yours, there isn't much to tell. I'm fabulously wealthy, of course, and I date a different handsome man every night."

"I'm not surprised. I wonder, could my name be added to the list?"

"Possibly. Though I'm currently booked for at least the next six months."

From his seat beside her, Julius Dumont leaned across Sarah and waggled his bushy eyebrows at me. "You know, I think you two kids are going to get on like a house on fire."

I laughed, trying to brush it off. I was afraid Julius would blow the ruse.

Dun Luce barged in. "I must say, you two look enough alike to be the same species."

I faked an air of outrage. "Oh? I suppose we non-Rhegedians all look alike to you. Is that what you're saying?"

His blue ears turned a shade of purple. "No, I ... No. That's not what I mean at all. Obviously, I note differences. Her hair is yellow. Yours is brown. Her species is much thinner."

I dropped a hand to my stomach. "Surely not that much thinner. I run. I bike."

At the other end of the table, Oren, Tracy, and Zastra were swapping crime stories while Aras Rune stared off into space with a bored expression.

Lucas returned with more plates, still averting his eyes. He sat one plate in front of Sarah.

"Thank you," she said.

Lucas replied, "You're welcome, Mom ... um ... ma'am" He glanced up at me with wide eyes and shuddered before again dropping his gaze. He gave the other plate to Julius and hurried out. Buad and Blan flew in with a plate they served to Udra Danril before flying off again.

Oren spoke up from the end of the table. "Mr. Luce, I believe we met once before. At an exhibition at the Kuggeheim if I recall."

Dun Luce bit his wide lower lip. "I'm sorry, Mr. Vilkas. I don't remember that. Not that it didn't happen. My memory is terrible sometimes."

I wondered if Oren was trying to spring a trap with that comment. If so, Luce had refused to take the bait.

Buad and Blan returned with a salad for Teragram. Lucas served Nurke and Tracy. So far Koval had not made an appearance.

The sewer king took a bite of salad, then scowled up at the covered canvas. He pointed his spork at it and said, "Bella, someday you and I need to talk about ownership of the Cormabite."

"Whatever do you mean?" Bella asked, her eyes intense.

"I mean I owned the *Self-Portrait* until it was stolen from me a year ago. I think you had something to do with that."

Bella breathed in sharply and turned a lighter shade of blue. Eyes around the table snapped up to take in this exchange.

Teragram gazed at the sewer king with shocked eyes. "Mr. Danril, what a thing to say to our host!"

"You stay out of this."

Julius said, "Hey, you can't talk to my wife that way. That's my job. Danril, you're a lout."

Danril snarled. "What? Why I have never been so insulted in my life."

Julius waggled his eyebrows. "Well, it's still early. I'll see what I can do."

Bella held up a hand. "Please. Don't argue. I don't know what painting you think you had, Udra, but the *Self-Portrait* has been in my family for generations. Isn't that right, Trub? You've seen it hanging here for years, haven't you?"

Nurke stared at his salad and said nothing.

Bella glared at him, then tried Luce. "Dun, you knew my father. Hasn't the *Self-Portrait* been here for years and years?"

Dun Luce looked up. "What? The Cormabite? Oh, yes. Well, since my grandpa's day."

Udra Danril's face darkened. With a harrumph, he turned to the other end of the table, "Well, Mr. Vilkas, in addition to recovering the painting, have you caught the scoundrels who took it?"

Oren said, "One of the thieves is dead."

"Is he? Then justice is served."

"Is it? I don't believe theft carries the death penalty on Rheged Prime. As to the other burglars, I have a hunch where one can be found. And the third is at this table."

"What?" Danril jerked his head left and right looking at everyone. "Who is it?"

Buad and Blan flew in with Zastra's salad and winged back out.

Bella said, "Is everyone served now? No, Ms. Rune's place is still empty. Forgive me, Aras. This table service is going entirely too slowly. My maid, Koval, was supposed to assist, but I haven't seen a blue bit of her." She rang the bell and called out, "Koval. Koval, where are you?"

The maid shuffled in from the kitchen, her eyes fixed on the floor. She moved to Bella's side, keeping her back toward the table as much as possible. "Yes, ma'am."

"Koval, you must help the others serve food."

"Sorry, ma'am, my shoulder is sore this evening."

"I am sorry to hear that, but you simply must help."

"Yes, ma'am."

At that moment, Udra Danril, who had been chasing a bite of salad around the plate, looked up. He froze, his spork in mid bite. "You there. Server."

Koval ignored him.

Bella said, "Koval, one of the guests has addressed you."

Koval half turned toward the sewer king.

"You!" Danril said it like a cuss word.

He sprang from his seat, grabbed his cane, and dashed limping around the table. Danril grabbed Koval by both arms and began shaking her.

Shocked expressions swept across the faces of everyone around the table. Everyone, that is, except for Oren. He was smiling.

## Chapter 39

# The Fight Scene

*Lucas*

Mom always told me my first job would probably be something in food service — maybe flipping burgers or cleaning tables. I never thought it would come at age seven on an alien planet. Yet here I was, dressed up like a server and ready to wait at table for a fancy dinner party. I could think of about a billion other things I would rather be doing, but if this made me part of the Galactic Detective Agency team, then I was ready to do my part.

The chef wearing a tall white hat slid something into an oven and wiped her hands on her apron. She called out. "Servers, gather round."

I stepped up to where the chef was standing. Buad and Blan flew over and perched on a counter. A bent old lady dressed all in black with one arm in a sling and her hair pulled up in a bun pulled herself off a stool and joined us.

The chef gave us our orders. Salad first, followed by soup, then the main course. We would finish with dessert. I hoped there would be some left over because it all looked good, and I was hungry.

Through the kitchen window we got a view of the guests as they came to the front door. Everybody was dressed up fancy. Especially my mom, who looked like a movie star.

From the other room, Ms. Balok called out for everyone to be seated. This was followed by a lot of noise from people shuffling around. That was when I heard it — an uneven tapping sound, *thump tap* pause, *thump tap* pause. It was the same tapping I heard in the kidnap house. I sucked in air.

Blan flew up in front of me. "Hey, kid, you look like you saw a ghost."

"I think I heard one. That tapping."

"What of it?"

"One of the kidnappers made a sound like that when he walked."

"I thought the kidnapper was an augment. There ain't no augments on the guest list."

"Not him. The other guy I couldn't see."

Blan spoke through the translator bots. "Hey, Oren, does somebody out there make a tapping sound when they walk?" He tilted his head. "Uh-huh ... Yeah. Lucas says ... Yeah, that's right ... What do you want us to do? ... Right. Sure."

Blan turned back to me. "One of the guests, Udra Danril, walks with a cane. Funny thing, Oren seemed to already know. He says to proceed with serving."

I said, "What if that guy tries to grab me?"

Blan said, "Forget about it. There's no way we let that happen."

I swallowed and nodded. "Okay. But I'm not serving him."

"Not a problem. Buad and me will take care of the creep."

A bell rang from the dining room. The chef snapped her fingers. "Now. Salads."

I stepped to the counter, picked up two plates, and passed through the swinging door into the dining room. I glanced up at the table and spotted the cane hanging over the back of a chair. The guy in the chair looked mean, but fortunately he wasn't looking at me. I kept my head down, served my plates, and got out of there as quickly as I could.

I returned to the kitchen and waited for Buad and Blan. "Should we tell Gabe and Zastra about the guy?" I asked. "Gabe is sitting right beside him."

Buad said, "Leave that to Oren. He's right there. He'll know what to do."

I served more plates. This time I caught Gabe's eye and tried to signal him with a jerk of my head toward the guy. I don't think Gabe got the message.

After my third trip to the dining room, I glanced out the window as I stepped back into the kitchen and froze in my tracks. Outside, leaning against a yellow tree was the augment who had grabbed me. What was he doing here?

Buad and Blan flew in behind me. Without a word I pointed out the window.

Buad chuckled. "Well. Looks like everything is gonna go down tonight — the robbery, the kidnapping, the whole shebang. Don't you worry, Lucas. We'll nab 'em all."

In the other room somebody yelled, "You!" Then there were raised voices, chairs screeching across the floor. We rushed in to find the guy with the cane shaking the bent server lady.

Ms. Balok yelled. "Mr. Danril, release my maid this instant!"

A fat guy sitting by Mom hauled himself up from his chair and grabbed the cane guy. He tried to pull him off the bent lady, but the cane guy turned and whacked him across the head with his cane. The fat guy tumbled backwards to the floor.

Then this other woman, not Ms. Balok, but a skinny woman with blue hair sitting beside Oren, ran to the fat guy. She kneeled beside him and said, "Are you hurt, baby?"

The fat guy shook his head like a wild man. "Aras! No!"

Meanwhile, the cane guy had turned back to the bent lady and wrapped his hands around her neck. That's when Detective Tracy jumped in, grabbed the cane guy and punched him. The cane guy went down in a heap.

Julius Dumont jumped up on his chair, his glass in one hand and a spork in the other. He dinged the glass with the spork and called out, "At the end of round one, Luce and Danril are down, and Tracy is ahead on points."

Tracy turned to the bent lady, and out of nowhere she stood up straight and kneed him in the gut. She didn't look as old now, and she sure didn't move like an old person. Tracy staggered back, then lunged at her and grabbed her.

Mr. Dumont spoke into the spork like it was a microphone. "And out of nowhere, folks, Koval the maid attacks Tracy in a surprise move. And here's another one. Dun Luce is up from the floor, attacking Udra Danril. It's a left hook. Then a right cross. And now here's Zastra, the Scrappin' Srathan, leaping right across the table into the fray. She's trying to separate Luce and Danril. Tracy is trying to help her while keeping the maid corralled with one hand. But the maid is kicking him. Ouch! That has to hurt."

"Julius," Ms. Dumont said, "sit down!"

The fat guy was trying to use his weight to push Zastra around. Buad and Blan flew in and pecked at the guy's neck and face. Pieces of him started coming off in their beaks and talons. There wasn't any blood or anything. His face was just coming off like pieces of rubber.

"Now, folks," Mr. Dumont said. "Aras Rune is on her feet. Is she joining the fight? No! She's running toward the door. And with her, also trying to make a quick exit, is Trub Nurke. But Gabriel 'The Grappler' Lake is after them, and so is the glamorous Sarah Moon."

Mom yelled, "Not so fast Nurke," and grabbed him by the shoulder.

Gabe caught the Aras woman. She turned and punched Gabe in the face where he was already bruised. Gabe yelled in pain but managed to hold on.

Mr. Dumont announced into the spork. "Aras Rune appears to be snared. No, wait, she isn't. She just pulled off a stunning martial arts move, dropping to one knee and flipping Gabriel Lake over her shoulder. Who knew she had that in her? Lake hit the floor hard. Can he get up? It's anybody's guess. Wait. Now he's grabbing Rune's leg and pulling her down."

The guy Mom called Nurke elbowed her in the stomach to break her grip. I could tell it hurt because Mom bent over in pain. That did it. He couldn't do that to my mom. I ran to the guy and started hitting him from behind. He backhanded me hard, and I fell to the floor. I licked my lip and tasted blood.

Mom came back with fire in her eyes, leaned back, and kicked the guy right in the chin. His head snapped back like a Pez dispenser. Way to go, Mom! I couldn't believe it. She was like Wonder Woman or something. They were still going at it when the door crashed open, and the augment rushed in.

"And a new pugilist has entered the ring!" Mr. Dumont said.

The augment glanced around the room and ran toward the cane guy who was still struggling with Zastra. He grabbed the cane guy and punched Zastra in the gut. Her hand slipped off the cane guy, and the augment picked him up and dashed for the door.

It didn't look like Zastra was going to be able to catch him before he escaped. Everybody else was fighting somebody, except for Oren, who couldn't fight because he didn't have a body. And except for Ms. Balok and Ms. Dumont who were sitting there looking horrified. And Mr. Dumont who was busy calling the fight. I had to do something.

I knew I couldn't tackle the big augment guy, but I might be able to pull the cane guy out of his arms. I grabbed the cane guy's leg and lifted my feet to put all my weight into it. Sure enough, he slipped from the big guy's grasp to the floor.

The augment turned and glared at me. "You again!" he said.

That's when I saw it. One of the chips in his head had a connector with a familiar shape, like the shape on the phased signal attenuator Jace gave me.

The augment stooped beside the cane guy and said, "Are you all right?" The cane guy nodded. The augment said, "I gotta deal with this kid."

Jace had told me the attenuator changes the power of a signal, like a volume control. I wondered what would happen to whatever that chip in the guy's head controlled if it got more juice. Whatever happened, he deserved it.

He stepped toward me. A grin, and not a happy one, spread across his face.

214

I dug in my pocket and pulled out the attenuator. It came out along with the badge Zastra had given me. The connector shape looked like a match.

The augment grabbed me and picked me up until we were nose to nose. "Where did you come from?"

Mr. Dumont yelled. "You, unhand that kid. Detective Tracy! Zastra!"

Jace had said the screw on the attenuator adjusted it up or down. I needed it up all the way. My arms were pinned in front of me. I kept my eyes on the augment while I tried turning the screw with my thumbnail. It wouldn't budge. What about the badge? I had used it as a wrench before. It was still in my hand. I slid the edge into the screw and turned. I hoped I was turning it the right way.

The augment's eyes narrowed to slits.

I said, "Hey, ugly, I've got something for you."

I wrenched my arm loose and jabbed the attenuator into the chip. The big guy let go of me and grabbed his head. He tried to swat at the gizmo, but now his arm didn't want to move right. He dropped to his knees, then slumped to the floor.

Mr. Dumont screamed. "And it's a knock-out for young Lucas! Hooray!"

Detective Tracy ran over, holding the maid lady with one hand while he handcuffed the augment with the other. "Are you all right, Lucas?"

"All right? Are you kidding? This is incredible!"

# Chapter 40

# Oren Takes the Stage

*Gabe*

"I should thank you, Mr. Danril, for helping us break the case." Oren said. "I had suspected Koval of being Carsta Rio. Your outburst confirmed it."

The fight was over. The tablecloth and most of the dishes had been pulled off onto the floor in the brouhaha. Oren's hologram was still sitting in the chair at the end of the table, all eyes now on him.

"Wait." I turned to gape at the maid. "Koval is who now?" She struggled in Dak Tracy's grip, her hair no longer neatly bunned.

After handcuffing the augment and Udra Danril, Tracy had run out of bracelets, leaving us to improvise restraints for any other dinner guests who still resisted. Zastra was standing over Dun Luce as he sat on the floor looking worse for wear with bits of his face coming off. Sarah and I had tied up Trub Nurke and Aras Rune with curtain ropes and set them down in chairs at the table. Nurke sported a red spot showing through his scraggly beard where Sarah had kicked him.

After getting in fights two nights in a row, I could feel fresh bruises popping up inside old bruises. Sarah, on the other hand, looked amazing despite the torn collar on her new dress. She had a flushed glow in her cheeks and a confident smile on her face. She sat casually in a chair beside Lucas, who was bouncing with excitement. Beside them sat the Dumonts. Buad and Blan perched on the table near Bella.

"Carsta Rio," Oren said, answering my question. "You remember our missing thief, the third person in the gang along with Mot Vagis and Krellan Kaktal."

"How did you come to suspect her?"

The holographic Oren swept a hand toward the recently repaired window. "The shot. You assumed, Gabriel, that Ms. Balok was the target. However, two other people were in the room at the time — yourself and Koval. I considered each of the possibilities, and I realized if Koval were Carsta Rio, shooting at her would fit with Krellan Kaktal being killed. It meant someone was picking off the gang members one-by-one."

Zastra said, "But by that same logic, couldn't Ms. Balok have been Rio?"

"Unlikely," Oren said. "Why should she steal from herself?"

"Insurance fraud."

"Possibly, but then why hire the Galactic Detective Agency to investigate the crime? She would want to file the insurance claim and move on."

I asked, "What happened to the third thief, Mot Vagis?"

Oren gestured toward Dun Luce. "He was with us the entire time in disguise. Mot Vagis kidnapped his employer and assumed his identity with the help of a suit built to make him appear much heavier. No doubt, it was the real Dun Luce who made those thumping noises you heard in his apartment, sounds that your host passed off as renovation. It is time he is unmasked."

I moved to Dun Luce. "Lucas, do you want to do the Scooby-Doo here?"

"Can I?" He ran over and pulled off the remains of the mask, leaving a young face and thin neck sticking up from the fat suit like a turtle peeking out of its shell.

I poked Vagis (aka Luce) with a foot. "Zoinks! Like wow, man. Hey, Vagis, now say, 'I would have gotten away with it too if it weren't for you meddling kids.'"

Mot's face was a question. "What meddling kids?" His voice was different now — less nasal, deeper. I tell you, this guy was a master thief *and* a voice actor.

"Lucas and me. We're the meddling kids."

Lucas giggled.

Mot scowled at me and turned to Oren. "What gave me away?"

Oren said, "The first clue was how highly you spoke of Mot — a little too highly for someone who abandoned you. Then there was how you referred to Dun Luce's grandfather as Grandpa. I'm old enough to remember the man. He was known far and wide by everyone, including his grandchildren, as Pop-Pop. Finally, our surveillance saw Aras Rune come to visit you. You exchanged terms of endearment — sweetie, baby. Dun Luce would not have done so. Dun Luce loves only food and art."

I said, "So those three stole the Cormabite. But why all the false identities?"

"I presume the personas were part of the plan. Rio took the job as Ms. Balok's maid and Vagis the job of Dun Luce's assistant to infiltrate the art community and pull off a series of robberies, including Ms. Balok's Cormabite and, no doubt, some of Dun Luce's artwork. I imagine once they pulled off the last heist, they planned to both disappear. You'll recall that Koval did disappear the day after the robbery. But it seems Mot Vagis decided to double-cross everyone, including his partners in crime. He vanished along with the Cormabite, taking Dun Luce's persona. Carsta Rio came back to work as Koval until she could figure out what to do."

Zastra said, "So that's why Krellan Kaktal was following us. He learned we were on the case and hoped we would lead him to either Mot or the painting or both."

"Most likely, you are correct" Oren said. "Unfortunately, the killer found him first."

Sarah said, "Who was it who was trying to kill them, Oren?"

"We know the *Self-Portrait* would be next to impossible to fence. They had to have a buyer already lined up. In disappearing, Vagis didn't merely double-cross his partners. He also double-crossed their buyer, the person who hired them to steal the Cormabite in the first place. That person wasn't going to tolerate being betrayed."

"Who?" asked Julius, on the edge of his seat.

"Udra Danril."

"What?" Danril said, "That's ridiculous. Outrageous. I have been beaten, handcuffed, and now accused of murder. You all will be hearing from my attorney."

"Pipe down," Tracy said.

Oren stretched a holographic hand toward the sewer king. "Mr. Danril believed Ms. Balok was behind the Cormabite being stolen from him a year ago. He hired the thieves to steal it back. When Danril didn't receive the painting, he hired the augment to hunt them down, recover the painting, and kill them."

Zastra said, "Then the augment killed Kaktal and took the shot at Rio in the guise of the maid."

"And kidnapped me," Lucas said.

"Correct," said Oren. "He was afraid you had caught enough of his conversation with Danril to expose the plot. He would have killed you too had you not escaped."

The augment spoke up. "For the record, I wasn't in favor of killing the kid. That was all Danril's idea."

"Shut up," Danril said.

"And could everyone quit calling me the augment. I have a name, for Zahn's sake. It's Dennis."

I said, "If the augment … I mean Dennis … killed Kaktal, who was the thin, covered-up person who was following him?"

"Carsta Rio," Oren said. "She was following Kaktal, hoping he would lead her to Vagis. None of our thieves trusted each other. I believe that's what later got her shot. After killing Kaktal, Dennis followed her home."

"How did she climb through the bathroom window in the café with her bad back?"

"If you'll notice, Gabriel, she is standing straighter now."

Oren was right. Koval, or Carsta Rio, now looked about ten years younger. That was one more question answered. I had still more. "How does Trub Nurke fit in?"

"You could say he lit the fuse. Danril told you he purchased the Cormabite six years ago from Nurke and owned it for five years until it was stolen. All that time Ms. Balok had the Cormabite hanging on her wall. The painting obviously could not have been in two places at once. Which meant that one of them was lying or else at least one of the paintings was a forgery."

"Nonsense," Bella said.

"I presumed you would say that. However, the matter of the Carafozzio indicates otherwise. My associates saw a painting in Dun Luce's apartment and then saw the same piece for sale in Mr. Nurke's gallery?"

"Yeah," I said, "And Bella told me she used to own it herself but sold it to Nurke."

"The Cormabite and the Carafozzio. Two sets of duplicate paintings. Both tie back to Mr. Nurke, who, in his own words, dabbles in painting."

Zastra said, "More like dabbles in art forgery."

"Correct," said Oren. "The final piece of that puzzle came from Lucas who noticed Ms. Balok composing a message to Mr. Nurke. She said she again needed his skills. What skills might she mean? Given the confusion with the paintings, a reasonable assumption is that she required his art forgery skills. We can infer that six years ago, Ms. Balok found herself in need of funds and had Trub Nurke forge a copy of the Cormabite."

"That's not true," Bella said. "Gabriel, tell them it's nonsense."

I said nothing, and Oren continued. "Which is why he rushed to see Ms. Balok when he heard of the robbery. He was afraid we might learn of the forgeries. Ms. Balok probably kept the original for herself but arranged for the copy to be sold as the original, which Udra Danril bought. At some other point she did the same with the Carafozzio, with the copy going to Dun Luce. She gets the benefits both of selling the art and keeping the art. Only with the Carafozzio she needed funds so much that she also sold the original to the studio."

I said, "Then our gang of art thieves moved in. Either Vagis or Rio could have placed the camera during the party to spy on the security code."

"Or Kaktal, who was there as a server. I believe those three also stole Danril's copy of the Cormabite a year ago." Oren's eyes went to Koval and the unmasked Mot Vagis. "How did you pull that off, by the way?"

Neither of them answered.

Oren shrugged. "It doesn't matter. The point is that Danril, thinking that Ms. Balok had his stolen painting, then hired the same thieves who stole the forgery from him to steal the original from her."

"Well, ain't that bursting with irony?" I said. "So the forgery led to the robbery, which led to kidnapping and murder. Like you said, generations of crimes. How is Holo Grenton involved? His card was in Kaktal's pocket."

Oren said, "Grenton was involved merely as a property agent. The gang rented a house on Pardus from one of Grenton's agents, planning to use the place as a hideout after the robbery. The clue was the number written on the card, two-one-eight-seven."

Through all this, Tracy had been taking in Oren's performance like he was listening to a true crime podcast, nodding, making occasional notes on his wrist device. Now he scratched his head. "We ran that number through all our criminal databases and found nothing."

Oren said, "You should have tried the Pardiun real estate database. One of several instances of that number was the listing of two-one-eight-seven Orion Avenue in the city of Volans. It is owned by Grenton's company and was recently rented to Krellan Kaktal for four people, I assume our gang of three plus Ms. Rune."

Tracy ran a hand through his hair and nodded. "Makes sense. I have just one question. Who all do I arrest?"

Oren said, "All of them. Except for the Dumonts."

Bella said, "Not me! I had no idea Trub was forging those paintings. I took them to him for cleaning and frame repair. I'm the victim here."

"That is possible," Oren said. "However, your reference to Mr. Nurke's skills tends to argue otherwise."

"Art restoration skills. That's all I meant."

"And what will your bank records say, Ms. Balok? Will the sentries find large influxes of cash about the time Dun Luce and Udra Danril bought the forgeries?"

Bella's started to jump from her chair. Sarah moved like lightning and pushed her back down, appearing to enjoy the task a great deal.

Blan said, "If Bella was having money troubles, how was she planning to pay us. We ain't cheap."

Oren said, "No doubt that was why she again needed Trub Nurke's skills. As for the crimes of the others, Mr. Nurke forged paintings and sold them as originals. Ms. Rune is, at the least, an accessory after the fact in the robbery. Her visit to Dun Luce's apartment and the terms of endearment they used with each other prove she knew it was Mot Vagis. Perhaps she was involved in the actual robbery itself. Mot Vagis and Carsta Rio are guilty of multiple thefts. Mr. Danril is implicated in the robbery and murder for hire schemes. And the augment — excuse me, Dennis — is the murderer."

Udra Danril said, "You assume. You believe. This is all merely a story. You have no proof for any of it."

Tracy said, "Oh, I think between bank records and interrogations we can dig up sufficient proof. I tell you what, the first one of you to turn on the others gets a deal."

Carsta Rio (aka Koval) didn't hesitate. "I will."

The faces of the others fell like they were all being simultaneously sucked into a black hole. In a way, they were.

# Chapter 41

# So Where's the Painting?

*Gabe*

Julius stood. "Well, if no one is going to arrest Tera or me, I believe I should be getting my wife home. I have to say, Mr. Vilkas, you put on quite a show. Add in a few musical numbers, and you could take it on the stage. Speaking of which, it's time we exit stage left. Come along, dear."

The Dumonts left, leaving us staring at each other. I asked, "So where's the painting, the Cormabite?"

Oren said, "Unless I am mistaken, Gabriel, it is in Dune Luce's apartment. Mr. Vagis, please give us the access code to the apartment to allow us to retrieve it."

"Why should I?" Mot said.

Tracy said, "Cooperating with us will help with your sentencing, and I suspect you're going to need all the help you can find."

Mot pulled a face. "D78362."

Tracy said, "I can have sentries there in minutes. We need to free the real Dun Luce."

"If you please," Oren said, "I would prefer you let my people do it. We were hired to recover the Cormabite, and I always like to finish what I start. Surely you owe me that much after I handed you everything else."

"Sure, if you insist. Though I'd like to point out that we would have worked it all out eventually even without your help."

"I agree. As I'm sure you will agree that it was preferable to stop the killing spree as soon as possible."

Tracy nodded, though with a scowl.

I asked, "Do you want Zastra and I to go?"

"Only you. Detective Tracy will need the others here to corral everyone until other sentries arrive."

"How about I take Lucas? He deserves to be in on the resolution."

"Certainly. And, Gabriel, be sure to give Dun Luce my regards. He and I met once."

"At the Kuggeheim?"

Oren smiled.

As Lucas and I headed for the door, Sarah said, "Go get 'em, tiger." I wasn't sure which of us she was talking to.

I had WALT summon a hover taxi for us. While we were waiting for it under the light of the twin moons, Lucas said, "Gabe, I'm sorry about stowing away and causing so much trouble and everything."

I rested an arm on his shoulder. "Yeah. I should apologize too for not taking you into space sooner. Up to now I wasn't able to arrange special trips. And, as you can see, these cases can be hazardous."

He looked up with a light in his eyes. "And awesome! That was amazing in there with everybody fighting."

The taxi came, and we set out through the dark streets. The driver, a Muc with a pig nose and bushy hair, glanced at us and asked, "Is that your son?"

I said, "Well. We aren't related by blood."

Lucas reached up a finger and touched a place at the side of my mouth where I was cut. Then he touched a matching spot on his face. "Kinda we are."

I laughed, which made the cut hurt a little. "Yeah, you're right. Blood brothers."

Some family you're born with. Some you make. Some you find along the way.

Of course, the hover taxi couldn't take us up the hundreds of feet to the sky suite, and we couldn't find a pod shuttle at that time of night. Fortunately, the building had an elevator, which was fine by me. I didn't want to walk across that vertigo-inducing landing pad in the dark.

The access code worked, and we walked in on a darkened apartment, the only light coming from the twin moons shining through the expanse of window.

I said, "Lights on," and the lights came up.

"Wow! Look at this place!" Lucas said. He ran to the windows and looked down over the city. "How high up are we?"

"We can admire the view later. First, let's find Dun Luce. Try all the doors."

We found him in a bedroom in the back stretched out on a huge bed, tied, and gagged. He was as enormous as Mot's disguise. He watched us with wild eyes as we worked at the ropes.

"Who are you?" He asked when I pulled off the gag.

"My name is Gabriel Lake. This is Lucas Gallo. We're with the Galactic Detective Agency. We were working a case that ended with Mot Vagis being unmasked and arrested."

"Thank you. Thank Oren Vilkas."

"We will. He's the one who reasoned out that you were back here somewhere. He sends his regards. Can you sit up?"

"I ... I think so. I don't know. I have been tied up like this for days."

"We can call medical help for you."

"Please."

I said, "WALT, have a medical team sent to Dun Luce's apartment."

"Sure thing, Gabriel," WALT said.

"They're on their way," I told Luce. "We need to recover a stolen painting hidden here somewhere."

"Do what you need to do. No, wait. Would you be dears and find me some food from the kitchen? The creep barely fed me at all."

Lucas and I located the kitchen and found some grub. Dun Luce devoured it.

I said, "Oren, Dun Luce is free. I think he'll be all right."

Luce called, "Are you speaking with Oren Vilkas? Please pass on to him my sincerest gratitude."

I said, "He says thank you. Now where is the painting?"

"Move to the room where you interviewed Mot Vagis."

I motioned to Lucas, and we returned to the room with the Jetsons chairs. "Okay, we're there."

"Do you see the polka dotted painting with the ornate gold frame — the one Zastra asked about the other day?"

"Yeah. It's right here."

"Does anything about the painting strike you?"

"Um ..." I wasn't exactly being struck by anything.

"It doesn't fit with any of Mr. Luce's other art pieces. Except for this one, they are all landscapes."

"Right. Right. I assumed he wanted to branch out."

"Possibly, but what do you discern about the frame?"

"It's fancy. Personally, I don't think it matches the feel of the painting."

"It does not. But more to the point, I recognized it as the same frame from the photo Bella showed you of the Cormabite."

"You mean … Well, I'll be. Hidden in plain sight."

I pulled the painting off the wall and flipped it over. Four sliding latches held the canvas to the frame. As I freed it, the polka dot canvas slipped off revealing the round black face of Pollock Cormabite.

Lucas said, "How come it looks like Marvin the Martian?"

"I know, right? It's nice having another Earth guy around who sees these things."

"There's Mom."

"Yeah, well, she's a girl, so …"

He nodded like a bobblehead doll. "Don't I know it?"

Minutes later, with the medical crew on hand tending to Dun Luce, Lucas and I were riding the elevator down, the Cormabite tucked under my arm.

I said, "During the fight I saw how you rushed to defend your mom. Well, I saw some of it. I was kinda involved in my own fight at the time."

He shrugged. "Turns out Mom didn't need much defending. I knew she was taking martial arts classes, but I never saw her do stuff like that."

"Me neither. I bet after this you'll do what she says the first time."

He made a toothy, wide-eyed expression that reminded me of the grimacing face emoji.

I said, "You know, seeing you try to help her made me realize something."

"What's that?"

"Well … um … the thing is, and this is a secret so don't tell your mom, but I'm planning to ask her to marry me. I haven't been able to yet. We keep getting interrupted with things like kids stowing away on spaceships and getting kidnapped and such."

Lucas's shoulders sank. "Sorry."

"That's okay. I realize now I need to do this first. Sometimes guys ask a girl's father for permission, but you're the one who takes care of her, the same way she takes care of you. And if we get married, you'll be every bit as affected by it as we will. I realize I won't ever really be your dad. But I want to be the guy who helps raise you, the guy you can talk to about stuff."

"Like how come there's an alien species that looks like Marvin the Martin?"

"Exactly. Stuff like that needs to be discussed. I mean, this could have serious implications for the universe. Are there Autobots on some planet somewhere? Is Krypton in the next solar system? Anyway, what do you say? Do I have your permission to ask your mom to marry me?"

He blinked and blinked again. Then he threw his arms around my waist, nearly knocking the priceless Cormabite out of my hands.

# Chapter 42

# Date Do-Over

*Gabe*

The next morning in the galley, Lucas was shooting me knowing glances and nodding his head in the direction of his mom while we munched on waffles. I mouthed to him the words, "Not now," with a stern expression. Fortunately, Sarah was focused on her coffee and an ache in her ribs where Nurke had hit her.

Oren's voice came over the speakers. "Detective Tracy is stopping by. Would everyone come to the office, please?"

"Let's finish up and go," Sarah said.

"Me too?" Lucas asked.

"Yes, you too. I'm not sure we could have solved this case without you."

Lucas beamed as he stuck a whole waffle quarter in his mouth to clean his plate. Sarah frowned at me like that was my fault.

We climbed to the office to find the whole gang there, even Jace, who was leaning back in my desk chair. He started to rise when we entered, but I waived him off and sat with Sarah and Lucas in the red leather chairs up front.

We didn't have to wait long for Dak Tracy to contact us over his wrist device and tell us he was outside the ship. Blan flew down and escorted him up. The square jawed detective was back in his yellow trench coat, dark suit, and ten-gallon fedora.

"Thanks for seeing me," he said, dropping into the chair beside me, "I wanted to stop by to give you a report. Carsta Rio gave it all up. The string of robberies. The fact that Udra Danril hired them to steal the Cormabite. She even knew about the forgeries. Turns out, Aras Rune had let the gang use the gallery one night to draw up their plans, and there was a half-finished copy of a Tim Brandt painting on an easel in the office. The only thing she couldn't tell us about was the murder for hire scheme since she was one of the intended victims. I would sure like to make that one stick since it's murder. In the end I think either Danril or the augment will turn on the other. Criminals always do. Even if they don't, we have them both for the kidnapping and Danril for the robbery. Believe me, they're all going away for a while."

"Even Ms. Balok?" Oren asked.

"Even Ms. Balok. You were right about the bank records. Large deposits to her account coincide with deposits to Trub Nurke's account and withdrawals from the people who bought the forgeries. She was in on it. I have to hand it to you, Vilkas. You had it all worked out."

Oren looked like a balloon about ready to pop.

I said, "One minor thing. I think Julius Dumont dropped off a painting the other day at the gallery … um … for a cleaning. Can you make sure the piece is returned to them without any trouble? They're a dear old couple."

"Sure thing." Tracy stood. "Well, that's the report. I want to offer you all my thanks. I don't care much about art forgeries, but I do love getting murderers and kidnappers off the street."

Blan showed Tracy out. When he flew back to the office he said, "Too bad about Bella. She was our client. Looks like we don't get paid now. This was a whole lot of work and danger for nothing."

A smile spread across Oren's face. "Ah. Well, that was something I wanted to mention. Dun Luce contacted me this morning. He was quite appreciative of our part in freeing him."

"How appreciative?" Zastra asked.

"Extremely so, and in a decidedly material and tangible sense."

Buad said, "That's all right then."

"You sly fox," I said. "No wonder you wanted us to free him instead of the sentries and for me to give him your regards."

Oren gave us a fake innocent shrug.

Jace said, "I guess the only thing left is to return these kids to Earth."

"Yeah, about that," I said, "Can we wait until after lunch?"

Jace said, "Sure. It gives me time to run the final checks before we take off. Why?"

"Oh, I want to take Sarah out on a lunch date."

Lucas said, "Can I stay here? I just want a taco." He shot me a wink.

Sarah cocked her head. She had to notice all the goofy expressions on everyone's face, especially Lucas's. They all knew why I was doing this. "Sure. I guess. What's the occasion, Gabe?"

"Only that we never got to finish our date the other night."

"Will you be okay here, Lucas?"

"No problem. Zastra promised to teach me some martial arts moves if we had time."

"Oh my. Well, be careful."

The meeting broke up, and Sarah and I walked back to my cabin.

"Now what do we do until lunch, Gabe?"

"I thought we'd take our time and walk to the restaurant — one more chance to see Rheged Prime." I paused. "Also, I was thinking. Your dress from last night got a little torn up in the fight. We could have the replicator fix it."

She raised an eyebrow. "You're saying you like the dress?"

"I do, and I'd like to take you out in it for a quiet dinner sometime … to a place where we won't end up in a brawl."

"That would be a refreshing change of pace. Not that these last few days haven't been … well, I won't say fun. How about …"

"Thrilling? Exhilarating? Electrifying?"

"More like spine-tingling … in both a bad way and a good way."

"I'll try to take it down a notch."

"Much appreciated. By the way, don't expect the dress for lunch. It isn't lunch attire."

"Yes, ma'am … or no, ma'am."

"And don't call me ma'am."

"No … um … Ms. Gallo."

"Now, if you'll excuse me, I need to get myself ready for our date."

I did the same, and a few hours later we were strolling through the streets of Tikal for the last time.

"Where are you taking me?" she asked.

"With Kah-Rehn's help I found a place near here with great reviews on WELP."

"WELP?"

"Apparently it stands for Write-ups of Entertainment and Lunch Proclamations."

"You're kidding me, right? You're making a joke."

"That's what Kah-Rehn told me. Search me. I don't even understand how alien acronyms can possibly translate."

"It appears they don't very well."

She took my arm, and we ambled on to the restaurant where we had a delightful meal in a patio surrounded by purple vines and blue flowers.

As we were finishing, Sarah said, "I hope they can still return us home in the wee hours. I need to catch up on my sleep. Not to mention that by going back to the night we left, I will have aged five days in one Earth day."

"You shouldn't worry about that. You look lovely."

"What about you? Are you ready to go home?"

"Almost. There's one item of unfinished business."

I paused and glanced around the room, assuming that the server or the manager or another customer or somebody would momentarily be coming up to interrupt me. Everyone, however, appeared busy with their own lives. I turned back to her.

"You know, I wish I had met you sooner."

"Why? So you could have seen me when I was younger and not a haggard old mom?"

"What? No. No! I only mean we could have more time. Seriously."

She chuckled. "I'll allow it."

"Still," I said, "we have all the time in the future stretching out before us." I eyeballed the room again. Still no interruptions on the horizon. I plowed on. "Going through this adventure with you and with Lucas has made me realize how much I care for both of you."

Her head dipped, and she looked at me questioningly over her glasses.

I said, "I think you and I make a great team."

"At what?"

"Hmm?"

"What do we do great as a team? Sleuthing? Fighting bad guys? Euchre?"

"You do play a mean hand of Euchre," I said.

"You're not so bad yourself, though you bid a bit too aggressively for my taste."

"I like going for it. Speaking of which — and what I'm trying to say is—"

A voice came from over my shoulder. "Are you ready for the check now, sir?"

There it was, that interruption I was expecting. Without even looking at the guy, I pulled the payment stick from a pocket and held it up. He took it and disappeared. A troubling thought crossed my mind.

"Um … that *was* the server, right?" I asked.

"Yes."

"Not some random guy running a con?"

"No."

"Good. Now where was I?"

"You were saying we make a great team."

"Yeah. You and me, Sarah. Me and you."

"Don't forget Lucas."

"How could I? He was amazing."

"He's still grounded. Sneaking out of the house. Stowing away. We can't have that."

"You're the mom."

"Need to nip that in the bud."

"Right. Right."

The conversation was drifting off topic. I needed to steer it back. I thought over my planned speech and dismissed it all. There was only one thing left to say.

I reached into my pocket, pulled out the ring, and held it up as I slid out of my chair to one knee. Her eyes grew large, her smile like fireworks on the fourth of July.

"Sarah, will you marry me?"

Would you like to make my day?
Review this book on Amazon and on Goodreads.
Your honest words would mean the world to me.

# Last Word and Free Stuff

Thanks for reading *The Cormabite Maneuver*. The book was a blast to write. This whole thing started when my grandson Gabriel, who is the namesake for Gabriel Lake, suggested I write one that featured Lucas. I figured, if it featured Lucas then some of it should be in his voice and from his perspective. So that's how I ended up attempting to connect with my inner seven-year-old. My wife says my inner seven-year-old doesn't always stay inner anyway.

Some readers will be too young to recognize Groucho Marx and Margaret Dumont in the Dumonts. If that's you, do yourself a favor and check out *A Night at the Opera* or *Duck Soup* or any of the Marx Brothers' movies.

I would love to hear what you think about the book. Leave a quick review of it on Amazon and/or Goodreads. Please! It genuinely helps move the book up the algorithm. It would also make my day.

Thank you to Kameron Robinson for a great cover design. And thank you to my readers who encourage me with reviews and just buying and reading.

Follow me on Amazon, to know when I have new releases. To do so, click the Follow button beside my picture on the Amazon page for any of my books. You can also follow me on Instagram at garyrandolphstoryteller and Facebook at GaryRandolphStoryteller.

Check out my website at grstoryteller.com. It has summaries of all my books and links to my blogs. I also do storytelling, and you can watch some videos of me singing songs and reciting poems.

While you're on the website, please sign up for my mailing list at the bottom of the home page. That way I can tell you when I'm releasing a new book, having price promotions, or doing a storytelling performance. I promise I won't abuse the privilege of having your email address. Nobody hates spam more than I do.

And something free for you. If you sign up for my mailing list, I'll send you *The Jewels of Eca*, an 8000-word story that tells how Zastra joined the Galactic Detective Agency. If you're a fan of the series, it's a tale you'll want to read.

# Other Books by Gary Blaine Randolph

## The Galactic Detective Agency

Gabriel Lake is just a regular computer guy from Indianapolis … until he is recruited into this series of lighthearted murder mysteries in space. Under the guidance of the brilliant Oren Vilkas, the Galactic Detective Agency hops from one weird world to another to take on quirky aliens and solve interstellar crime.

The complete series is available on Amazon at amazon.com/gp/product/B08XN1BL1G

Book 1 – A Town Called Potato

Book 2 – The Maltese Salmon

Book 3 – Return of the Judy

Book 4 – The Big Sneep

Book 5 – Murder on the Girsu Express

Book 6 – The Cormabite Maneuver

Book 7 – Trouble in Paradox

Book 8 – The Wrath of Kah-Rehn (coming late 2024)

# Pelham and Blandings

Pelham G. Totleigh is an unlikely hero. His species, Haplors, are smaller than most others in the galaxy. And as his Aunt Agutha constantly reminds him, he is hardly the smartest or most industrious of Haplors. He also has an unfortunate habit of stumbling his way into the most outrageous and hilarious predicaments. Fortunately, his faithful valet Blandings has enough brainpower for both of them and is always there with a brilliant idea and an excellent cup of tea. This series is a loving tribute to and re-imagining of the Jeeves and Wooster stories of PG Wodehouse. Join Pelham and Blandings on their comic misadventures through space.

The series is available in both paperback and e-book formats on Amazon at https://www.amazon.com/dp/B0BYPLWPBV

Book 1 – Viva Lost Vogus

Book 2 – The Importance of Being Pelham

Book 3 – The Code of the Totleighs

# Alien World

If you were stranded, all alone on an alien world, if you had to hide your identity and try to blend in, how would you do it? What would it cost you? What would you long for most?

Not a comedy — well, there are some funny bits — *Alien World* is an exploration of what it would be like to be an alien stranded on Earth and forced to live out decades there, trying to blend in while staying one step ahead of the military that is hunting him.

Available on Amazon at https://www.amazon.com/dp/B085SYG3L7